Academic Curveball

Academic Curveball

Braxton Campus Mystery Book 1

James J. Cudney

Acknowledgments

Writing a book is not an achievement an individual person can do on his or her own. There are always people who contribute in a multitude of ways, sometimes unwittingly, throughout the journey from discovering the idea to drafting the last word. *Academic Curveball: A Braxton Campus Mystery* has had many supporters since its inception in June 2018, but before the concept even sparked in my mind, others nurtured my passion for writing.

First thanks go to my parents, Jim and Pat, for always believing in me as a writer, as well as teaching me how to become the person I am today. Their unconditional love and support have been the primary reason I'm accomplishing my goals. Through the guidance of my extended family and friends, who consistently encouraged me to pursue my passion, I found the confidence to take chances in life. With Winston and Baxter by my side, I was granted the opportunity to make my dreams come true by publishing this novel. I'm grateful to everyone for pushing me every day to complete this third book.

Academic Curveball was cultivated through the interaction, feedback, and input of several beta readers. I'd like to thank Shalini G, Lisa M. Berman, Didi Oviatt, Misty Swafford, Tyler Colins, Nina D. Silva, and Noriko for providing insight and perspective during the development of the story, setting, and character arcs. A special call-out goes to Shalini for countless conversations, helping me to fine-tune every aspect of the setting, characters, and plot. She read every version and offered a tremendous amount of her time to help advise me on this book over several months.

I'd also like to thank my editor, Nicki Kuzn at Booktique Editing, for helping fix all the things I missed along the way. She's been a wonderful addition to the team and has been very focused on making this book a success. Between coaching and suggesting areas for improvement, she's guided me in all the right directions.

Thank you to Next Chapter for publishing *Academic Curveball* and helping pave the road for more books to come. I look forward to our continued partnership.

Welcome to Braxton, Wharton County
(Map drawn by Timothy J. R. Rains, Cartographer)

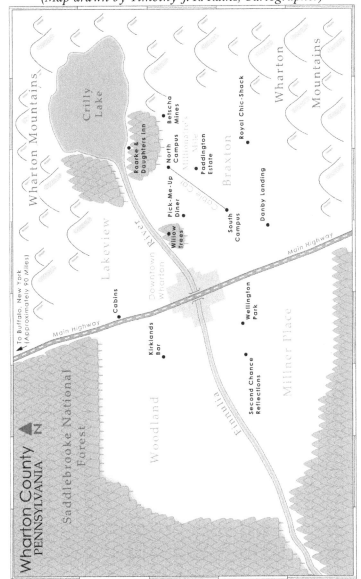

Who's Who in Braxton?

Ayrwick Family

- *Kellan*: Main Character, Braxton professor, amateur sleuth
- *Wesley*: Kellan's father, Braxton's retiring president
- *Violet*: Kellan's mother, Braxton's admissions director
- *Emma*: Kellan's daughter with Francesca
- *Eleanor*: Kellan's younger sister, manages Pick-Me-Up Diner
- *Nana D*: Kellan's grandmother, also known as Seraphina Danby
- *Francesca Castigliano*: Kellan's deceased wife
- *Vincenzo & Cecilia Castigliano*: Francesca's parents

Braxton Campus

- *Myriam Castle*: Professor
- *Fern Terry*: Dean of Student Affairs
- *Connor Hawkins*: Director of Security, Kellan's best friend
- *Maggie Roarke*: Head Librarian, Kellan's ex-girlfriend
- *Jordan Ballantine*: Student

- *Carla Grey*: Student

- *Craig 'Striker' Magee*: Student

- *Bridget Colton*: Student

- *Coach Oliver*: Athletics Directo

- *Abby Monroe*: Professor

- *Lorraine Candito*: Wesley's Assistant

- *Siobhan Walsh*: Communications Department Assistant

Wharton County Residents

- *Ursula Power*: Friends with Myriam

- *Eustacia Paddington*: Nana D's frenemy

- *Alton Monroe*: Abby's Brother

- *April Montague*: Wharton County Sheriff

- *Marcus Stanton*: Braxton Town Councilman

- *Officer Flatman*: Police Officer

Other Visitors

- *Derek*: Kellan's Boss in Los Angeles

- *Mrs. Ackerton*: Abby's Neighbor

Overview

When I decided to write a cozy mystery series, I adhered to all the main rules (light investigations, minimal violence or foul language, no sexual content, murder happens off-screen, protagonist is an amateur sleuth, and set in a quiet, small town). Some authors push the boundaries with variations, and in the Braxton Campus Mysteries, I followed the same route... just differently. Kellan, my protagonist, is a thirty-ish single father, whereas traditionally a woman is the main character. Children aren't often seen in most series, but Kellan's family is important to the story. Kellan is also witty and snarky, but intended in a lovable and charming way, just like his eccentric grandmother, Nana D. Both are friendly, happy, and eager to help others, and they have a sarcastic or sassy way of interacting and building relationships... hopefully adding to the humor and tone of the books.

Cozy mysteries are different from hard-boiled investigations, thrillers, and suspense novels; the side stories, surrounding town, and background characters are equally important to building a vibrant world in which readers can escape. I hope you enjoy my alternative take on this classic sub-genre.

Chapter 1

I've never been comfortable flying. My suspicious nature assumed the magic suspending airplanes in the sky would cease to exist at some master planner's whim. Listening to the whirr of a jet propeller change speeds—or experiencing those jolting, mysterious *pockets of rough air*—equaled imminent death in an aluminum contraption destined for trouble. I spent the entire flight with my jaw clenched, hands clutching the armrests, and eyes glued to the seatback in front of me, impatiently hoping the diligent crypt keeper didn't claim another victim. Despite my uncanny knack for grasping anything mechanical and Nana D always calling me brilliant, I was entirely too doubtful of this mode of transportation. My gut promised I'd be safer plummeting over Niagara Falls naked and in a barrel.

After landing at the Buffalo Niagara International Airport on a miserable mid-February afternoon, I rented a Jeep to trek another ninety miles south into Pennsylvania. Several inches of densely packed snow and veiled black ice covered the only highway leading to my secluded childhood hometown. Braxton, one of four charming villages surrounded by the Wharton Mountains and the Saddlebrooke National Forest, felt impenetrable from outside forces.

As I changed lanes to avoid a slippery patch, my sister's number lit up the cell screen. I paused *Maroon 5* on my Spotify playlist, clicked accept, and moaned. "Remind me why I'm here again?"

"Guilt? Love? Boredom?" Eleanor chuckled.

"Stupidity?" Craving something of substance to squelch the angry noises radiating from my stomach, I grabbed a chocolate chip cookie from a bag on the passenger seat. The extra-tall, salted caramel mocha—free, courtesy of a pretty red-haired barista who'd shamelessly flirted with me—wouldn't suffice on its own. "Please save me from this torture!"

"Not gonna happen, Kellan. You should've heard Mom when I suggested you might not make it. '*He's always inventing excuses not to return home more often. This family needs him here!*' Don't worry! I calmed her down," shouted Eleanor over several dishes and glasses clanging in the background.

"Did she already forget I was here at Christmas?" Another cookie found its way into my mouth. I was powerless to desserts—also known as my kryptonite—hence why I'd always thought they should be a major food group. "Two trips home within six weeks is one too many by my count."

"How did our darling siblings invent acceptable excuses to skip the *biggest social event* of the season?" Eleanor said.

"I gave up competing with them years ago. It's easy to get away with things when they're not disappointing our parents like the rest of us."

"Hey! Don't take me down because you can't escape the awkward middle-child syndrome." Eleanor placed me on hold to deal with a customer complaint.

My younger sister unhappily turned thirty last month, given she *still hadn't met the right man.* She also insisted she wasn't morphing into our mother, despite every hour of every day steamrolling those figments of her imagination into oblivion. Truth be told, Eleanor was the spitting image of Violet Ayrwick, and everyone saw it but them. *Twinsies*, as Nana D always taunted with the cutest lilt to her voice. Eleanor would definitely be at our father's retirement party, as there wasn't a snowball's chance in you-know-where of me going to that boondoggle by myself. The man of the hour had been the president of Braxton College for the last eight years, but upon turning sixty-five, Wesley Ayrwick stepped down from the coveted role.

Eleanor jumped back on the line. "Was Emma okay with you visiting by yourself this time?"

"Yeah, she's staying with Francesca's parents. I couldn't sign her out of school again, but we'll *Facetime* every day I'm gone."

"You're an amazing father. I don't know how you do it on your own," Eleanor replied. "So, who's the woman you plan to meet while gracing us with your presence this weekend?"

"Abby Monroe completed a bunch of research for my boss, Derek," I said, cursing the slimy, party-going executive producer of our award-winning television show, *Dark Reality*. Upon informing Derek that I needed to return home for a family obligation, he generously suggested adding extra days to relax before everything exploded at the network, then assigned me to interview his latest source. "Ever heard the name?"

"Sounds familiar, but I can't place it," Eleanor replied in between yelling orders to the cook and urging him to hurry. "What's your next storyline?"

Dark Reality, an exposé-style show adding splashy drama to real-life crimes, aired weekly episodes full of cliffhangers like reality television and soap operas. The first season highlighted two serial killers, Jack the Ripper and The Human Vampire, causing it to top the charts as a series debut. "I've got season two's massive show bible to read this weekend… ghost-hunting and witch-burning in seventeenth-century American culture. I really need to get a new job. Or kill my boss."

"Prison stripes wouldn't look good on you." Eleanor teased me frequently.

"Don't forget, I'm too handsome."

"I'm not gonna touch that one. Let Nana D weigh in before I crush you for saying something so pathetic. Maybe Abby will be normal?"

"With my luck, she'll be another bitter, scorned victim rightfully intent on justice for whatever colossal trauma Derek's inflicted," I replied with a sigh. "I vote she's another loose cannon."

"When are you gonna interrogate her?"

I'd meant to schedule a lunch to get the basic lowdown on Abby, but I barely made the flight cutoff at the gate in the last-minute rigmarole. "Hopefully tomorrow, if she isn't too far away. Derek confirmed she lives in central Pennsylvania. He has no concept of space or distance."

"It's getting busy here. Gotta go. Can't make dinner tonight, but I'll see you tomorrow. Don't commit any murders until we chat again. Hugs and kisses."

"Only if you don't poison any patrons." I disconnected the phone, begging the gods to transport me back to Los Angeles. I couldn't take the stress anymore and devoured the last two remaining cookies. Given my obsession with desserts, the gym had never *not* been an option. Exercise happened daily unless I was sick or on vacation, which this trip didn't count as. There would be no beaches, cabanas, or mojitos. Therefore, I wouldn't enjoy myself.

I navigated the winding highway drive with the heater set to die-from-sauna max and the wiper blades on maniacal passive-aggressive mode to keep the windshield clear of heavy sleet and snow. It was the dead of winter, and my entire body shivered—not a good thing when my feet needed to brake for deer or elk. Yes, they were common in these parts. No, I hadn't hit any. Yet.

No time like the present to suggest a meeting to Abby. When she answered, I wasn't surprised at her naivety regarding my boss's underhanded approach.

"Derek said nothing about meeting anyone else. You got a last name, Kellan?" Abby whined after I'd already explained who I was in the first minute of the call.

"Ayrwick. I'm Kellan Ayrwick, an assistant director on the second season of *Dark Reality*. I thought we could review the research you prepared and discuss your experience working in the television industry."

A few seconds of silence lingered. "Ayrwick? As in... well... don't a few work at Braxton?"

I was momentarily stunned how a groupie girl would know anything about Braxton. Then I speculated she currently attended the college or previously went to school with one of my siblings. "Let's have lunch tomorrow. One o'clock?"

"Not really. I wasn't prepared to chat this weekend. I thought I'd fly out to Derek in the next few days. The timing is off."

"Can't we meet for a brief introduction?" Derek sure knew how to pick the dramatic ones. I could picture her twirling her hair and blinking her empty eyes despite not knowing what she looked like.

"I'm in the middle of an exclusive exposé about a crime in Wharton County. Might be something to pitch to Derek for... well, it's too early to say anything." Her voice went limp. She'd probably forgotten how to use the phone or accidentally muted me.

"Is this what you proposed to him for a future season of *Dark Reality*? I'm more interested in true crimes and investigative reporting. Maybe I could help with this scoop." Once I realized she was in the same county as me, I tried all angles to snare a meeting.

"Are you Wesley's son? He's got a whole slew of kids."

My mouth dropped two inches. Nana D would've counted the flies as they swarmed in, given how long it remained open. Who was this girl? "I don't see how that's relevant, but yes, he's my father. Do you attend Braxton, Abby?"

"Attend Braxton? No, you've got a few things to learn if we're going to work together." She laughed hysterically, reaching full-on snort level.

"Great, so we can meet tomorrow?" The woman's tone annoyed me, but perhaps I'd misjudged her based on Derek's normal taste in women. "Even thirty minutes to build a working relationship. Are you familiar with the Pick-Me-Up Diner?" Eleanor ran the joint, so I'd have an excuse to step away if Abby became too much to handle. My sister could arrange for a waiter to dump a bowl of soup on Abby, then lock her in the bathroom while I escaped. There was nothing more I disliked than foolish, clueless, or vapid people. I'd had enough of them while dating my way through a sorority years ago. If I ran into one more *LA valley girl*, I'd let Francesca's family, the Castiglianos, take control of the situation. Scratch that, I never said those words out loud.

"No, sorry. I'm gonna be tied up, investigating all the nonsense going on around here. I'll see you on campus tomorrow night."

I shook my head in frustration and confusion. I clearly heard her stifling an obnoxious laugh again. If she weren't a student, why would she be on campus? "What do you mean *tomorrow night*?"

"The party celebrating your father's retirement."

Derek would owe me big-time for this ordeal. If he didn't watch himself, I'd give her his real cell number and not the fake one he initially dispensed.

"How do you know my—" A harsh tone beeped when she disconnected.

I continued on the main road into the heart of Braxton, tooting the horn as I passed Danby Landing, Nana D's organic orchard and farm. I was especially close with Nana D, also known as my grandmother, Seraphina, who'd turn seventy-five later this year. She kept threatening to bend our town's councilman, Marcus Stanton, over her lap, *slap his bottom silly,* and teach the ninny how things ought to be done in a modern world. It's my second job to keep her in check after the incident where she was *supposedly* locked up in jail overnight. Lacking any official records, she could continue to deny it, but I knew better given I was the one who had to convince Sheriff Montague to release Nana D. I hoped never again to spar toe-to-toe with our county's ever-so-charming head law enforcer, even if it's necessary to save Nana D from prison. I felt certain *that* had been a onetime card I could play.

The sun disappeared as I parked the Jeep at my parents' house and scampered toward the trunk to get my bags. Given the temperature had slipped to the single digits, and the icy snow wildly pelted my body, I hurried to the front door. Unfortunately, fate opted for revenge over some past indiscretion and struck back with the vengeance of a thousand plagues. Before long, I skated across a sheet of ice like an awkward ballerina wearing clown shoes and fell flat on my back.

I snapped a selfie while laughing on the frosty ground, to let Nana D know I'd arrived in Braxton. She loved getting pictures and witnessing me make a fool of myself. I couldn't decipher her reply, given my glasses had fogged over, and my vision was equivalent to Mr. Magoo's. I searched for a piece of a flannel shirt untouched by the falling sleet or the embarrassing crash to the ground and wiped them dry. A glance at the picture I'd sent caused the most absurd guffaw to erupt from my throat. My usually clean-cut dark-blond hair was littered with leaves, and the four days of stubble on my cheeks and chin was blanketed in mounds of snow. I dusted myself off and rushed under the protection of a covered porch to read her text.

Nana D: *Is that a dirty wet mop on your head? You're dressed like a hooligan. Put on a coat. It's cold out. I miss you!*
Me: *Thanks, Captain Obvious. I fell on the walkway. You think I'm normally this much of a disaster?*
Nana D: *And you're supposed to be the brilliant one? Have you given up on life, or did it give up on you?*
Me: *Keep it up, and I won't visit this weekend. You're supposed to be a sweet grandma.*
Nana D: *If that's what you want, go down to the old folks' home and rent yourself a little biddy. Maybe you two can share some smashed peas, green Jell-O, and a tasty glass of Ovaltine. I'll even pay.*

After ignoring Nana D's sass, I ran a pair of chilled hands through my hair and entered the foyer. Though the original shell of the house was a wood-framed cabin, my parents had added many rooms, including a west and an east wing bookending the massive structure. The ceilings were vaulted at least twelve feet high and covered in endless cedar planks with knots in all the right places. A pretty hunter-green paint coated three of the walls where the entranceway opened into a gigantic living room. It was anchored by a flagstone fireplace and adorned with hand-crafted antique furniture my parents had traveled all over the state to procure. My father was passionate about keeping the authenticity of a traditional log cabin while my mom required all the modern conveniences. If only the *Property Brothers* could see the results of their combined styles. Eleanor and I referred to it as the *Royal Chic-Shack*.

I dropped my bags to the floor and called out, "Anyone home?" My body jumped as the door to my father's study creaked open, and his head popped through the crack. Perhaps I had the paranormal and occult on my mind, knowing *Dark Reality's* next season was unfortunately in my foreseeable future.

"It's just me. Welcome back," replied my father, waiting for me to approach the study. "Your mother's still at Braxton, closing on the final admissions list for the prospective class."

"How's the jolly retiree doing?" I strolled down the hall toward him.

"I'm not retired yet," my father countered with a sneer. "I finished writing my speech for the party tomorrow evening. Interested in an early preview?"

Saying *no* would make me a bad son. Eleanor and I had promised one another at Christmas we'd try harder. I really wanted to be a bad son today—just kidding! "Sure, it must be exciting. You've had a bountiful career, Dad. It's undoubtedly the perfect example of oratory excellence." He loved when I stretched my vocabulary skills to align with his. I shuddered thinking about the spelling bees of long ago.

"Yes, I believe it is." My father squinted his eyes and scratched at his chin. No doubt he was judging my borderline unkempt appearance. I'd forgotten to shave and taken that classic nose-dive on the ground. Sometimes I preferred the messy look. Apparently, so did that airport barista!

I ambled to his desk, studying the frown lines forming around his lips. "Everything okay, Dad? You look a little peaked."

"Yes... a few things on my mind. Nothing to trouble you with, Kellan." He nodded and shook my hand—standard, male Ayrwick greeting. At six feet, my father stood only three inches taller than me, but the dominant Ayrwick genes made him look gargantuan. Lanky and wiry, he hadn't worked out a day in his life, but he also never needed to. His metabolism was more active than a thoroughbred, and he ate only the healthiest of foods. I was *lucky enough* to inherit the recessive Danby genes, but more on those cruel legacies another time.

"I'm a good listener, Dad. Tell me what's going on." I felt his bony hand pull away and watched his body settle into the worn, mustard-yellow leather chair in front of the bookcase. It was his only possession my mother hadn't yet replaced—purely because he'd threatened divorce. "It's been a while since we've talked."

My father stared out the window. I waited for his right eyebrow to twitch, signaling the onslaught of a battle, but the high arch never came. "We're having some problems at Braxton with a blogster. A bunch of articles or post-its, whatever you call them these days... trash is what I'd like to say." He closed his eyes and leaned back into the chair. "This isn't the way I pictured my pre-retirement weeks."

I stifled a laugh, hoping not to drive another decisive wedge between us. He'd opened up a little more than usual, and it didn't matter if he used the wrong terms to explain whatever fake news propaganda had developed at Braxton. "What's the blogger saying?"

"Someone has an ax to grind about the way I've supported parts of the college. He claims I'm favoring the athletics department by giving them more money this term." My father crossed his legs and cupped his hands together. His navy-blue corduroys and brown loafers seemed out of place.

Was he taking retirement seriously? I'd normally seen him in suits, or occasionally a pair of Dockers and a short-sleeve polo when he'd meet friends at the country club for a round of golf. I hoped it didn't mean he'd be wearing jeans soon. The shock of suddenly embraced normalcy might bury me in an early grave before that doomed airplane.

"Is the blogger going after you specifically or Braxton administration in general?"

My father quickly typed a few words on the iPad's keypad and handed the device to me. "That's the third message in two weeks. The links for the rest are at the bottom."

It's unlike my father to worry about this type of nonsense, but he'd become more sensitive about people's opinions as he grew older. It seemed the opposite of what I thought ordinarily happened as one aged. Nana D was the first to spill whatever was on her mind or laugh when others said anything negative about her. She almost delighted in their criticisms of her behavior. I couldn't wait to get old and say anything I want the way she did!

I scrolled through the recent post. The explicit focus on my father alarmed me the most.

Wesley Ayrwick, in his archaic and selfish ways, has struck another blow in eradicating the true purpose for Braxton's existence. His continued support for a failing athletics department while neglecting the proper education of our beloved student population has made it impossible for me to stand down. A recent six-figure donation was carelessly handed over to Grey Sports Complex for improving the technology infrastructure of the athletic facility, returfing the baseball field, and securing a modern bus for the players traveling to opposing teams. At the same time, the communications, humanities, and music departments suffer with minimal software programs, deteriorating equipment, and lack of innovative venue spaces for live performances. When asked about the decision to split the anonymous donation ninety percent to ten percent in favor of the athletics teams, President Ayrwick claimed they'd been waiting longer and were in danger of not being able to compete in the upcoming sports season. This is the third occurrence of his favoritism in the last two months, which clearly explains why the petition to remove Ayrwick from office sooner than the end of this semester is gaining momentum. Let's hope we can say goodbye to this crooked figurehead before Braxton's ship has sailed too far adrift from its proper course. Retirement must already be on the old coot's brain, or perhaps he's just one of the worst presidents we've ever had. My fondest wish is for Wesley Ayrwick's memory to be buried and long forgotten by the end of this term.

"What do you make of it?" he hesitantly asked.

A quick perusal of the earlier posts revealed similar sentiments, all fixated on my father for some perceived sense of unfair balance with the generous donations bestowed upon Braxton. The last line read like a death threat, but that might've been my imagination running wild since learning the startling truth about the Castigliano side of my family. "Who's the anonymous donor? Are you responsible for choosing where to allocate the funds?"

My father wrinkled his nose and raised his eyebrow. "No, you know better. When it's anonymous, even I'm not supposed to know. Sometimes the benefactor has a specific request on where to distribute the money. I can offer my insight and suggestions, but the Board of Trustees and its budget committee ultimately decide where the funds go."

"I meant you have some influence." I stepped into the hallway to drop off my keys and wallet on a nearby bench. "Should it have gone to the athletics department?"

My father's scowl indicated his annoyance over my lack of unconditional support. "Yes. While I agree the purpose of a college education is to prepare for life in the real world, to study and learn a trade or a skill, it's also about developing interpersonal relationships and opening one's eyes and mind to more than amassing facts." He crossed to the window, shaking his head back and forth, clearly distracted by something. "Sports build camaraderie, teamwork, and friendships. It provides opportunities for the college and the town to unite in support of their students. Leads to a stronger foundation and future."

I couldn't argue with his logic and pondered the past as I kicked off my shoes. "You've put that rather well. I believe you, Dad. Not to change topics, but I had a question about Abby Monroe. She mentioned attending—"

He never heard me as the door to his study slammed shut. I'd been home for ten minutes and already stuck my foot in my mouth. Between our off-the-charts intelligence and arrogant, stubborn streaks, neither of us could back down nor develop a normal relationship. I'd never learn how to bond with the indomitable Wesley Ayrwick. At least I could count on my quick wit and devilishly handsome face to make things seem better!

I dragged the luggage to my old bedroom, which my mother had once fretted over, harboring some foolish notion I might move back home. Did she really think a thirty-two-year-old would want to sleep in a room still wallpapered with *Jurassic Park* and *Terminator* paraphernalia? Before settling in to digest Derek's show materials, I scurried downstairs for a light meal. The incident in the study had left me zero desire to eat dinner with my parents. I'd just turned the corner when I heard my father's voice on the house phone.

"Yes, I read the latest post. I'm aware of our predicament, but we've already discussed it. Terminating the employee isn't an option."

It seemed the posts were causing major troubles, but my father had previously acted like he didn't know who was behind the blog.

"I understand, but I've no intention of revealing this secret. I'm only keeping quiet because of the benefit to Braxton. If they discover the truth, we'll figure out the best solution. For now, I can handle a little hot water. You need to calm down," my father advised.

It sounded like the blogger was telling the truth about underhanded chicanery. Was my father involved in a potentially illegal or unethical situation?

"You should've thought about it before taking a foolish approach to... now wait a minute... no, you listen to me... don't threaten me, or it'll be the last thing you do," he shouted angrily.

When he hung up, I ducked into the kitchen. Between the elusive Abby Monroe's connections to Braxton, the ruthless blogger publicly denouncing my father, and the hostile call I'd just overheard, this weekend might turn out more eventful than expected.

Chapter 2

When I stirred on Saturday morning, thick paste coated the insides of my mouth. The room was dark, and a low-rattling noise emanated from the far corner. I sat straight up in bed, smacked my head into a wood beam, and freaked out that I'd gone blind and a possum had snuck into the walls. I soon determined the obnoxious sound was the hissing of the radiators delivering much-needed warmth to the room.

Once the initial shock of my surroundings wore off, I stretched and grunted at the crunch in my lower spine from sleeping on the firmest mattress known to man. Between jet lag from the red-eye and the time difference, I'd dozed off early but woken up several times throughout the night. I checked my phone only to learn it was a few minutes shy of noon. That's also when I saw a message from my father chastising me for not bringing Emma home. Based on the timestamp, it'd come in the previous night shortly after I'd overheard his argument. Did he know I'd been listening outside his office?

Wesley Ayrwick was not a frequent complainer, and if he elected to vent, it was only on important topics. The last time I'd pressed him for thoughts on something vital, he revealed how much he'd disliked my wife, Francesca. This had occurred when I asked for his help to plan her funeral after she'd been hit by a drunk driver in West Hollywood two years ago. Francesca and I had left her parents' house on Thanksgiving in separate cars, as she'd been staying with them while I was working on an out-of-town film project. I'd always be thankful Francesca's mother, Cecilia Castigliano, had strapped Emma into my car's safety seat that night. Thinking about the alternative scenario consistently brought me to tears. I wasn't anywhere ready to talk about losing my wife at such a young age, nor being a single parent, so let's allow that to sleep longer.

After brushing my teeth, I called to check on Emma, but she was swimming in the neighbor's pool. Her grandparents would contact me as soon as she returned home. I'd only been away for twenty-four hours, yet it felt as if a part of me was lost whenever we were apart. The connection felt fuzzy, as though the distance prevented me from truly knowing whether my six-year-old daughter was okay. I'd give up a lot of desserts to swing her in my arms right now. Or watch her dance to some silly cartoon on her iPad. My heart melted at the pure innocence of her smile.

Before summoning the courage to start the day, I tossed on some clothes and descended the staircase two steps at a time. Walking around the house in only my snug black boxer briefs wasn't an option. I trotted into the kitchen and brewed a pot of coffee, noticing my mother preparing lunch. I still needed to ferret out the detailed agenda for tonight's retirement party.

"How's the best mother in the world doing?" I embraced her the way only a son could remind his momma she's loved. Her shoulder-length auburn hair was pinned back with the jade butterfly clip Eleanor had given her for Christmas, and her face looked like she'd started applying makeup on one side but had forgotten the other half. I'd bet money on today's slipshod appearance resulting from something Nana D had done.

"Oh, Kellan! I wanted to come home early last night, but... the rehearsal for the party... talking to the planner about the seating chart... a near disaster. Do you know she had Nana D sitting next to Councilman Stanton at a table in the back row? I've told that planner ten times if I told her once... Marcus will make an important speech and needs to sit at the main table with your father. Nana D can't be anywhere near him based on their last public argument when she called him a—"

I interrupted before my mother prattled on for hours, bless her soul. "Got it. Makes total sense. You did the right thing, but I thought Nana D declined your invitation?" I suddenly remembered reading a text before falling asleep where Nana D clarified she'd rather spend an afternoon with her mouth crammed full of lemon wedges, her fingers pricked by a thousand tiny needles, and her feet glued inside a bumblebee's nest than attend another Braxton event for my father. "And what's with the crazy portrait-of-a-lady-with-two-faces look?" I cocked my head to the side, reached for the fruit bowl at the end of the island, and stepped a few inches away, certain she'd swat at me for that comment.

My mother, somewhere in her mid-fifties, had feverishly obsessed over her appearance for as long as I could remember. Despite my father telling her she's beautiful, or how he had to prevent all his friends from hitting on her, she put herself down. Even when my father explained how all his golf buddies called him a cradle robber because of my parents' ten-year age gap, she still went on a two-week hunt around the world for the latest wrinkle prevention products and anti-aging miracle cures.

"Whaaat? That woman is gonna be the death of me. She called while I was putting on my face and wanted to know if your father had changed his mind about retiring. She'd heard some rumor about his real intentions, then asked who wrote the scathing blog post. Any idea what she's talking about?" She ducked into the half-bath and applied a colorful powder to her right eyelid.

"We'll chat when you're done. Beauty first," I quipped, changing the topic and preparing a sandwich. "So, Nana D's not going? That's gonna make this party a lot less interesting."

My mother's lack of awareness surrounding the blog posts surprised me. She read everything about Braxton she could get her hands on—it was important to know what's being written about her college to prepare for questions from prospective or current students. Then again, she could've been craftily testing me to see what I knew and wasn't confessing. Often the little charade of trickery we played in the Ayrwick family got complicated—somewhere between a game of *Who's on First?* and *Russian Roulette.*

My mother smacked her lips together like a blowfish. "What did you say, Kellan?"

"Nothing. I'm glad to be home." Eleanor would have to agree that I'm being such a good son.

She retreated into the bathroom while I devoured the sandwich. When she reappeared, her face sparkled. Eleanor better watch herself, or people might ask questions like *who's the older sister* between the pair of them. Maybe I'd even start that rumor. It'd been an ice age since I stung Eleanor with a perfect zinger.

"What's the plan for tonight?" I blurted out while swallowing the last crumb of my sandwich.

"We'll greet early arrivals for the five o'clock cocktail hour. Then we present your father with a service award, and a few folks make speeches between six and seven. They'll serve dinner between seven and eight. Everyone can mingle afterward for an hour before it ends." She collected her breath, then popped a strawberry in her mouth. "I need to take lunch to your father. Please get there early. He wants to introduce you to people."

"Eleanor and I plan to arrive exactly at five. Cross one less worry off your list." I had to motivate her sometimes, or she'd fret over the tiniest things. "We'll be on our best behavior."

My mother kissed my cheek before ascending the stairs to deliver my father's meal. "I'll always worry about my children. Even Gabriel, despite not hearing from him for over seven years. Hugs and kisses!"

As she exited, I caught my reflection in the window and rolled my eyes at her lipstick marks. If I survived the night, I'd exact revenge on Nana D for avoiding it all. I sent her a text to remind her she'd promised to bake me a cherry pie for brunch tomorrow. There was no better dessert, especially the way Nana D prepared them with the cherries on top and the crust only on the bottom. She'd attach little pastry donuts on the side, so we could pull them off and dip them into the cherry filling. Mmm, delicious. Don't get me started on pie.

Nana D: *Arrive by 10. Have fun without me tonight. Please piss off your father for me.*

Wow! She had it in for him. I returned to my bedroom and dove into the show bible sitting on the night table. The next page was Abby's email to Derek from a week earlier. It read:

I'm so glad you selected me to provide the research on Dark Reality's *next season. I received the contract and will send back a signed copy next week. When do we meet again? I had so much fun drinking cocktails with you last month. You're adorable in that recent picture you sent from Tahiti.*

I have tons to share re the birth of witch covens in Pennsylvania and the Beguiling Curse of 1689. Should I book a flight to Hollywood soon? Will the network cover first-class tickets? This is the beginning of a lasting partnership. I've also stumbled upon something controversial going on in my hometown. It's worthy of a future season for our TV show, but I've got more research to do. I'll keep you posted.

How come I keep getting your voicemail? Can you please try to reach me tonight? I'll be home waiting for you to respond. In case you need my cell number, it's...

Derek had gotten himself into trouble again. Ever the talented rascal, Derek was known for dumping his crazy groupies on colleagues and getting everyone else to do his job for him. The last girl he'd assured a walk-on part on the set of *Dark Reality* hopped a series of red-carpet ropes during a season-one screening party, claiming Derek had promised her a front-row seat. When security called him over, my boss looked her right in the eyes and said, "*Never met this woman. Kick her out.*" I was there. I saw the confusion plastered on her face. I also noticed him blink twice, then his lip quivered. Derek had a *tell* I'd pegged from the first day we met.

Between yesterday's call and this email, a decisive picture of Abby Monroe popped into my head—twenty-six, blonde, hourglass shape, perky, and bubbly. She hadn't even known Derek blew her off and put me in the middle of this explosive atom bomb. I scrolled through the call log for Derek's number and patiently waited to connect. What was I walking into with Abby Monroe? Although I'd done most of the work on the first season, my name wasn't listed in the credits, nor were my contributions recognized by anyone at the network. Since I was way more experienced and intelligent—or maybe the better word was *talented*—than Derek, I'd learn everything I needed to earn my own award and escape his drama.

"Wussup? You should see the waves at this hour. Primo!" shouted Derek.

I'd forgotten he was in Hawaii and quickly converted the time before realizing the sun was just rising over countless breathtaking beaches. For some reason, I'd been gifted with the ability to retain way too much useless knowledge. "Oh, I hope I'm not waking you up."

"I haven't gone to bed yet, Kel-baby. We're about to rent surfboards. You should be here, man."

Any traces of guilt I had about rousing him from a blissful slumber disappeared, knowing he's the one who'd sent me on this foolish diversion. "No can do, Derek. Trying to pin down your source is proving to be difficult. How is Abby Monroe connected to Braxton?"

The waves intensely crashed against the sand as he mumbled about paying for rental surfboards. Someday I'd learn to extricate myself from these situations, but until then, it was best not to get on his nasty side. The last time we'd had creative differences, he hired my replacement to trail me all day, threatening to cut me loose if I didn't acknowledge his authority.

"She's a piece of work, ain't she? Never would have guessed Abby looked like that. You meet her yet? Thanks for dealing with this one, Kel-baby." He ignored the question about Braxton.

"It's Kellan." I'd told him before not to call me Kel-baby. It reminded me of a high school girlfriend who'd forced me to watch every episode of *Saved by the Bell* one summer, trying to perfect her acting skills. I'd had enough of the *Kelly Kelly Duo* and never again would someone mistakenly call me *Kel* or *Kelly* as a nickname. "What's Abby look like? Is this another awful Tinder date I should know about?"

"Dude, I'm innocent, I swear. She's hot for an older babe. And it's about time you got some—"

"Stop right there. My personal life is off limits," I said, knowing he irritated the most patient of people. "How much do you know about Abby?"

"I was going to say *attention*. You're acting holier-than-thou lately, and it's time you took off that faulty halo and engaged in some fun. Seriously, man. Let loose and take some risks while the network's paying for your trip. I gotta jet. My date's getting antsy, and these waves are fierce."

"Wait! Answer my question about Abby."

"I barely know her. We met at a conference in New York City last month. I gave her my number and email address. Didn't you read the show bible with all the open questions? Abby needs to fill in those blanks. I'm counting on you, Kel-baby. Later."

"You mean you gave her your fake number, right?" Various methods of revenge formulated in my head. I wanted to remind *Derek-baby* what people said about payback, but halfway through my witty comeback, he hung up.

Derek was the second person since I'd arrived in Braxton who'd chosen that route. Was I doing something wrong? What happened to proper manners? There were rules. One person initiated a good-bye sequence, and the other held it up to share remaining thoughts. There's an awkward moment how to end the call, and then you both said goodbye at the same time before the actual disconnect. Either I was getting old, or other people were getting crazier. I mentally added it to the list of things to ask Nana D the next time I saw her. Despite her age, she had all the answers about the new etiquette system of my generation's people.

Hoping to shake off the conversation and alleviate the knots in my back, I went for an hour-long run in Braxton's fresh mountain air. Many parts of the town—topping out at about three-thousand citizens—offered natural, untouched beauty everyone had protected for three hundred years. Shortly before Pennsylvania had become a state, my ancestors developed the sheltered land where the Finnulia River emptied into Crilly Lake at the base of the Wharton Mountains. Though the landscape was intoxicating, I had little time left before the party. I returned home, showered, and dressed for the event.

Promptly at four thirty, I stood outside Memorial Library, assuming Eleanor would be late. Inevitably, there would be some crisis at the diner—a lost car key or a last-minute wardrobe change. It's lucky my sister's saving grace had always been she's the most intelligent, loyal, and caring person in my life. If not, her constant tardiness and indecisiveness would drive me batty and send me running in the opposite direction.

The Paddington family originally erected Memorial Library. A fire damaged the first floor in the late 1960s during a Vietnam War protest that had gone off the deep end. The powers-that-be in charge of the campus at the time had rebelled against old-world charm and preserving history. The result was a cheap repair of the antiquated structure and an institutional, utilitarian-looking addition reminding everyone of a grammar school cafeteria gone wrong. It needed to be demolished and redesigned more than our town's government.

While waiting for Eleanor, a woman on a cell phone wandered past me. She was explaining how she'd already finished marking the exam and was on her way to enter the results in her grade book. It sounded like an unhappy student was trying to change the professor's mind about his or her grade. The last line I caught before she was out of range made me laugh, thinking about how far someone would go to demand a better mark. *"Yes, come to my office at eight thirty. But trust me, you won't alter my decision. Nada. Zilch. You're killing me with this persistent pressure and the multiple diversion tactics,"* she chastised.

My gaze switched to several students milling in and out of Memorial Library, surprising me how popular it was on a Saturday evening. Although I'd been a decent student during my time at Braxton, I had reserved weekends for fraternity parties, off-campus troublemaking excursions, and strenuous visits with my family. Saturday nights at a library were uncool a decade ago. It seemed much had changed.

I considered following a student inside to gander at the dreary interior décor, but stopped when two snowballs slammed into my shoulder. Not one to back down from a challenge, I ducked to the ground to gather a handful of snow and steadied myself to throw a powerful curveball. Had an immature student taken advantage of my distraction, or was the professor using me to express her frustration with the caller?

"So, he *can* clean himself up for the proper occasion," taunted my sister, throwing another snowball. "I'd have placed a bet you'd wear the usual jeans and a gray t-shirt tonight."

Nope, my expensive black suit and herringbone topcoat looked quite dapper. I rolled both eyes in her direction several times with enough emphasis that they almost got stuck on the final lap. "Funny! I'd have placed a bet you wouldn't be here until five thirty, so you could tell Mom it was my fault we were late."

Eleanor meandered over and gave me the biggest hug I'd received since the last time I was in town. "I miss you so much. Why do you leave me here in this boring arctic tundra alone with our parents? Can't you work from Braxton part of... oh, fine, I'll stop. The stars are telling me not to pester you anymore tonight."

I agreed about the arctic part. I'd never get used to it, especially after gazing at palm trees and listening to ocean waves in Los Angeles. When we separated, I scanned her shocking and brilliant transformation. Her curly, dirty-blond hair was pinned to one side of her head with a bright crimson bow matching the color of her dress. She wore heels, which I hardly ever saw her in for two reasons—one, she was a tad clumsy, and two, she claimed it made her tower over potential male suitors. We were the same height, but in the sparkling Christian Louboutin stilettos she'd chosen, I couldn't reach her on the tips of my toes.

I only knew the brand and type of shoes because Francesca had trained me well. We spent many Sunday afternoons window shopping up and down Rodeo Drive, guessing the prices of everything she loved but for which she refused to pay full cost. Despite being raised with money, my wife had loved a good bargain.

"You could always move to the West Coast if you can't hack it here." I smiled at how grown-up my baby sister looked in her red-sequined gown. She possessed a unique fashion sense, imposing her own spin on each outfit. Today, it was the dark-gray sash worn across her hips. Eleanor had always been sensitive about inheriting the Danby bone structure and found ways to either accentuate or hide it—whichever improved her look, depending on the garb and the position of the moon that day. She was a fanatic about horoscopes, astrology, and numerology. "Or consult that crystal ball of yours to see what's in store for your future."

"Oh, shut your trap door. Someday we'll live closer together. The cards have already decided so. Tell me, who do you think will be there tonight besides the usual stuffy colleagues and friends? I've had a premonition about something dark happening. Not sure who's in trouble, but someone's aura is dust!"

As she said her last line, thunder struck in the nearby Wharton Mountains. We both jumped. Our eyes bulged with indeterminate shock. "Yeah, let's get to the party before you invoke some sort of ancient curse on us. You've got the worst luck lately."

Chapter 3

Eleanor grabbed my hand, leading us toward Braxton's main entrance gate. As we walked, I summarized the incendiary blog posts and our father's mysterious phone conversation.

"I hope the blogger does nothing to embarrass Dad tonight," Eleanor said.

"He can take care of himself." We agreed not to confront him since it wasn't our business.

Braxton's campus was spread out across two parts of town and connected by a charming, antique cable car service covering the one-mile distance in between. The trendy transportation system functioned like an airport trolley between terminals—leaving North Campus every thirty minutes to make the return trip back and forth to South Campus. When the weather cooperated, it was a brisk fifteen-minute walk to reach either end. Quaint shops, the occasional college bar, and student rental housing lined the streets.

"Even though most of the primary academic buildings and student dorms are on North Campus, I've always found South Campus more idyllic." Besides hosting the executive offices and the campus coffeehouse, The Big Beanery, South Campus also housed the music, humanities, and communications departments. Paddington's Play House and Stanton Concert Hall were the big entertainment attractions keeping me from being bored as a student.

"True. I'm looking forward to seeing Mom's artisanal handiwork. She thought it would be a fun twist to rearrange all the tables in Stanton Concert Hall to face the center of the room. Even brought in a temporary dance floor and a raised platform for the speeches." As the cable car arrived, Eleanor filled me in on her exciting day at the Pick-Me-Up Diner. Braxton's baseball team had caused a big ruckus at their impromptu lunch. "It was odd when the cheerleading squad showed up too. They should've been discussing strategies to win the opening game."

"Aww, were you jealous? Did it stop you from flirting with the players?" I was on fire today.

"Bite me, Kellan. Even Coach Oliver couldn't control them when he handed out the team's newest college jackets. The burgundy and navy-blue colors looked like a cool design."

I quipped, "We both know the real reason the team's onset annoyed you is because cash-limited students are notorious for leaving no tips."

When all the passengers disembarked, Eleanor and I squeezed into a two-seater near the back plastered with characters from Marvel comics. Each year, the graduating class presented a gift to the college to redesign the cable car as their outgoing mark on Braxton.

"Bring back any memories, *gladiator-man?*" asked Eleanor.

I'm ashamed to admit my class had chosen a Spartan theme since the movie *300* had just hit theaters. At the unveiling ceremony, they forced me to wear an extremely short, body-hugging tunic while wielding a plastic shield and spear. I'd almost died of embarrassment when the fabric split open as I kneeled for a picture. I hadn't looked as handsome back then as I did now. Yep, you gotta get used to this humor!

We arrived at Stanton Concert Hall, aptly named for Lavinia Stanton, an elderly spinster ancestor of Marcus Stanton's who'd left her entire life savings to Braxton in the early twentieth century. A lippy security attendant greeted me, snapped my picture, and typed in a few commands on a keypad. Thirty seconds later, he returned a badge with a bunch of codes and symbols.

"Can you make the machine explode when you create Eleanor's ID?" I asked the attendant, who unfortunately didn't find me hilarious. The process completed flawlessly.

The guest list topped out at two hundred colleagues, family members, and friends. I skimmed the expanse of the room with a fleeting thought that I could pick out Abby, but no one matched the imagined description.

My mother had outdone herself. She transformed the hall into a full-on party atmosphere complete with authentic, old-fashioned lampposts retrofitted as conversation tables where we could eat endless amounts of hors d'oeuvres; ornate beverage carts rolled around by penguin-clad waiters serving a fizzy blue cocktail; and a fine mist spraying jasmine from the ceiling. Eleanor went in search of our parents while I tested the aqua concoction. A bit tart for me, but I saw the appeal.

While mingling, I caught up with my former art professor and shook hands with Councilman Marcus Stanton—his palm was so clammy I'd never wipe off the pungent pool of sweat. The handshake was also too weak for a real politician. No wonder Nana D had it in for him.

When an incoming text vibrated, I hoped it was Abby, but it was from my daughter, Emma. She was back from the neighbors and wanted to tell me she missed me and loved me. I sent a video of a papa bear cuddling with his baby bear—our way of sharing a hug when we weren't in the same place together. She was intelligent and intuitive for her age and loved our quirky relationship. Six going on sixteen!

Before putting away the phone, I texted my father's assistant. Lorraine Candito had served as my father's right-hand woman for twenty years, including following him from his prior position at Woodland College across the river. I was certain she was the only reason I'd gotten birthday cards or frequent packages from my father. My mother was too busy and had her own way of showing how much she cared, but Lorraine was like a favorite aunt you could always count on. My phone buzzed with her response:

Let's connect after dinner. Need to get your gift. I left it on my desk.

Curiosity brewed, then I remembered something from Christmastime. She'd probably bought me a present with the new Braxton logo. I texted back a confirmation and caught sight of my father approaching from the dance floor.

"Let me introduce you to someone, Kellan," he began. A woman with short, spiky gray hair followed nearby. Her natural black shade had faded and rather than dye it, she'd accepted the graceful aging process. I commended her. If my hair color ever began to change, I'd be the first in line at the salon. I could be a bit vain about these things. Although her hair was striking, her pursed lips and icy stare stole my attention's focus.

I reached my hand to her, hoping the councilman's sweat had dissipated, or she'd be in for her own unpleasant shock. "Pleased to meet you... Mrs.... Miss...?"

My father continued talking when she failed to engage. "This is Dr. Myriam Castle. She's a professor in our communications department and has been at Braxton for... what, three years now?"

As she nodded, the temperature of the air between us distinctly dropped. It wasn't just the crisp, stark power suit molded against her thin frame. The deep and pointed collar of her pink dress shirt covered her entire neck and had a small opal and silver broach clasped over the top button. The lines on the shoulders, sleeves, and pant legs were as sharp as a knife blade, but the sensible black pumps convinced me she was a no-nonsense gal.

"Yes, three at the beginning of this last term. Are you enjoying the party the college has so thoughtfully thrown? It must have cost quite a small fortune to put on this show, but you are beloved around here for your... *generosity*," she replied with a tartness one only experienced when tasting something exorbitantly sour. "*Men's evil manners live in brass; their virtues we write in water.*"

I glanced from her to my father, anticipating an insightful and punishing retort. She'd quoted Shakespeare's *Henry VIII* in her petulant dig about virtues. Could she be the blogger? The acerbic tone of her words matched the profile of the anonymous villain.

"Oh, Myriam, ever the clever one. I'd love to chat, but I must prepare for my speech. I hope you'll have a splendid time despite it coming so unnaturally to you," my father replied.

As he walked away, a snicker formed on his lips. Maybe I *would* have some fun at this party. "I see you have quite the banter. I trust it's in good humor."

"Wesley Ayrwick and I have an understanding. He is aware of my contributions to the college. I am aware he'll be replaced imminently." As a server passed, Dr. Castle dropped her empty glass on a tray and grabbed a fresh one. "So, how do you know our fine president? Do you work at the college?"

Ah, she didn't know I was his son. I thought I'd leave out that fact to see what else I might learn. "I can't remember when we first met. Years ago, but it's all a little fuzzy. To answer your last question... no, I live in Los Angeles and am back in Braxton for a few days." I considered my options for extending the conversation about her opinions of my father, then realized I should take advantage of my opportunities. I had little time left before the speeches started. "Dr. Castle, are you familiar with Abby Monroe?"

My new friend cleared her throat and slid her glasses down the bridge of her nose. "My night keeps improving. Is that why you've attended this party? A guest of Monroe's?"

"On the contrary. I've never met the woman. Might you point her out?" I could tell Dr. Myriam Castle was an expressive woman. All her gestures were over-exaggerated, and her words offered two, maybe even three levels to them. "If you know what she looks like, that is."

"I've had the unwelcome privilege to meet Monroe many times. I'm not one to push my opinions on other people, Mister...?"

She hoped I'd fill in my surname, but it was more fun leaving her with the short end of the stick. "Oh, but I'd love to hear your thoughts. Please, feel comfortable sharing whatever's on your mind." I noticed a moment where Dr. Castle considered my words, then saw my father step to the podium.

"Monroe thinks the world of herself and has made it clear to everyone at Braxton how she got her job. An intelligent, savvy young man should easily recognize the elevator does not go all the way to the top floor in that woman's head." As she pivoted to leave, the boom of the microphone resounded.

I found it funny the way she called the woman *Monroe.* "It was a pleasure meeting you, Dr. Castle. I look forward to chatting again soon, but we need to gather around the center floor." I extended my hand in the stage's direction and watched her head lift higher and her nose wrinkle as though something odorous wafted by.

"Trust me. Stay clear of her. While you're in town, also be careful not to associate too closely with the Ayrwicks. They might be on top right now, but it won't be for long, I'm confident."

I shrugged and stepped in the opposite direction. Wait until I told Eleanor and Nana D all about Dr. Myriam Castle. Would they know any gossip about the woman? I needed to find out what this feud was all about. I sent a text to Abby asking when we could meet. She confirmed quickly, suggesting *nine in the foyer,* when the party ended.

My father's speech was better than I'd expected, as was Councilman Stanton's brief but remarkable words. Perhaps I could overlook the flimsy handshake if his verbal skills were a strong counterbalance. Dinner was relatively tasty—chicken cordon bleu, rice pilaf, and steamed asparagus. I saw a vegetarian dish at a few tables too. Kudos to my mother for remembering other people's needs and preferences. Ever since she'd developed a shellfish allergy, she became much more attentive to food choices.

I'd already sampled one fizzy blue drink and one glass of champagne earlier and was now standing near a portable bar cart, contemplating a third, when my sister approached. "Guess whom I ran into?" she sang in an awkward, jovial tone. "Don't turn around. I'll give you three chances."

I thought I'd met everyone at the party given how often I introduced myself in the last few hours, except of course for Abby, the one person I wanted to come across. Could my luck be changing? "Ummm... The Queen? Meryl Streep?" She's my favorite actress. A guy could dream, right? "Pink?" I had a crush on her for years, yet it was highly unlikely she'd show up for a retirement party. Now that I'd exhausted my three guesses, the silly game could end, and I could turn around.

"Wrong! It's Maggie Roarke. You remember her, right?" Eleanor teased while hopping up and down like an overzealous Easter bunny.

The room stood still, and I was transported back a decade. Even the song playing in the background felt like I'd leaped through time and was sitting on a giant comfy couch at The Big Beanery, listening to Michael Bublé croon while Maggie and I sipped cappuccinos and ate biscotti. I hadn't seen my best friend and former girlfriend since we'd broken up at our college graduation. "Maggie, I can't believe I didn't notice you earlier. You look... you look...." I wanted to say fantastic and gorgeous, but after ten years, it didn't seem appropriate.

"I look marvelous, Kellan. It's okay, you can say it." Her luscious straight brown hair was pulled back across one shoulder. There was a radiant shine making her more attractive today than when we were in our early twenties. She looked confident and decisive, traits she'd always envied but struggled to find in the past. "You're as handsome as ever."

When I leaned in to embrace her, instinct took over. I kissed her cheek, and my body flooded with an unusual yet familiar warmth. Alabaster skin shined, and deep brown eyes peered back at me, almost making her look like a frozen statue or an elegant piece of porcelain. "I'm sorry. It was a surprise to see you. A welcome surprise."

Eleanor chimed in, sensing she should give us a moment alone. "Oh, there's Mom. I've been looking for her. I'll be back." As she stepped away, a quick pinch at my waist confirmed she'd planned the setup. Retaliation for my earlier comments about her crystal ball search for the future. Score one for Eleanor tonight. At least she joined the playing field.

"I agree," Maggie replied. "You must be so excited your father is retiring. Will your mother leave next? They should travel the world after working so hard for Braxton. I'll miss seeing them."

Maggie and I had separated when we attended different graduate schools. We tried to maintain a friendship, but we were both secretly upset with the other for not trying to make a long-distance relationship work. We'd emailed that summer, yet once she left for Boston, all communication stopped. It suddenly occurred to me what she'd said about missing my parents. "Great seeing you, but what brings you to the party, Maggie?"

"Oh, you don't know? I started working at Braxton this semester as the new head librarian. I moved back from Boston after the job fell into my lap. Do you remember Mrs. O'Malley?" Maggie announced it was too loud near the rest of the crowd, so we stepped to the far corner.

Mrs. O'Malley had been the head librarian for over thirty years when we'd attended Braxton—a fixture who knew everything and everyone on campus. She'd once caught Maggie and I making out behind the ancient microfiche machine and rather than scold us for getting intimate in a public place, she embarrassed us for picking the oldest piece of equipment in the building as our romantic hiding place. She told us even she had the intelligence to take Mr. Nickels, the cable car's engineer, to the downstairs reference section where no one had ever gone. Imagine a sixty-something lovesick woman shaking her finger at two college seniors over that.

"I haven't thought about her in forever. I guess she retired." I wasn't a granny chaser, but I'd felt a weird attraction to Mrs. O'Malley after she'd told us about her illicit affair.

"Last fall. I'd gotten the strangest call. We'd kept in touch over the years, and she wanted me to know about her plans to leave Braxton. Mrs. O'Malley was the primary reason I earned my advanced degrees in library studies. She invited me back to talk about the changes happening at Memorial Library, then had me meet with your father to discuss the position. Three weeks later, I gave notice to my job in Boston."

I couldn't believe how much Maggie had changed. Gone was the little mouse I used to know and adore. I always wondered what would've happened if Maggie and I had decided differently that day.

"That's awesome. I'm thrilled and also a trifle shocked my father never mentioned it."

"Or your mother. She and I meet for coffee when I can take a break from the library, or when she needs to get away from prospective students pressuring her for an acceptance decision." Maggie brushed several bangs from her soft and stunning features. "You know nothing about our weekly walk from South to North Campus along Millionaire's Mile?"

Behind the main road between campuses were larger estates where families like the Stantons, Greys, and Paddingtons lived. We had nicknamed it Millionaire's Mile long ago, and it was a key attraction in Braxton for visitors and new students who wanted to learn about the history of the town's wealth.

I shook my head. "I'll find out later. Now that I know you're back in Braxton, let's grab a coffee. I'll be in town for a week, maybe more." We chatted about the last decade, and I discovered her husband had tragically died of a brain aneurysm several years ago. My heart broke for her at having to go through the devastating loss of a spouse, but it was also a moment where our connection flourished like when we'd dated in college. It was in that instant I felt a sense of security about the future, as though reestablishing a friendship with Maggie might help me move forward.

I glanced toward the hall's entrance, where my father's assistant dashed into the room. Even at this distance, something looked off. Lorraine's blue dress was slightly askew, and her eyes darted erratically. She was clearly agitated and looking for someone. In the distraction, I failed to hear Maggie's response.

"Kellan, where did you go?" Maggie tapped my shoulder. "I'd love to meet at The Big Beanery to catch up on life post-college. Emma sounds delightful."

My gaze returned to Maggie. "We should do it. Definitely," I countered and rattled off my cell phone number. "Do you know my father's assistant, Lorraine?"

"Yes, such a sweet woman. I wonder if she's retiring now that your father will leave Braxton this semester."

It hadn't occurred to me, nor could I remember my father saying anything. "She's walking this way and looks quite unraveled. I hope the food's not making people sick."

Maggie and I turned toward the entrance and waited for her arrival. I spoke first. "Lorraine, it's so wonderful to see you. Everything okay?"

"Your father... dead body...." Lorraine struggled to respond, then slumped to the floor.

Chapter 4

While I reached for Lorraine's left arm, Maggie propped her against a table. "What's wrong? Are you ill?" I worried she was having a stroke or heart attack. She looked practically catatonic.

"I'm afraid your father... have you seennn hhhim?" Her breathing labored, and a look of terror possessed her face. Though her skin was usually quite pale, she looked nearly translucent.

What did she mean by *a dead body*? She'd aged ten years in those moments. I pulled out my phone and pressed the button to dial his cell. "What's going on, Lorraine?" Maggie briefly slipped away and returned with a glass of water. People had begun to leave the party. My phone verified it was exactly nine o'clock. The call went to voicemail. I didn't leave a message, as I had no idea what to say.

"I saw... ummm... someone needs to... check on... now!" She pointed out the window and covered her mouth. Exaggerated expressions produced unfortunate wrinkles on her forehead. "I'm sorry... such a shock."

"What?" I grew fearful over what she might have seen. "Did something happen to my father?"

Maggie rubbed Lorraine's back to comfort the panicked woman. "Talk to us."

Lorraine finished drinking her water. "I went back to the office to get your Christmas present. It was so lovely, and... but then I...."

I nodded. "That was thoughtful, thank you. But surely that's not what has you so upset." I had no clue what caused her to approach hyperventilation mode. "What about my father?"

"I couldn't find him, that's why I came to you. Went to the back door... closer to my desk... working there temporarily... finish all the construction." Lorraine paused and let out a deep breath. Her hazel eyes shifted and filled with wild anxiety. "I got the key to unlock it... saw it was partially open."

I wasn't sure what she'd meant by temporarily working elsewhere, but I didn't want to interrupt her baffling train of thought. "Okay. Did you go inside?"

"No, I couldn't. I tried to push the door open... wouldn't budge. It only moved an inch... crack wasn't wide enough to stick my head through. That's when I ran around to the front of the building... used the main entrance."

"Keep talking, tell us everything." Maggie's gaze went broad with confusion.

Lorraine composed herself. "I walked through the hallway to the back of the building. I thought I could open the other door leading into the stairwell from the inside, but it wouldn't move either. Something was sitting on the platform, preventing both doors from opening."

"Right. It's such a tight space. Two people can't open the doors at the same time since they both open inward," Maggie responded. "Then what?"

Lorraine explained she'd gone up to the second floor to look down the stairwell and see what was on the other side of the doors. While she painfully told us everything—probably suffering from shock over what she'd seen—I wondered why my father had left the party. Had he gone to meet someone? Why wasn't he picking up my calls? Was there really a dead body?

"Somebody fell down the stairs. I could see blood. I thinkkk they hit their head. Might be deaddd," Lorraine stuttered with a wicked shiver.

Maggie stifled a scream. Her body twitched from the tension. She'd been leaning against me as we comforted Lorraine. "Who was it?"

Lorraine's eyes opened wider. "I was too afraid to go down. Will you checkkk the building next door?"

Maggie offered to stay and take care of Lorraine while I went to the other building. My stomach sank in fear something horrific had happened to my father.

"No, I have to come with you," Lorraine murmured. "I locked the front door after I left. I... I... didn't know what to do and just came running over here."

Lorraine had either drank too many fizzy blue concoctions or was imagining things in the dark, but intuition told me something real had genuinely frightened her. The three of us left the retirement party and scrambled toward the temporary office space. Meeting Abby would have to wait. I encouraged the ladies to run faster, eager to see what had happened to my father or someone else.

"I'm going as fast as I can," Lorraine noted.

Heaviness settled in my chest, and a sharp pain jabbed my gut. Please don't be my father. I wasn't ready for him to get sick or die. When Maggie, Lorraine, and I arrived at the building, it became clear she'd been referring to Diamond Hall, where I'd spent many hours attending literature, art, and media lectures. It hadn't occurred to me when Lorraine said the building next door she'd meant *literally next door* to Stanton Concert Hall. My father's normal executive office building was farther away near the cable car station. Was the threatening call I'd overheard the previous night that serious?

Diamond Hall, an old colonial-style mansion, had been converted into a series of classrooms and departmental offices a few decades earlier. A limestone facade mined from local Betscha quarries in the 1870s covered all three stories of the impressive building. The well-manicured primary entrance contained a winding slate path, burgundy shutters adorning large, crisscross lattice windows, and giant rhododendron bushes growing in the front gardens. On the first floor were four large classrooms, each capable of seating at least thirty students, two single bathrooms, and a small supply closet. In the front entrance was a staircase set between two center walls taking visitors to the upper floors, and in the back was another small stair-case—previously a servant's access passage—allowing professors direct access to their offices without having to go through the main classroom area.

"Show me exactly where you saw a body, Lorraine," I directed with increasing trepidation in my voice. "We should call 9-1-1, but I'd like to verify what you saw before we—"

"It's a body. I know what I saw, Kellan," Lorraine interjected with a much calmer voice than when she'd first informed us. "Follow me."

We ran up to the second floor where ten or twelve oddly shaped offices—typically the center of many vocal professors arguing about who deserved the biggest space—resided. While there was no staircase accessing the third floor from the back side of the building, a narrow one in the front led to a cozy library and common area for students working on a group project or a professor holding a special lecture session. Based on what Lorraine had told me on the walk over, my father recently commandeered the third floor during the renovations on his office. Since the top floor was only large enough for his furniture, given the peaks of the slanted roof and the built-in library shelves, Lorraine sat in a central open section on the second floor between the two staircases.

My stomach twisted in agony. There was a good chance my father could be at the bottom of the stairwell. All three of us crossed through the second floor past Lorraine's desk and looked at the swinging door to the back stairwell. "Did you leave it open?"

She shook her head. "I thought I'd closed it. Maybe I ran out and didn't pay attention. The body is inside. Step into the vestibule and look down to the right."

I'd seen a few dead bodies in the past. It had never bothered me until they called me to the morgue to verify Francesca's identity on Thanksgiving. I still remember the fear moments before they lifted the sheet. I ultimately couldn't do it and stepped out of the silent and frigid room, grateful to my father-in-law for taking on the responsibility. I had to be brave and determine if Lorraine were losing her mind or if there was any truth to what she'd seen. I tiptoed into the vestibule with my eyes closed, turned to the right, and felt my composure fade. I slanted my head at the angle I thought would align with the bottom platform and opened my eyes.

The way the body laid on the floor all tangled up was the most horrid part. Two legs were folded under the person's upper half, and his or her head was trapped between twisted hands and arms. That's when I breathed a sigh of relief. It wasn't my father. It was the woman I'd seen outside the library on the phone while waiting for my sister.

I'd been quiet for too long, prompting Maggie to screech, "What's going on, Kellan?"

I peeked my head around the corner of the wall and observed a shaky Maggie and Lorraine holding hands. "Yes, someone's down there. I can't tell if she's breathing."

"Please go check, Kellan. She could be hurt," begged Lorraine while puttering with several pieces of costume jewelry on her wrist.

I shuffled down the steps. Something told me the victim was a goner. When I reached the platform, there wasn't a lot of room to move around, but I stretched my nervous hand to the woman's neck.

"Is she alive? Should I call 9-1-1?" Maggie asked.

"No, she's dead. There's no pulse, but we need to call them, anyway."

Lorraine yelled back at me. "I'm on my way down. I'm well enough to assist."

Maggie dialed the emergency line and explained the situation on speakerphone. When Lorraine reached the last step and stood a few inches from me, she grabbed my elbow. "Can you turn her head? I think I recognize her."

"Not a good idea. If she's just unconscious, we could cause spinal damage." This wasn't the night I'd expected. I wanted something livelier than a boring retirement party where I listened to dull speeches and met my father's insipid friends and colleagues—not dealing with a dead body.

Lorraine leaned forward over my shoulders. I cautioned her to avoid the patch of blood on the stairs. The woman must have smacked her skull hard when she fell, to cause it to bleed like that. Just as I thought Lorraine was going to back away, she gasped. "Oh, my word! I know her."

I wasn't in the mood to comfort someone else over death right now, especially if they were friendly with the person. I merely wanted to give a statement and locate Eleanor. "Ummm… who is she, Lorraine?"

"Abby Monroe," squealed Lorraine with a series of "It can't be, it can't be" wails.

Maggie bellowed to us from the top of the stairwell. "The ambulance is on its way. The cops are coming too. I should call Connor."

When I first heard the name, my immediate thought shifted to my other former best friend and fraternity brother, Connor Hawkins. He and I had stopped chatting around the time we'd all graduated ten years ago too. "Hold up, Maggie. Lorraine thinks she knows who this is." Tonight was becoming way too creepy.

"I couldn't tell from way up top, but I saw her at the party earlier wearing this same outfit. Dean Terry remarked how well that sapphire blue empire-cut blouse matched her eyes. And that skirt… Abby always wears pencil skirts." Lorraine nervously pulled at her blond curls.

"Are you sure? I've been looking for Abby Monroe all evening," I said.

Lorraine wobbled her head. Based on the peculiar expression on her pale face, my news had confused her. "Why were you meeting her? Maybe we should wait for the cops upstairs. I feel a little weird standing so close to… you know… ummm—"

"The body?" I tossed both hands in the air. Things were not going well since I'd returned home to Braxton. "I'll explain another time why I was meeting her." As we both climbed the stairs to the second floor, Lorraine awkwardly grinned back at me.

When we arrived, Maggie rested her hand against her forehead. "Connor will be here any minute. He'd just gotten to the retirement party to wish your father well."

"Ummm… Connor who?" Given the number of times I'd been surprised already that night with Maggie returning to Braxton, finding

Abby at the bottom of a stairwell, and meeting the peculiar Myriam Castle, I had an inkling Maggie's Connor would be our Connor from years ago.

"Connor Hawkins. Don't you remember anyone, Kellan?" shot her somewhat sassy response. The drama of finding a dead body was causing everyone to be irritable and short-tempered.

"Did I hear my name?" boomed a deep voice across the hall. A darker-skinned man a few inches taller than me walked past the central admin area and hugged Maggie. They whispered something and shared an intimate connection.

Yep, it was the same Connor. But it was also an extraordinarily different Connor. This Connor obviously spent his day working out at the gym or popping steroids. "Is that really you?" I asked in puzzlement, looking from him to the stairwell hiding Abby's lifeless body.

"Kellan, what are you doing here?" He wrinkled his brow and jolted his head sideways.

"Well, yeah, it seems kind of obvious being that it's my father's retirement party." I hadn't meant to sound like a jerk, but I was a bit off-kilter given everything happening that evening.

"I know… I meant at Diamond Hall," Connor said authoritatively.

A desperate sense of loss surrounded me. Connor, Maggie, and I had been inseparable all throughout college. When Maggie and I had broken up, he took her side and told me how stupid I was to let her go. What had happened to him after Braxton?

I responded, "Lorraine found the body and sought help. I was the nearest person she could find." Visions of Francesca's last moments plagued me. I couldn't think straight.

Connor moved uncomfortably in his light tan suit and striped Braxton tie, but it was a powerful offset to his cocoa-touched skin. His mother was from the Caribbean, and his father was a South African sailor on leave from the navy when they'd met. Connor had inherited the best features from both and was always considered charming and gorgeous by the girls who melted anytime they heard his accent. Back in school, he'd been in decent shape, but he could now pass for a twin to Adonis. "I can't believe you're here. And Abby is there. How did...?"

Maggie tapped her foot. "Although I'm sure you boys can't wait to catch up, maybe Braxton's crack security team could do a quick check on the body randomly hanging out at the bottom of the stairs?"

"It's Abby Monroe, the chair of the communications department," Lorraine insisted.

"I'll go check. Are you sure she's already dead?" Connor added with a pointed stare.

I nodded. "Pretty certain. You're a security guard now?"

"No, he's your father's *head* of security for the college. Do you not know about that either?" sniped Maggie. The shock was overwhelming all of us.

I swallowed my tongue and pride. My parents had some explaining to do. "Let's not get into that right now. Did she trip over something and hit her head?" Nobody responded. As Connor descended the steps, I turned to Lorraine. "Are you okay? Did you know Abby well?"

Before she could respond, two people strutted across the second-floor office space. A familiar, mid-thirties blonde in a pair of dark jeans, an ill-fitting tweed coat, and standard-issue beat-walking shoes announced, "I'm Sheriff Montague. There's been a report of someone falling down a flight of stairs?" She turned to her colleague, a male cop with a crew cut, an enormous nose that must have been broken several times, and a pair of furry earmuffs. "This is Officer Flatman."

"I'm down in the stairwell, Sheriff Montague," shouted Connor.

While the two newest arrivals followed Connor's voice to the body, I thought about what Abby's death would mean to Derek's plans for the second season of *Dark Reality*. I should have called him right away, but I had no information other than she'd died. I also tried to reach my father, but he didn't pick up again. I called my mother.

"Kellan, I've been looking for you for nearly an hour. Please don't tell me you left already," my mother said in a shrill voice. She should have been an actress instead of Braxton's admissions director.

"No, I'm… outside. Is Dad around? I need to talk with him about something… important." I didn't want to alarm my mother, given how easily agitated she'd become since my arrival.

"I was looking for him myself, but he got pulled into an urgent meeting and said he'd find me at some point tonight. You know your father, even in near-retirement, he still feels obligated to remain a workaholic."

I mumbled something to my mom, making it sound like I agreed with her, and told her I'd be back to the party as soon as possible. I turned to Maggie and Lorraine to verify what they were doing. Lorraine chatted on the phone with someone, but I couldn't determine his or her identity. Something about urgently returning a call that evening to discuss what she'd found.

Maggie sat on a guest chair opposite Lorraine's desk and fiddled with her earlobes. She'd always played with them when nervous or worried about something life changing. "It's awful to know she fell down the stairs, and no one was here to help her. I hope she didn't experience any pain."

I was about to reach out and wrap my arms around Maggie when Connor bounded into the room. "Okay, so Sheriff Montague asked me to tell you three not to leave. She has some questions about the order of events tonight, but she's still finishing a cursory review of the body. It's definitely Abby Monroe. I saw her leaving Stanton Concert Hall about a quarter after eight while I was doing my nightly walk through campus."

Lorraine perked up after finishing her call. "Is she really… dead?" A trail of mascara stained her cheek.

Connor nodded. "Yes, Mrs. Candito. The coroner will be here in a few minutes, but she's been dead for under an hour. I've seen this type of thing before."

Connor's response made me curious what he'd been up to the last ten years. What was going on between him and Maggie? My concentration broke when Lorraine burst into tears. Maggie comforted her.

Connor strode toward me. I didn't know whether to grab his fingers using our secret fraternity greeting or hover there in silence. I was grateful when he made the first move—a typical handshake, no double tuck and punch like the old days. "What a way to reconnect tonight, huh?"

"Yeah, feels like a nightmare. Over a professor falling down a flight of steps and dying."

Connor rubbed his temple. "Tragic, but it's far worse. She didn't just fall down the steps."

I thought I'd misheard my former best friend, but his panicked expression revealed I hadn't. "What do you mean? How can it be any worse than death?"

"It wasn't an accident." Connor stared at me, deliberating what he should and shouldn't reveal.

My eyes popped open like a deer caught in headlights. "Did she try to kill herself?" Though I felt both stupid and silly about the question, I barely knew anything about the woman. Anyone who hooked up with Derek was slightly off her rocker.

"No, that's not what I mean. Sheriff Montague wouldn't want me to say this, but the blood on the ground came from a deep gash behind Abby's ear. There were some metal flakes mixed throughout her hair in the middle of the wound."

"Wouldn't that be from when she hit the steps?" I scanned the room, filling with edginess over being around another dead body.

"Nope. She had a giant egg on the front of her head where she hit the steps. The wound on the back of her scalp was a much harder blow. Plus, there's nothing on the stairs or the floor that has any metal. It's all solid marble. We're looking at a murder tonight, Kellan."

Chapter 5

"Maybe your old man snapped his lid and killed that mischievous woman?" Nana D said as I scooped a forkful of cherry pie between my drooling lips. Given the cops had kept me on campus until two in the morning, I'd gotten minimal sleep. I was surprised to make it to Danby Landing on time.

"My father, Braxton's presidential killer! Wharton County News at eleven," I spat out between bites with a boisterous chuckle. Nana D's had it in for my father for as long as I can remember, but she's equally free with the barbs against my mother, her own daughter. "You're not supposed to know it was murder. I don't think Sheriff Montague wants that released."

"Listen here! I've got my finger on the pulse of this town. I knew before *you* it was murder," taunted my five-foot-tall nana while dropping another piece of pie on my plate. "Eat up."

"How's that possible?" Was she about to tell me she was psychic like Eleanor? All we needed was two of them in the family. Maybe they could get their own show like the *Long Island Medium*.

"I've got my ways. All part of my master plan. Keep up on the news, stay connected to hear all the gossip, and find out what's happening around town." Nana D slurped her coffee while fastening her nearly three-foot-long braid to the top of her head. She waffled between wearing her red tresses loose and tying them in a braid around the crown of her noggin—as she called it—depending on her activities for the day. It had to be dyed, but Eleanor's best guess was a henna rinse.

"Why did you call her a *mischievous woman*?" I recalled the conversation I'd overheard about a student's grades when Abby had been inches away from me the previous night.

"I never much cared for that tart. Sneaky type. Hassled with me over the price of a bushel of apples. I'm certain she filled her pockets with three extra grannies at the farmer's market last weekend."

"What else can you tell me about her?" I asked after updating Nana D on my reasons for trying to meet the late professor. "Anything bad enough for someone to want to murder her?"

Nana D loved her gossip and gave as good as she got when unearthing everyone's secrets. I didn't know how she did it or whom she bribed, but if there were information to be found, Nana D was the first in line. She's like the Mata Hari of the Americas, and I was even certain she knew the dance. Nana D had pushed her boundaries ever since my mother pressured her into semi-retirement from running Danby Landing on her own. In its heyday, the farm was the most productive, income-generating business in the entire county, but as the industry changed and the maintenance costs doubled, she sold off parts to a real estate company who built Willow Trees, a senior citizen's residential complex. With the new freedom, she'd taken on the role of community watchdog, ensuring she kept everyone in line. I swear she carried a stun gun just to watch people dance for her own pleasure sometimes.

"Murder's a funny thing, Kellan. Sometimes it's premeditated, but there's also the spur-of-the-moment killing when you can't control your emotions. I thought about murdering Grandpop a few times. Run him down with the tractor or stab him with the pitchfork while baling hay. Always too much of a mess to clean up, so I let him live." She snatched a piece of crust off the pie and dipped it into the cherry filling. "Mmm, I've surpassed myself again."

She'd never really thought about killing Grandpop. They'd been sweethearts since they'd fallen in love at thirteen at a drive-in movie theater. "That was kind of you not to kill him. I'd have missed spending all those summers with Grandpop if you offed him before he died of that heart attack."

"I miss that delicious man every day. The things he could do to my body just by winking at me. Did I ever tell you about the time he—"

"Stop, Nana D. I don't want to hear about it." I dropped my fork and covered my ears before they bled uncontrollably. "What about Abby?"

"That's what's wrong with you kids today… always so politically correct and sensitive about making love. Lost your emotions." Nana D washed our plates in the corner sink of her quaint kitchen.

"Focus, Nana D. I'm curious what you know about Abby or who might want her dead."

Nana D wrinkled her nose and squinted her eyes. "She was the type to piss off the dangerous people in this world by asking too many questions. Someone pushed her down the stairs to shut her up."

"I don't know how you know these things, but I trust your instincts," I consented, then grabbed a dish towel and began drying.

I filled her in on the events at the party before stumbling across Abby Monroe in the stairwell. Nana D planned to start a petition to have the councilman removed from office because of his sweaty hands. She'd try anything to get Marcus Stanton out of office ever since he'd served her with a summons for improper waste removal at the farm. Nana D might have dumped a bucket filled with manure from her tractor's front-loader over the fence into his backyard last year, claiming the machine had malfunctioned. Unfortunately, it occurred during his family's Labor Day barbecue, and they'd been standing on the other side of the fence when it happened. I'm still unsure how or why their war ever started. "I've got to head downtown to the Wharton County Sheriff's Office to sign some statements. What are your plans today, Nana D? Harassing Councilman Stanton? Prank calling Ms. Paddington again?"

Nana D stuck out her tongue and made childish noises. "Didn't I tell you I started teaching music lessons again? Gotta fetch my old clarinet before she gets here." Nana D wrapped foil around the pie and placed it on the shelf in the refrigerator. "Keeps me young spending time with the college kids."

"Really? No, you hadn't mentioned it. I was thinking about teaching Emma to play the clarinet. She loves music and seems agile with her fingers. Maybe she'll follow in your footsteps."

"Well, you never could play worth a darn, could ya?" Nana D slapped my cheek until it hurt. "Talent might have skipped a few generations, but you sure got Grandpop's good looks. You probably drive all the girls crazy too." Nana D and Grandpop used to hold concerts at Danby Landing, entertaining the visitors and employees each weekend. Grandpop played the piano and guitar while Nana D sang and played the clarinet. She'd given it all up when he died, informing everyone it was *their thing to do together* and *all good things end, eventually.*

"Maybe so," I replied as the doorbell rang. "Want me to get that?"

"Yes, please, that would be Bridget. Go introduce yourself while I get the clarinet and make a call about a meeting I have later today," Nana D replied, winking and smirking.

"What are you up to now?" I narrowed my eyes and leaned my head in her direction. "More trouble?" I pictured news reporters showing up at my father's door and asking why he killed one of his professors, or a fake college student calling my mother to tell her he'd fallen in love with her and would do *anything* to attend Braxton. Nana D played way too many jokes on them in the past.

"Go get the door. Make yourself useful and quit being a party-pooper, love." Nana D disappeared down the hallway while I scurried through the living room and opened the front door.

Standing on the porch was a girl harboring an odd expression on her face—a cross between dumbstruck confusion and a pouty, angry elf. Not that I'd ever seen a real-life elf, but her ears were pointy, and she had these big, bright eyes that seemed to glow. I was afraid she might change shapes in front of me. "Hello," I said curtly and cautiously.

"You're not Seraphina," questioned the elf. "Am I too early again?"

I shrugged as I didn't know what time she was supposed to be here. She wore striped red and white leggings and an oversized green parka. Granted, it was freezing outside, but the outfit truly reminded me of the Elf-on-a-Shelf appearing every Christmas in the Castigliano mansion for my daughter, Emma. I wanted to ask why the elf couldn't use magic to answer her own question, but since I didn't know her, it might sound a tad obnoxious of me. Was she a good or a bad elf? I had enough crazy juju already and didn't need the vengeance of a nasty imp. Given Nana D expected someone for music lessons, there was a decent chance she was Bridget. "Not that I know. Come on in."

The elf stepped through the entryway and waited for me to say something else. "Ummm... so...?"

"Are you here for the Vespa driving lessons?" Perhaps I'd inherited too much of Nana D's wit. "We're bandaging up the last student, but don't worry... we put the bobcat back in its cage."

"If that's humor, I feel bad for you." The elf removed her coat. "I'm Bridget. Who are you?"

Bridget was a petite girl who seemed capable of holding her own. Besides her elf outfit, she had chestnut brown hair pulled back in a ponytail, emerald green eyes, and minimal makeup. It dawned on me this might be another romantic setup. Nana D had tried to match me up with a traveling horse groomer over the Christmas break until we learned not only had the woman already been married, but she was wanted in two other states for bigamy.

"Are you for real or is this part of Nana D's hoax?" I had to know if I was about to be played by my clever grandmother. It might've been early enough to convince Bridget, the elf, to join my team.

Bridget hung her coat on the rack, pushed past me into the living room, and dropped her backpack on the coffee table. "You're weird. You must be Kellan. Seraphina told me about you at last week's lesson."

So, the elf was smarter than she dressed. "Yes, I guess you must be normal if she's told you about me. How long have you been playing the clarinet?"

"I'm twenty-one. Started when I was nine. I'm sure you're capable of doing the math." As she sat on the couch across from me, she pulled out a couple of reeds and several sheets of music. "Are you gonna listen in and harass me today? Cause I didn't sign up for a super judgy audience."

I shook my head. I had places to be and needed to update Derek about Abby. With the retirement party over and no more source for season two, I could head back to Los Angeles early. Although the crime buff inside me wanted to do my own investigation into Abby's murder, it was secondary to escaping my parents. "Nope. Just visiting my nana. I'm leaving soon."

"So, I see you've met," Nana D announced, holding the clarinet behind us. "Behaving yourself, Kellan?"

I feigned a look of shock. "Of course, I always do."

Nana D glanced at Bridget, who responded, "He's been a perfect gentleman. I can see the resemblance between you two. He's got your humor and your nose. Like a little button." Bridget nervously laughed and reached for her bag.

"Well, I need to make a few calls, Nana D. I'll check in with you later. Anything with your *afternoon meetings* that I need to prepare for?" I questioned with a growing angst and curiosity.

"Not at all, dear. I'm not up to anything, at least nothing that your mother should worry about."

"Or Dad? I've heard he's a bit shaken about the... issue... from last night." I suddenly remembered I wasn't supposed to talk about it, per Sheriff Montague.

"Nothing for him to fret over either. Now skedaddle, please. I've got more important people to spend my time with." Nana D shoved me out the door before I could say goodbye to Bridget.

I drove to the sheriff's office and signed my official statement. In Wharton County, there was one sheriff and a few detectives to cover all the towns, including Braxton. Local police in each town ensured smaller crimes were addressed and minor ordinances were obeyed while the sheriff's office handled major crimes, specifically murder and grand larceny. The sheriff was out on an interview, but Officer Flatman who'd been on campus the night before was glad to assist. Stepping away from his desk, I saw a notation on a post-it about contact with an Alton Monroe. Next of kin? Something to follow up on.

Eleanor lured me over by offering to prepare an amazing meal. Ten minutes later, I sat at a corner booth at the Pick-Me-Up Diner and devoured my ham and cheese egg white omelet with avocado on the side. I needed something healthy to offset the two pieces of pie I'd already eaten for breakfast. Gone from last night was the relaxed sister who'd rocked a gorgeous dress, and in its place was a serious worker-bee in a pair of stained khakis, Keds, and a faded black polo shirt. Her hair was still pinned up, but she hardly had any makeup on today. Working in a diner would prevent a clean and spiffy appearance.

"Mom and Dad were meeting with Braxton's public relations director about the accident. Dad told me a bit about Abby. Poor woman, I can't believe she fell down the steps and died."

"Did Dad know her well?" I considered revealing what Connor had shared about it not being an accident. Bad enough Nana D had figured it out, I couldn't let it slip again.

"She'd been the chair of the communications department for many years, but they didn't get along well. After a few months, Dad decided she didn't properly represent Braxton. By then, they'd already granted tenure, which meant he had no simple way to get rid of Abby," Eleanor said.

A server cleared the plates, impressing her boss by wiping the table, asking how everything tasted, and suggesting different dessert options. I declined, knowing I'd already have to run twice as long that afternoon.

"What's the latest word on the over-achieving end of our family?" I asked Eleanor, who kept in contact with our older siblings much more than I did.

"Eh, Penelope seems happy, though there are days I wonder if she might not be looking for an excuse to have an early mid-life crisis," Eleanor replied.

"She has her hands full with the kids. But she loves it all, and I can't imagine she'd have given up any part of her life." I secretly knew Penelope was hoping to buy a larger stake in her real estate firm. "What about your brother?"

"Hampton's your brother too, no matter how much you two fight," she replied. "And with Gabriel refusing to talk to any of us, we can't ignore him."

"Yep, I should behave more brotherly to the Hampster." Don't even ask why I call him that, as it's been his nickname forever. Hampton, four years older than me, was a lawyer in Tulsa and married to an oil heiress who never let him go anywhere.

"He's coming to town soon to share news," Eleanor said. "I bet his wife's pregnant again."

I cringed at the thought of four kids under the age of six. "Speaking of Dad, did Mom say where he disappeared to last night? I tried to contact him. He never answered his phone." It was odd that he didn't even text me back, but I figured he got caught up in controlling the release of any information to the media. "Connor thought—"

"No, I left shortly after the party ended." Eleanor looked peculiar when her face flushed a deeper shade of red. Did she know something she wasn't telling me?

"I see. How about Connor working at Braxton? I was surprised to hear about that."

Eleanor shuffled across the booth. "Yeah, big changes, huh? Well, I need to check on a couple of things in the kitchen, which means you need to jet. I'll call you later. Hugs and kisses."

We said our goodbyes, which felt a little awkward given how abruptly she hightailed it out of the booth. I texted Maggie to see if she wanted to meet for dinner, but she had plans already. Instead, she suggested I stop by Memorial Library the next day. I confirmed, then bit the bullet to call Derek.

Astonishingly, he answered on the first ring. "How's the research going?"

"Not so well. There's been an incident," I said, angst rising inside my body. I couldn't tell him she'd been murdered, but it suddenly crossed my mind that he'd pawned her off on me. Could things have gone sour between them, and he was somehow involved in her death?

"Do tell. You know I'm counting on you to help put this background material to bed, so we can start this project as soon as possible, right?" replied Derek.

"Abby died last night." I pondered what kind of response I'd receive to my news. Would he be nervous? Relieved? Cool and collected?

Derek laughed hysterically. "That's a great one, Kel-baby. First time I've heard that excuse to get out of a work assignment. Awesome way to make me laugh, dude."

Not a reaction I'd considered. "Seriously, ummm… appears she fell down a flight of steps."

"Wait, you're not joking, are you?" he replied.

"No."

"That's insane. Didn't you talk to her yesterday?" He stopped laughing and listened to me.

"We were supposed to meet last night, but then I stumbled upon her dead body with a friend of mine on campus." I updated Derek about Abby working as a professor at the college, what Myriam Castle and Nana D had said about her, and the little I'd learned from visiting the sheriff's office that morning.

"Do whatever you can to get her research notes. I texted her earlier to give them to you." Derek didn't seem too phased about her death, but he also thought I'd have access to her personal things. "I guess I won't be getting a reply, huh?" He laughed again, but this time with a more sinister tone.

"And exactly how am I supposed to do that?" Perhaps I should ask *him* where he was last night.

"You're the wannabe investigative reporter, Kel-baby. Break into her office or tell the cops she left something behind for you about a project you were working on together. I need this to be your top priority. We have to film season two as soon as possible, dude."

Derek was the typical sleaze who made me doubt my career working in Hollywood over the last few months. "Listen, I know this is important. I'll see what I can do. I guess I'll be coming back to Los Angeles sooner than we planned."

Derek was unusually silent on the phone before finally responding. "Why don't you stick around for her funeral? Meet her contacts and find out who else she worked with. Take advantage of the situation. Get the scoop on her death too. Builds a good side story for the show. Research professor falls to her death while working on *Dark Reality*. Think of the ratings, Kel-baby!"

His last comment lit the proverbial fire under me to finish my time with him as quickly as possible. "Yeah, good plan. What hotel are you staying at? I'm thinking about visiting Hawaii next month." I had no intention of going to the tropical islands, but how much did I know about this man outside of work? Was he really where he said he was?

"Royal something, can't recall. Good chatting. Gotta run. Get that scoop. Your job depends on it!"

Before I responded, Derek hung up on me. What an idiot! I needed to quit, but I was close to getting my name on the credits for a full season, and this would be the exact bonus to staking a claim to my own show in the future. It wouldn't be difficult to check if Abby had any notes in her office. Attending the funeral with my family was a good show of faith.

Since Maggie was on my agenda the following day, I'd add in visiting Lorraine. She'd have information on Abby's funeral arrangements. I also wanted to touch base with Connor to determine what he'd been up to for the last ten years. Ever since Francesca's death, I'd pushed away all our friends in Los Angeles and spent my free time with Emma. I hadn't truly connected with a group of guys since my days in the fraternity. Abby's death reminded me too much of the lost man I'd become when my wife died two years ago. While in town, I could reconnect with some old buddies and solve a crime!

Chapter 6

After my five-mile run later that afternoon, I found my father sitting in his office drinking a glass of Macallan scotch and watching the sunset over the Wharton Mountains. It looked like the bottle I'd given him at Christmas was at least half empty, which meant for once he'd enjoyed one of my holiday gifts. I declined his offer since scotch after a run never settled well in my stomach. I was also starving and needed to eat something before I passed out. "Maybe next time. I'm gonna heat some party leftovers for dinner. Are you hungry?"

"I had an early meal with your mother before she went back to the campus. The final deadline is this week for notifying students who've been accepted for the next term. Not that I'll be the one welcoming them to Braxton," he replied in a somber tone while swallowing a mouthful of liquor. I could hear the melancholy oozing through the burn of the scotch.

It hadn't occurred to my overworked and distracted brain he'd be sad to retire. If I'd worked tirelessly for forty years, sitting on my rear end doing nothing for a few months would be a welcome change. *"That's the problem with this younger generation. Can't put in a full day's work without complaining,"* Nana D would likely chastise. "Chin up, Dad. You've got a lot to look forward to after the big day. The new president will want you to stick around to help settle in, right?"

He nodded. I waited for him to keep talking, but the scotch and the silence in the room overtook the possibility of him leading our conversation. "Any traction with the search for a new head honcho?"

"The Board finished all the interviews and asked me to meet with the final two candidates again this week. I'm not at liberty to provide details, but they've been considering internal and external options. I'm partial to one candidate. We're doing separate group panels with them both tomorrow before we make the final decision." He swung the chair away from the window and narrowed his eyes. "How long are you planning on staying this time, Kellan?"

I'd been theorizing when he'd ask that question. He'd suggested a few times over the Christmas break it'd be beneficial for Emma to be around both sets of grandparents. I thought for a moment he'd discovered my late wife's dirty family secrets, but if that were true, he'd not yet revealed it to me. "I'm trying to figure that out. I have work that might keep me here for the rest of the week."

"I see." He clicked his tongue against the roof of his mouth.

"So, I was trying to get hold of you last night after finding Abby's body at Diamond Hall."

My father cleared his throat. "The ringer was off, so I could enjoy the party in peace. I didn't realize you'd been desperately trying to find me," he replied in a bitter tone, pouring another scotch and opening his laptop.

Ouch! I wasn't sure what I'd said to deserve his scathing retort, but I'd obviously hit a nerve. "I wasn't desperate. Just curious about who killed Abby Monroe."

My father dismissed me through a combination of shrugging, lifting his eyebrows, and ignoring me as he typed away on the computer. I wanted to find out where he was and whom he'd threatened on the phone the night I arrived, but I took my cue and ate dinner in the kitchen by myself. Should I abandon the investigation or jump in deeper to protect someone I knew?

* * *

I'd fallen asleep in bed the night before while surfing the internet and reading the show bible for a second time, but at least I'd been able to ascertain several interesting facts about the late professor, or *Monroe,* as Myriam Castle referred to her. I'd researched that churlish woman too.

Abby had spent most of her life specializing in broadcasting and media studies, following a similar post-undergraduate degree path as me. As near as I could figure, Abby was at least fifteen years older than me. Although I'd made it to Hollywood, she'd worked in the academic world her entire adult career, hopping from college to college until settling at Braxton nearly ten years ago. She started right after I'd graduated and was promoted to chairman of the communications department when the incumbent retired. At Braxton, the communications department included media and broadcasting, literature, theater, writing, public relations, and art majors. Abby taught three courses this semester—Intro to Film, History of Television Production, and Broadcast Writing.

It surprised me to discover Myriam Castle was one of the professors who worked for Abby in the communications department. Her specialty was literature and theater productions, which made sense given her exaggerated facial expressions at the retirement party. On paper, Dr. Castle was clearly more qualified to be running the department, but Abby had been put in the role before Dr. Castle joined Braxton. No wonder there was tension between the women. It would be an interesting discussion with my father when he graciously stepped off his high horse and spoke to me again.

I'd also found a website where Abby referred to co-authoring articles in a widely published journal with her husband, Alton Monroe. The news filled in a blank from a scrap of paper I'd seen on Officer Flatman's desk at the sheriff's office. Could Alton be someone to provide a copy of Abby's *Dark Reality* notes? I cross-checked the names with online directories and located an address on the north side of the county. I made a note to swing by while on campus meeting Lorraine and Maggie later that day.

I braved the near-freezing temperature and dodged a few icicles dropping off the roofline as I hopped in the Jeep. Twenty minutes later, I found a lucky parking spot down the street from the Braxton Campus Security (BCS) office.

The last time I'd been there was after a rival fraternity, the Omega Delta Omicrons, complained we were having a loud party our senior year. I'd spent forty-five minutes trying to convince the previous security director not to report us to Fern Terry, the Dean of Student Affairs, but he wouldn't budge. I'd left his office after a few less-than-kind words that evening and found myself with a slap on the wrist the following morning when Dean Terry told me my childish word choices had disappointed her. Was she one of the two final candidates vying for Braxton's presidency? Maybe I should stop by the administration office to check if she still worked on campus. I hadn't seen her at the party, yet I assumed she would've shown up if she was employed at Braxton.

As I walked up the cobblestone pathway, I considered what kind of security director Connor would be. He was always the goody-two-shoes who cautioned not to let the fraternity get into trouble, but he'd protect me from taking the fall on my own when we'd been caught doing something wrong. Not that any wrongdoings happened often, but Connor was a dependable and honorable guy. In theory, it made sense that he went into security work, yet I had trouble imagining him sitting on the opposite side of college administration.

I stepped into the foyer of the single-story security building and gave it the once-over. Little had changed, possibly a coat of fresh paint and a series of new digital cameras and computer systems. Connor stepped out of his office, no longer looking uncomfortable in a tan suit and Braxton tie; now he busted out of his sports coat and jeans. "Kellan, I didn't expect to see you today. What's going on?"

"Got time for a cup of coffee? My treat." I hoped he'd take me up on the offer. When he nodded and told a student worker to call him promptly with any issues, I realized Connor had become an admirable and responsible adult.

He suggested The Big Beanery on South Campus. I was more than happy to visit our old stomping grounds. The car ride took less than five minutes because he was in a BCS vehicle, and everyone stopped to let him through the streets first. Must be good to have that kind of power—even come in handy one day if I needed his help.

When we arrived, Connor grabbed a table while I ordered two black coffees. I'd wanted creamer in mine, or even a cappuccino, but when he mumbled something about too much sugar, I followed suit and pulled up a chair across from him. "So, working in security at Braxton. That's quite a leap from what we used to do on campus ten years ago, huh?"

His laugh was hearty and deep. "Ten years is a long time. People mature. You've done some changing yourself. Seems like you even frequent the gym now."

"Well, no competing with you, man. You look like a brick wall!" I assumed he could throw me across the room. Not that I'd do anything to encourage it, but I'd be glad to have him on my side in any bar fight or street brawl. I had an urge to call him *Double-O-Seven.*

"I've always wondered what happened to you. We sort of lost touch, huh?" he asked after taking a giant sip of his coffee. His eyes continually scanned the room behind me as if he were looking for someone. It's probably a normal thing for the head of security to always check out his surroundings. "Gotta admit, it pissed me off when you left town that summer. I know you went off to grad school, but you were my best friend back then."

"Yeah, I felt bad about it. Life has this funny way of making decisions you don't understand at the time. When I look back, I had some growing up to do, didn't I?" I suspected Connor carried a grudge over the past. I might have a harder time trying to reestablish a friendship than expected.

A few students waved at him. It looked like a girl was trying to flirt. If he noticed, he ignored her. We reminisced about our last decade. Connor had spent a year living in Anguilla with his mother's family to rebuild after a series of devastating hurricanes took its toll on the people living on nearby islands. He'd also worked as a police officer in Philadelphia for several years, then left the force after dealing with too many violent gang fights and deaths. It was a year ago when he'd heard about the opening at Braxton.

"Married, kids?"

"A daughter." I always hated that question. It's never easy telling someone you lost your wife to a drunk driver. They inevitably felt uncomfortable about asking, then you felt weird for delivering the awful news. No one should feel bad except the idiot who stepped into his car after drinking a six-pack and thinking he was totally fine to drive. To this day, they hadn't caught the hit-and-run driver.

We covered more basics. He was still single, dated on and off through the years, but nothing serious. I got the distinct impression when Maggie came up that he'd been smitten with her since she'd returned from Boston. While I was in no frame of mind to consider anything more than rebuilding a friendship with Maggie, somehow the thought of her being with someone else didn't sit well. I changed the topic to Abby's death.

"I'm not sure I'd have the latest. Murder is the authority of Wharton County. Sheriff Montague's been in contact to discuss protocol, but we haven't established all the boundaries." Connor confirmed they were still searching for signs of a struggle other than the gash in Abby's head.

"True. I just meant how were you handling it from Braxton's perspective." I signaled to the young waitress clearing a table nearby that we wanted two more cups of coffee. If Connor would share any information, I knew from experience, he needed caffeine.

"Sheriff Montague wants everyone to think it was an accident. Braxton's public relations department was quite pleased to take that approach." Connor slurped the remnants of his coffee.

"Murder won't help the upcoming admissions cycle," I said with a laugh. "Did you know her?"

"Met at a few college functions. She stopped in to discuss things from time to time. Abby had it in her head that because I was from the

Caribbean, my family practiced voodoo. She wanted me to hook her up with my shaman. What a kook! I don't even know what a shaman is."

The waitress dropped off the coffee refills and asked, "Who do you think will end up leading Saturday's big game, Director Hawkins? Striker our man? Or is Jordan gonna overtake him?"

I'd not been sure which sport they were talking about until remembering Eleanor's story at the Pick-Me-Up Diner about the baseball team. "Those the two choices for pitcher?" I tossed out my question, though her gaze barely left Connor's lips.

Connor replied, "Yep. Striker was last season's star, but his teammate, Jordan, suddenly jumped into the race based on his new curveball in the pre-season games. It's a close match."

When I went to hand her a ten-dollar bill, she waved me off. "Nah, we don't charge Director Hawkins. He checks on us from time to time to make sure we're doing okay." She backed away, nearly tripping over her own feet because she couldn't peel her focus off Connor.

"Someone thinks you're cute, huh?"

"Drop it, Kellan. She's a kid."

"I know. Seems like you're *king of the hill* around here these days. I'm happy for you."

"Yeah, I didn't ask for it. Just doing my job. I should head back soon. You need a lift?"

I declined. I planned to find Abby's house, and the access road to her neighborhood was closer to South Campus. "Before you go, do you think there's any chance I could look in Abby's office? It sounds funny, but I was supposed to meet her about some information for my boss, and I didn't get to before she died. We think it's somewhere buried on her desk." I felt awful asking for a favor from Connor after all these years, but I wasn't doing anything overtly wrong. Abby did the research for us, so we were getting back something owed to the network. I couldn't convince myself I wasn't stretching my justification, especially since the contract had never been signed.

"I don't have a problem as long as Sheriff Montague clears it. She might want an officer to be present." Connor stood, then smiled as someone walked to the table. "Speak of the devil."

"Devil? Something you care to explain, Connor?" Sheriff Montague's arms were crossed against her chest with the look of a woman ready to pounce. Whether it was to kiss or chastise him, I couldn't tell. Based on appearance, she was only two or three years older than us.

Connor excused himself, indicating I could fill in the blanks. As I pointed a hand to the open seat across from me, Sheriff Montague sat and said, "That is one fine man there."

I spat out a mouthful of coffee, then apologized and made excuses about it being too hot. "What Connor meant, Sheriff Montague, is I need to collect some papers from Abby's office regarding a project we were working on together. May I get in there?"

The sheriff had only moved to Braxton two years ago. I never got to know her. Did she remember me from the one time I bailed out Nana D? It didn't seem like she'd made the connection, but I'd think someone in her position as county sheriff wouldn't forget too many faces, especially not one associated with the frequently vocal Seraphina Danby. I got my answer rather quickly, after soaking up the spilled coffee and stopping myself from commenting on her motorcycle helmet hair.

"Your family might have some control in Braxton, Little Ayrwick, but let me assure you, I won't be pressured into any special circumstances or favors. I've got a murder investigation to lead, and I will run down anyone who gets in my way." When she finished, she stared at me like I might be dinner that night. I wasn't sure whether to wet my pants or put up a fight.

"You don't mince words, sheriff. I'm sorry if I came across the wrong way. When it became clear this wasn't just an accident, I worried it might have something to do with research Abby Monroe was handling on my television show, *Dark Reality*. Are you familiar with it?"

Surprisingly, that loosened her attitude. "That's your show? I watched the whole first season. My girlfriends and I can't get enough of it!" she replied in a syrupy tone as her eyes bulged wider.

Wow, I'd lucked out in that department. If I played my cards right, I could make an ally out of Sheriff Montague. "Yeah, definitely, I could get you a couple of tickets—"

"Cut the beeswax, Little Ayrwick. I don't watch the show. I've got better things to do than burn my eyes to their core from reality TV garbage. No offense since that's your thing."

Ouch, did I misjudge that one! "You got me there," I replied with my tail between my legs. "Seriously, I'll help the investigation however I can. Do you have any suspects?"

"A few. I'm not here to give you a tough time. I'll take all the help I can get, but you're a private citizen. We're not usually in the business of giving out that kind of information." She cupped her hands together and cracked both sets of knuckles, considering my offer as she stood. "We're focusing on a few people who had the means and the opportunity. We're still searching for the motive. I'm meeting with a witness who overheard a fight between Lorraine Candito and the victim."

I couldn't hold back my shock. "Lorraine? She wouldn't hurt a fly. I've known her for years, and I can vouch for her. Gentler than a Girl Scout or a newborn puppy. She might nibble from time to time, but there must be some misunderstanding."

Sheriff Montague shook her head vigorously. "A student worker Connor met this morning claimed to overhear the words '*over your dead body*' coming from Lorraine Candito's lips."

I'd been certain the fear on Lorraine's face was genuine. Could it have been guilt? "I'm meeting with Lorraine this afternoon. I can ask her about it if you'd like a second opinion."

"Leave the investigation to us, Little Ayrwick. I'll be in touch about access to Abby Monroe's office. Have yourself a good day." She adjusted one of her sleeves, glared at me a second time with laser eyes to ensure I got the message, then idled toward the counter to order something to go. Her sturdy gait and minimalist approach to dressing or wearing any makeup clearly showed she'd cared little about her appearance. Would it be wrong of me to ask Eleanor to give her a makeover in the hopes she'd win Connor's affection? I could think of no one else better to put a smile on the sheriff's face.

I wanted to warn Lorraine, but it wouldn't put me in good standing with the sheriff. It seemed most advantageous to give April Montague time to meet with the student worker and Lorraine before I dug any further. I'd pissed off enough people since returning to Braxton. It was time to let my spectacular curb appeal charm the rest before I found myself on the wrong side of town and living in a doghouse. In ten years, I'd foolishly forgotten what went on in a remote village.

Chapter 7

Abby's house was only a twenty-minute walk if I stuck to the path along the waterfront. Although still mighty cold, any snow on the ground had melted away, and since I wasn't likely to get to a gym that afternoon, the extra cardio was more than welcome. When I arrived at her street, I made a right and ambled past the first few houses before finally finding one with a number. Most of the homes in the immediate vicinity were three-bedroom ranches on small parcels with fenced-in front and backyards for children and dogs to play, less any worry about balls rolling into the street or wild animals roaming in from the mountains. The occasional bobcat had been sighted years ago, but as the area became more urbanized, the wildlife retreated further into the Wharton Mountains.

Abby's place was the second to last one on the left, a charming brick-fronted home with green shutters and a white door. As I neared the entrance, a four-door blue sedan crept down the driveway. I dropped to the ground to make it look like I'd been tying my boot laces. The driver reached into the mailbox, rifled through a few envelopes and a magazine, then took off down the street. He'd left the mail in the box. Had he been in the house?

I placed him in his mid-to-late forties, balding, and toying with facial hair. It was mostly grown in, a mixture of brown and gray surrounding his mouth and chin. Perhaps the goatee was making a comeback, or maybe he was hoping to lead the pack. Brother? Roommate? Could this be the husband, Alton? I hadn't seen a picture of Abby's spouse, but I'd gotten a good visual while this man was checking the mail.

If the *Dark Reality* notes weren't at her office, it was possible they'd be at her home. It wasn't like I was the kind of guy who'd break into the place to find them. Sheriff Montague would undoubtedly haul me to jail just for her laughs and revenge. When I was certain the blue sedan turned the corner, I stood and casually brushed off my pants. I was about to check for anything of interest in the backyard when someone startled me.

"May I help you?" asked a heavyset woman in a raspy voice and a peach-colored house dress. It was a little cold to be outside without a coat, but more power to her for being brave.

My eyes darted to the piece of mail in her hand, and I attempted to read the name. Even with my glasses, I could only decipher a few letters. "You must be Mrs. Ackerman, the neighbor my friend Abby talks about all the time."

She pulled back, slightly confused, then smiled. "Abby talks about me? How sweet of her! It's Mrs. Ackerton, handsome. And who might you be?" She pursed her lips and straightened her shoulders.

Wow! I was grateful for my quick thinking and stroke of luck. "Oh, I'm Justin. We work together at the college. I was just stopping by to check the mail for her while she's away."

Mrs. Ackerton shook her head and made a tsk-tsk sound with her tongue. "That explains why I haven't seen her lately. It worried me, especially when I saw that police car here yesterday. There wasn't a robbery, was there?" Mrs. Ackerton closed the lid on her mailbox and adjusted a hair curler. "Sorry, I'm not all fancied up for you at the moment."

"No robberies I've been told about." It seemed she wasn't aware Abby had died over the weekend, but she was awake enough to flirt with me. "I saw a car drive away while I was fixing my laces and thought maybe I'd missed her or her husband," I replied, ignoring the broccoli in her teeth.

"No, her husband don't live here no more. Noticed the car a few times, but I'm not sure I've ever gotten a good look at the person to say that's who's been sleeping here. If I see Abby, I'll mention you stopped by, Justin." She reached out her hand and grabbed my bicep. "I love a strong man."

"Do you think he was a friend of Abby's?" I asked, fishing for information. "She didn't tell me anyone else would stop by while she was away. I kinda thought I was the only—"

"Oh, I don't know if it was anything romantic. Don't reckon I'll ever understand relationships these days. I suppose playing the field is part of the game, eh? I hope she wasn't stepping out on you, Justin." She elbowed me a few times before heading back up her walkway.

Did she think I'd date someone like Abby? We said our goodbyes, and I began my excursion back to campus to meet with Lorraine. Along the path, I thought about whether Abby's death was a lover's quarrel gone wrong. Had her husband found out she was having an affair, or did her boyfriend get angry she wouldn't leave her husband? That's when I realized I still didn't know the exact cause of death. Connor had told me about the gash on her head, but it couldn't have been from hitting the steps. There was some other object that had knocked her out first. Maybe I could convince the sheriff to tell me what they'd discovered onsite.

Before I knew it, I found myself about to ascend the front entrance of Diamond Hall. My mother was exiting the building and waved at me.

"Hey, Mom. Fancy seeing you here. Were you visiting Dad?" I asked, noting how cute it was they'd still spend part of their day together on campus. She'd miss him when he retired.

"I thought Lorraine could tell me where he was, so I could surprise him for lunch, but apparently Sheriff Montague asked him to return to the precinct again. They have a lot of questions about his relationship with Abby Monroe."

"Did you ever find out where he went at the end of the retirement party?" I hoped she could fill in the information my father had conveniently left out.

My mother paused before offering an awkward, non-committal answer. "You know your father. He doesn't think to tell me where he goes. I'm worried about him lately. Something's not quite settled."

"What do you mean? Something to do with his retirement?" I thought about the phone call too.

"Well, not exactly," she replied, visibly drained and in need of a break. "He and Abby didn't have the best of relations. Your father tried unsuccessfully to remove her as department chair. I'm afraid Sheriff Montague thinks your father has something to do with her death." After glancing upward to the building's side windows, she covered her mouth as if she'd been shocked to say something out loud about the incident.

"Dad's hard to take sometimes, but he'd never hurt someone physically. He's more a master of verbal insults." I thought about his behavior the last few days. He'd become more strange, pensive, and closed-off despite my first chat with him. "Did Sheriff Montague accuse him of something, or are you reading between the lines?"

"Talk to him, Kellan. I can't make sense of it." My mother tilted her head to the side and began welling.

"Oh, don't cry, Mom. Everything will be okay." I pulled her in for a hug and patted her back. It was a rare moment to see my mother collapse.

"You were supposed to meet Abby, right? You could do a little investigating. See what she'd been doing recently or find someone else that detective could harass."

"April Montague is not a detective, Mom. She's the Wharton County sheriff. I'm sure she knows how to do her job. Asking Dad more questions could simply be to help find other suspects," I said, uncertain whether I believed my own words. Sheriff Montague had it out for my family in the past.

"Please, Kellan. I ask little of you. I know I keep begging you to come back home, but the least you could do while you're here is poke around. Isn't that what you do for a living? Research? Figure out what happened in a crime and then write a show all about it?"

While it was a cursory explanation of my job, she had a point. "Sure, I'll see what I can learn by asking some questions... starting with Lorraine. I'm on my way to see her. Was she particularly busy?"

My mother shivered from the wind. "Yes, a little frazzled. I got the impression she knew something but wasn't comfortable telling me just now. I'm sure you can get her to talk. Lorraine always had a soft spot for you."

"Is there anything you remember about the night of the party that might identify whom Abby was meeting at Diamond Hall?" She'd delayed chatting with me until nine, I presumed to give her time for her mysterious eight thirty meeting about a student's grades.

"I don't know if it has anything to do with Abby's death, but I saw someone walking around the side of the building. I'd stepped outside to find your father when I noticed Coach Oliver."

It was the second time I'd heard that name. "Who's Coach Oliver?"

"Our athletic director. He oversees the school's sports teams, practice fields, venues, and Grey Sports Complex, our main athletic facility. He's a nice guy, but that man seems a little obsessed with winning all the games rather than keeping the students focused on their studies."

"What time did you see him?"

My mother tapped her foot against the concrete steps. I could see the wheels turning inside her head as she thought about the night's events. "About eight thirty. I waved to him, but he was on his phone. He seemed distracted. I'm certain he planned to stop by the party, but he never showed up."

"Point out exactly where you saw him," I instructed her. She noted the far corner near the oak tree and bench on the narrow path toward Glass Hall. Coach Oliver had been near the back entrance of Diamond Hall, where the lighting was dim.

"Surely, you don't think he had anything to do with Abby's death, do you?" A grim expression overtook my mother's face while she moaned in an overstated fashion.

"I'm not certain. The woman I was supposed to meet with is dead. You're worried the sheriff assumes it involves Dad. Now you tell me you saw someone near where Abby died under mysterious circumstances. Did you inform Sheriff Montague?"

A blank and disconnected look told me she hadn't. "No, I didn't think to. Should I call her?"

I shook my head. There didn't seem to be any reason to share the news. I'd see if it were anything important before putting another family member in front of the persistent sheriff. Upon recovering from her worries, my mother walked toward the cable car to return to North Campus.

Exactly what I needed, another reason to put myself in the line of fire with the sheriff. I grew curious whether coach Oliver had authored the blog post or was the call I'd overheard in my father's study.

I climbed the steps and entered Diamond Hall. A string of yellow plastic tape blocked the entrance to the second-floor staircase. A sign indicated all classes were moved to Memorial Library. Lorraine called to me from the other side of the hallway. "Kellan, I'm over here."

Lorraine explained Sheriff Montague had quarantined the second and third floors for the balance of the week. Although they'd removed Abby's body and the cleaning crew had finished sanitizing the stairwell, the sheriff didn't want anyone in the building's top two floors while they searched for evidence. No students were allowed except a few workers who helped Lorraine with the daily administration in the communications department.

"So, there's no news yet?"

Lorraine leaned in and whispered, "Sheriff Montague is going through Abby's office. They're not telling me anything. It's awful."

I guessed I wouldn't be offered the chance to see Abby's belongings. I didn't expect the sheriff to take me up on my proposal, despite it making things much easier. "What's being said to students?"

"Full cooperation with local law enforcement to understand how Abby Monroe tragically fell to her death. We're expediting the investigation, and the building is off-limits until next weekend." Lorraine advised that she was given office space on the second floor of Diamond Hall because the communications department's office manager had gone on maternity leave earlier that year. Rather than fill the vacancy for the three months Siobhan would be away, Lorraine was asked to support my father and the professors since she'd temporarily be working in Diamond Hall. Knowing my father's impending retirement meant less work, Lorraine had agreed to handle the additional responsibilities and work from Siobhan's desk.

"I'm sorry you got stuck with all that. Holding up okay with the sheriff?" I asked.

"I've never found a dead body before. I'm so glad you were there to help me, Kellan. I haven't been able to sleep much." Her hands clasped together while rubbing her palms with nervous fingers.

"Lorraine, someone mentioned overhearing a conversation you had recently with Abby. Something about you issuing a veiled threat against her. I'm not entirely sure what that meant, but I wanted to ask you directly."

Lorraine sighed loudly. "Foolish of me. It was nothing. Honestly, the student worker simply misunderstood what I'd said."

"What do you mean?" I had to extract the explanation from her.

"I guess you'll find out, anyway. It wasn't common knowledge, but I knew Abby Monroe outside of Braxton. We were disagreeing about something… personal. It had nothing to do with her death. I could never hurt anyone." She glanced to the side and fiddled with a few papers.

"Does Sheriff Montague think you did something to Abby?" My mother seemed to be under the impression my father was a suspect. Could Lorraine be one too? "How did you know Abby?"

"My brother, Alton, had served her with divorce papers, but she wouldn't sign them for an entire year. Abby was a vindictive woman."

Lorraine filled me in on their history. Abby and Alton had been married for five years when he'd gotten fed up with her selfish attitude. He tried to mend the relationship, and even Lorraine had talked to Abby about the issues. In the end, Alton determined it was best to split up. The argument Lorraine had with Abby the prior week was about the divorce. Abby had threatened to ask for a larger amount of alimony if Alton wouldn't give her the rights to an upcoming book they'd planned to co-author.

"Someone overheard me saying '*It'll be over your dead body that I let you take anything else away from Alton.*' But I didn't mean it literally, Kellan. You've got to help me figure out what happened to Abby." Her hollow cheeks flushed, and she slammed her head against the desk.

There was something in the tone of Lorraine's voice, the imminent fear over what would happen if the cops couldn't find Abby's actual killer. She might always be suspected of the crime. As far as I knew, she had no children or a husband. Someone needed to protect her from any accusations cast in her direction. "I don't know the specific time Abby died, but surely Sheriff Montague understands you only slipped away from the party for a few minutes to stop by the office."

"Someone killed Abby between a quarter after eight and a quarter to nine. She'd only been dead a brief time when I'd first found her body. I can't find anyone who saw me at the party after eight o'clock."

"It'll be harder to prove you didn't do it, that's true. Do you know what they're hunting for upstairs?" The murder weapon had to be part of the search. I really wanted to know what it was.

"An officer said they'd swept the whole place but couldn't find anything. I still don't understand what they're looking for. I thought someone pushed her down the stairs."

Lorraine wasn't aware the gash on the back of Abby's head had come from a brutal blow. Either she was playing dumb or genuinely didn't know someone had hit Abby before she fell. I didn't think it was my responsibility to tell her, so I changed topics. "Is your brother holding up well enough?"

"Alton's my half-brother, we only share a mother. That's why we have different last names. I haven't been able to get in touch with him. He left last week for a remote research trip. No cell connection," Lorraine replied, dabbing her swollen eyes with a tissue. "I'm not sure he knows Abby is dead."

If Alton was away, then he couldn't be responsible for Abby's death. The sheriff would check his alibi, to be certain. The guy near Abby's house popped back into my head. "Was Abby seeing anyone new recently? If she was divorcing Alton, maybe there was a new man in the picture."

Lorraine shook her head. "I didn't keep tabs on her love life. Alton didn't care either, he just wanted out. They tried maintaining a friendship, but she was too egotistical."

I told Lorraine to think positively and cooperate as much as possible with the sheriff during the investigation. The truth had to come out at some point, and Sheriff Montague would realize Lorraine had nothing to do with Abby's death. I couldn't picture her as the killer. Unfortunately, that meant the sheriff might still suspect my father.

I checked the time and realized I still hadn't visited Maggie or eaten lunch. After stopping at the campus cafeteria, I would head to Memorial Library. I needed to learn what Maggie knew about the athletic director, theorizing she could figure out a way to introduce me to Coach Oliver.

Chapter 8

I caught the cable car back to North Campus. Students shared pics and tweets on their phone, arguing about which pitcher should start that Saturday. I'd been a baseball freak for years, but living in Los Angeles was difficult for a Phillies fan. Eventually, I'd given up quarreling over baseball and instead picked up football as my sport of choice. As the cable car pulled in, a light bulb went off in my head about how I could introduce myself to Coach Oliver.

I exited the cable car and took the shortest path to the cafeteria in the student union building. Lunch was winding down, so I got in and out quickly with two chicken salad croissants and a bag of salt and vinegar potato chips, Maggie's favorite.

No one at the library's reception desk stopped me from entering the building. Student workers busily studied or looked up naughty things on the reference computers. I made a right at the history section and found Maggie sitting behind her desk in the corner office. She smiled and pointed at the adjacent chair. The décor was truly in need of an update.

"I brought snacks, if you're hungry?"

"You're a savior! The staff meeting ran longer than expected, and I forgot to bring lunch. Please tell me those are potato chips?"

"It'll cost you," I said with a beaming smile. "My fees have gone up since senior year."

"I've never forgotten your silly games, Kellan. You always knew how to make me relax when the day had worn me out." She shifted a few books to the side of her desk and cleared a place for us to eat. "What's the price today? Study guides for an exam? Write an essay for you?"

"Inflation, baby. We're looking at a hundred-dollar bottle of champagne, or at the very least, an advanced copy of the latest Follett novel. I know you have connections as a librarian."

"As if I'd share it with you before I read it. I hardly think a bag of salt and vinegar potato chips is worth that much effort." Her eyes twinkled at me, and for a moment, I thought she caught me staring at her.

"True, I jumped the shark with that request, didn't I? Okay, today's a freebie, but next time, watch out. I won't be as easy with you."

We chatted about her new role at Memorial Library. She'd throw a magnificent costume ball later that semester for residents of Braxton, to receive more donations for the renovations. Although her predecessor was a fantastic librarian, Mrs. O'Malley hadn't embraced the technology curve as much as she should have. The college severely lacked access to the latest library hardware and software.

As we finished eating, Maggie surprised me by bringing up Abby's death. "Connor tells me they're announcing later today that they're close to identifying the killer. I guess they must reveal it was murder at that point, huh?"

I don't know whether I was more concerned they might apprehend someone I knew, or that Maggie had further demonstrated how close she and Connor had become in the last few weeks. "Really? I talked to him this morning. He mentioned nothing about an arrest."

"He called a few minutes ago. I'm glad we connected this year," she said with a rising glow.

A student worker popped in to ask if he could leave fifteen minutes early for an unplanned baseball practice. Maggie let him go and wished him luck on Saturday's game.

"So, what exactly are you and Connor these days?" Better to know than feel like I'd been left in the dark.

Maggie coughed and took a big swig of water. "Connor and… ummm… we are… well, what makes you ask, Kellan?" I'd seen that look on her face before, although in the past it was much more innocent.

"Yeah, I mean, you both lost touch like we did. Are you friends again? Are you colleagues who chat from time to time? You know what I mean." I didn't want to ask outright. I'd been clear enough with an open-ended question, but Maggie wasn't sure or didn't feel comfortable discussing it.

"I'd say we're friends. Good friends. He's been a big comfort since I returned. Connor's helped me figure out how to move on without my husband anymore." Maggie fiddled with the books on the desk, then stood. "I should get back to work. I'm so glad you came by today."

Ouch! I was being kicked out again, but Maggie's directness impressed me. "We must do this again soon. I should get going too. I need to swing by Grey Sports Complex to talk with Coach Oliver."

Maggie shifted her head sideways. "What's that about?"

"My mother thought I should meet him. That's all," I lied. Not that I didn't trust Maggie, but I wasn't sure it would amount to anything given the awkward moments we'd just shared. "What do you think of him?"

"He's a solid coach. Loves his job, but not a big supporter of the whole educational purpose for student enrollment at Braxton. That's why I let that pitcher leave early. If Jordan showed up late, Coach Oliver would penalize him in front of the entire team."

"That's cruel." No wonder I stayed away from playing sports back in college. I wouldn't have accepted it and gotten myself into trouble. I had a minor issue with authority figures in my teens and early twenties—the downside of being too clever for your own good.

"A bit, but he's trying to instill some discipline in the team. They had a rough year, and he wants to get a few of them into the minor or major leagues after graduation."

"I don't agree with his approach, but perhaps his heart's in the right place," I said.

"Listen, Kellan, it'd be nice to have dinner before you leave town. Call me when you have a free night?" When she grabbed my hand, a shock ran through my system.

I smiled my biggest smile since arriving back in Braxton. "Definitely. I'll call you soon, Maggie."

"I never could resist those baby blue eyes of yours." she said with a wink, giving me the shivers.

Ten minutes later, I stood outside Grey Sports Complex, a giant series of three-story buildings connected by a common, central entranceway. Above the front reception doors on the second floor, an enclosed courtyard with a ten-foot-tall statue of the college's founder, Heathcliff Braxton, loomed larger than life. Although you could see the top of the statue from the ground, the peaceful garden surrounding it—used by students in the spring and fall for outdoor physical education lectures—was only accessible from the second floor.

I rehearsed my planned conversation with Coach Oliver. *I'm a professional, I can do this*, I convinced myself while entering reception. There were two couches and a table, three doors besides the one I came in, and a television screen on the wall showing various camera positions throughout the building. I saw the baseball field, a swimming pool, what appeared to either be a tennis or volleyball court—the camera had a weird angle—and the fitness center. I looked around the reception area to determine where to go, but someone stopped me in my tracks. "May I help you?"

I heard the voice but couldn't find the corresponding body. I searched all around me in the small room, but I was alone. "Ummm… I'd love to introduce myself, but where exactly are you?"

"Please state your name and whom you are here to see."

Someone was way ruder than she needed to be. "Kellan Ayrwick. I am here to see Coach Oliver. Seriously, where are you hiding?"

"Notifying Coach Oliver. Please hold." The girl wasn't anywhere in the room, leading me to question my sanity.

Annoyed she wouldn't reveal herself, I tried all three of the doors. They were locked. Two minutes later, the middle door opened. After

I walked twenty feet down the hall, another voice said, "May I help you?"

Oh, not this again. I was about to use some foul language, but then it occurred to me I heard a *male* voice this time. Maybe he could help me find Coach Oliver. When I reached the steps, a familiar man approached—the same guy in the blue sedan outside Abby Monroe's house. All my worlds were colliding in that one moment.

After the initial shock wore off, my entire plan to meet the athletic director flew out the window. I tried the first approach I could think of. "There was a voice that spoke to me in reception. I'm not crazy, or at least I don't think I am, but I told the girl I was looking for Coach Oliver."

The man laughed and extended his hand. "You've come to the right place. That would be me."

Luck must be on my side today, but that only connected a few of the dots for me. "Oh, terrific. Then I'm heading in the right direction. I'm Kellan Ayrwick. Could you explain what happened back there?"

"Ah, we're testing out some technology. Rather than pay a student to sit out front all day and check identification cards for who can enter the building, we've installed new facial recognition software. It didn't know who you were, so the system asked you to identify yourself. When I heard you state your name, I released the door to let you in." Coach Oliver told me to follow him to the third floor.

I remembered the blogger had mentioned something about technology for the athletics department. "Is this for sports teams? I saw something similar at my father's party the other night."

Coach Oliver responded, "Ah, you're their son. Your mother volunteered to use it to track entry at the retirement party. We're eventually hoping to use it around the college but initially at the sports games to help with access control and improved security."

While what he said made sense, I still didn't grasp fully how it functioned. "So, does that mean I was speaking to some robot or computer back in reception?"

"Yes, a camera snaps a photo when someone enters the building. We match it against the system to grant access. Eventually, we'll record your movement throughout the facility, but for now, the facial recognition software is only installed in the reception area." We'd reached the third floor, and he made a left down the hall. "Our new fitness center is down the other hall to the right."

"What else have you installed so far?"

"We have one camera near the fitness center and several around Grey Field. They're currently fitting voice-activated controls for the lighting on the third floor in my office and nearby conference room. Just the minimum until we finish testing it next week. The system isn't yet fully functional."

"Cool stuff," I replied, unconvinced of its potential value on campus. "Braxton seems like such a small school to need all these advanced systems."

"It's a way to move toward the twenty-first century. We need to look like we're at the front of the curve if we want the right people to notice us," he replied hesitantly and breathing more heavily.

"Happy with it?" I wondered who was expected to notice them. Potential students?

"Everyone forgets their identification cards. Facial recognition has helped our operations, although a few people have gotten in without proper access. We're working out the kinks. I only use the system's features for tracking player performance and interacting with potential team sponsors and sports management companies."

"How did you get the financial support for such an expensive technology?" I became the blogger taking aim at anyone supporting the athletics department.

"Not sure. I guess the Board of Trustees ultimately found the funds." Coach Oliver started sweating once we reached his office. Was it the two flights of stairs or the questions about the money?

"Those anonymous donations must have helped with the improvements to the playing fields." While Coach Oliver considered my words, the bags under his eyes indicated he hadn't slept in a few nights.

"No clue who donated the money, nor can I say much about the security side of it. Our security director can fill you in on that. How can I help today?" He absentmindedly scratched his balding head.

Oh, true. I had a reason to meet him before I'd realized he was the same guy I'd seen at Abby's place. "I'm in town for a few days and sorely missing the gym, but there aren't any true fitness centers in the area. Could I use the college's facilities while I'm in Braxton? I wouldn't ask but—"

"Ah, yes, that would be totally fine. Your parents are good people, I'd do anything to help them. Your father's a big supporter of the athletics department. I'll add access to your identification card and account, so you can use the fitness center. We're open twenty-four hours a day, seven days a week." He pulled out his phone and typed a few commands while leading me toward the fitness center down the hall. "Are you attending our opening game this Saturday? Expecting a full crowd." The excitement in his words leaped from his mouth. For someone who potentially killed Abby or just lost his friend, it was curious. Either he was a great actor or something else was going on behind the scenes in this mystery.

"I heard about a big rivalry between two pitchers. What was it, Striker and Jimmy?" I kept my tone simple, looking disinterested and as though I were making normal conversation.

"Jordan Ballantine, last year's relief pitcher. I used to bring him in, in the seventh or eighth inning whenever Striker tired out or gave up too many hits. I spent a lot of time with Jordan over the summer. His new curveball came out of nowhere. That kid might come close to a hundred miles per hour. He's got a chance of making the major leagues, but Striker's the current top dog."

"Sounds like a healthy competition. Decided who will start?"

"Got one more practice this week, then I'll make a big announcement on Friday at the pep rally," Coach Oliver replied, noting he had to finish working on a few things. "Come by the fitness center anytime. Top-notch facility here, just bought a few new pieces of equipment that'll work wonders for those delts of yours." He slapped the back of my shoulder with heavy force.

I couldn't let him go that easily. "I appreciate it. My mom thought you'd be able to help. She was upset over missing you at the party. Thought she saw you walking that night, but you were looking the other way or something. I guess you never made it, huh?"

Coach Oliver startled like a fox caught in the henhouse. "Saw me? Really? Hmmm... I got to the party and met your sister, Eleanor, in the lobby... on her way out."

I let him squirm. When he didn't seem to recall or offer anything further, I triggered his memory. "I think she said you might have been right outside Diamond Hall."

"Ah, yeah," Coach Oliver said with a slightly higher pitch to his voice. "I just remembered. I was late dropping off the schedule for the upcoming week. President Ayrwick, I mean your father, likes a hand-delivered copy of the weekly sporting event schedule each Friday, so he can plan accordingly. I ran into his assistant, and she offered to drop it off for me."

Lorraine hadn't mentioned this to me, which seemed odd. Surely, Coach Oliver wouldn't lie about something I could easily disprove. I didn't want to alienate him, so I nodded and smoothed over the conversation. Maybe he'd admit to knowing Abby. "Oh, that makes sense. My father is particular about his schedule. Such a shame about what happened to that professor."

"Definitely. It's always hard to hear someone's died, but to know they had an accident at such a young age, that's worse. She had a lot of life left in her."

Given he opened the door, I stepped further inside. "I take it you knew her well?"

"No, I wouldn't say that. I bumped into her occasionally. She'd attended an event or two. Staff functions. That's all I remember. I need to run, Kellan. I hope you'll join us for the game on Saturday."

"Thanks again," I said as he scampered down the hallway. I'd made him edgy and caught him in at least one, maybe two lies. I poked my head in the fitness center and quickly determined the newer machines had cost major money. I had to agree with the blogger that something was unusual about the anonymous donations and their distribution to Grey Sports Complex.

I texted Nana D to ask if she wanted company.

Nana D: *I'm busy. I've got a life. Unlike some people. Hugs and kisses.*
Me: *Why don't we schedule a meal?*
Nana D: *Go find a cow to tip or a pile of bricks to rearrange if you're bored. Or call Bridget.*
Me: *Perhaps you're pushing things a little too quickly?*
Nana D: *Don't ignore me. Move on at some point. I say that with love. Yes, to brunch soon.*

Was everyone sarcastic? And why did Nana D feel the need to keep setting me up with weird women? How about a normal one for a change... like Maggie... wait, was I even ready to date again?

Chapter 9

On Tuesday, I woke early and pushed myself to visit Grey Sports Complex for my first workout in five days. Jordan, the student employee who worked at Memorial Library—and Striker's new competition—ran on a treadmill. A pretty blonde raced furiously on the stationary bicycle. When I walked past both, I heard Jordan call out, "You're gonna beat your record, hot stuff!" She smiled at him, and they both focused on their workouts.

Rather than address a specific body part or group, I tested several of the new machines and acclimated to the equipment. Although I wouldn't stay in Braxton long, it would be helpful to take advantage of the opportunity.

When I arrived home, I scarfed down an early lunch—chocolate whey protein shake with almond milk, peanut butter, strawberries, and flaxseed. *'Don't knock it til you try it,'* I remembered the juice-maker telling me back at my home gym. Ever since that introduction, it'd become my new standard lunch on workout days. I unlocked my iPad, opened the *FaceTime* app, and contacted my daughter. As expected, she accepted the call without her grandmother's help and waved hello to me.

"Hello, my precious girl. Good morning to you."

"Daddy! Where are you?" Although Emma knew how to hold the device properly, so the camera caught her face, she couldn't stop from bouncing up and down on the couch in excitement.

"Slow down, baby. I'm gonna get seasick."

"Sorry. But if you bounced too, maybe we'd both look like we were super still."

I found little fault with her logic about not getting seasick. Maybe she was onto something. "What did you eat for breakfast?" I noticed blueberry stains on her lips. She loved to eat fruit and didn't seem to care for desserts. I often questioned if she were truly my daughter.

"*Bear Berries.* Ummm... Grandma said we could go to the zoo. They have a new baby giraffe."

Emma was in her *obsessed-with-animals* phase and wanted to go to the zoo every weekend. I suggested other sites like the planetarium or the beach, but nothing had taken the zoo's place in months. At some point, you had to give in if you wanted to maintain your sanity as a parent.

I told Emma about Nana D playing the clarinet years ago. She asked to take lessons after the next zoo trip. When her cartoons came on, she tossed the iPad to her grandmother. Cecilia waved hello and asked when I'd be back. Not another person adding to my list of aggravations.

While Francesca's parents were fantastic grandparents, they were horrendous in-laws. Were they still in-laws if I wasn't married to their daughter anymore? My point—they were amazing to Emma when Francesca died. But a few months after the burial, once life somehow got normal again—as normal as it could be for a thirty-year-old widower with a four-year-old daughter—I started seeing unfortunate changes. Vincenzo and Cecilia Castigliano showed up uninvited at my house with a request to keep Emma overnight, claiming they missed their daughter and wanted to feel close to her. One afternoon, Happy Tots Day Care called to say Emma's grandparents wanted to sign her out for the afternoon. I tried to keep an open mind about the Castigliano behavioral changes, but on the one-year anniversary of Francesca's death, Vincenzo snuck into my office to inform me he and Cecilia had decided it would be better if Emma moved in with them. I'd always known Vincenzo brokered shady business deals, but I never knew the extent until that night when Francesca's sister revealed their father was part of a Los Angeles mob. I started asking around, and a colleague pointed out the Castigliano family weren't just *part* of a Los Angeles mob. They were the main family who *ran* the Los Angeles mob.

Although I was non-confrontational, I needed their help since I was a single parent and wasn't planning to move back to Pennsylvania. I made it clear Emma was never to be placed in any dangerous situations given the *family business.* Vincenzo had shrugged and grunted, then said, "*I don't know what you talk about. We run a lovely import-export business. Very quiet and safe.*" We'd come to an agreement, but if they ever stepped out of line, I wouldn't be afraid to do something more drastic.

After I hung up, I dropped my head to the counter and closed my eyes. I was weary and needed a moment of silence. Too bad that wouldn't happen.

"Good afternoon, Kellan. It's about time you woke up," my father commented as he stood over me with a glass of water and a plate full of scattered whole wheat toast crumbs.

"I've been up since at least eight. Don't forget that's like five to me with the time difference. I haven't yet adjusted." I wish I knew whether he was serious or simply enjoyed pushing my buttons.

"You're young enough it shouldn't matter. At your age, I already had—"

"What are you doing home, anyway?" I couldn't compare our lives anymore. He'd always win. "Has retirement already begun?"

"As your mother and Lorraine told you yesterday, I can't return to my office until the sheriff finishes searching the building. It's easier to get most of my work done at home in the mornings, then go on campus for meetings in the afternoon. I won't be using the temporary office anymore and asked the facilities department to put my furniture in storage until they complete the renovations."

"Does Lorraine report everything she tells me back to you?" I'd have to be careful how much I spoke my mind in front of her. "She's concerned about what Sheriff Montague wants from you."

"Nothing you need to worry about, Kellan. The sheriff and I are on good terms with this whole debacle. I'm confident they'll do the right thing soon," he replied. "While you're here, I need to speak with you about something."

Oh, great. If he asked how long I'd be staying again, I'd pack my bags that afternoon and hop the next flight no matter the cost or location, even if Derek fired me. Speaking of Derek, I owed him a status update. "What's on your mind? I have some questions for you too, Dad."

"Go ahead. You first." My father perched on a stool at the kitchen island and glared at me.

"Where did you go the night of the retirement party? Mom's worried about you. Something's weird around here." I didn't want to bring up the call I'd overheard yet.

"Well, since you've put that so eloquently, Kellan, I was doing my job. Not all of us have the freedom to come and go or choose what projects we work on. I had an impromptu conversation with the Board of Trustees about something urgent near the end of their meeting."

"They meet on Saturday night. Who does that?"

"If you must know, they were discussing their final recommendations on the new president before the panel interviews. Their meeting was held after they all stopped by my party." He turned his hands over, so both palms faced upwards, then pulled them back to his body and crossed them in his lap.

I had the sudden urge to mock him. I didn't, as it wouldn't win me any favors. "Anything new from the blogger? I couldn't remember the site name to check myself."

"Yes, there was another post on Sunday talking about the opulence of my retirement party." His color faded as he spoke, making me debate if he were more human than I'd given him credit for. "Your mother and I paid for that party out of our pockets. The Board wanted to cover all costs, but we insisted they'd already bought me a wonderful going away present." He handed me his phone to read the post:

If you weren't in attendance at Saturday night's grand ceremony, you missed a soirée fit for royalty. Between the exotic scents and rare foods dripping in excess, I found everyone's admiration for Wesley Ayrwick to be so sickening, I couldn't force myself to stay exceptionally long. I'd hoped to share photos, but a security attendant who treated us like criminals stopped any camera or video recordings. Are we supposed to bow to our king? He should've spoken less about the baseball team's new uniforms and more about the questionable source of the anonymous donations frivolously spent in all the wrong places. Stop by Grey Sports Complex to test the ridiculous new systems that were integrated into our curiously modernized athletic facility. I managed to overhear quite a conversation about an upcoming special visitor to campus, and a well-known community citizen might shake in their boots once I reveal what's been going on behind our backs. Look for my next post to disclose all the details of these shady shenanigans.

When I asked my father if there was any truth to the post, he changed the subject. He noted how students found the blogger to be a funny distraction but gave his or her messages little consideration. I recalled the conversation where Myriam accused him of spending the college's money in ways he shouldn't have. He'd let her believe Braxton covered the costs of the party and never attempted to defend himself. Was he learning how to be less combative with other people, just not me? "Do you think Myriam Castle is leading this crusade against you?"

"Doubtful. Myriam and I spar from time to time, and she doesn't particularly like me, but she's not someone to hide behind her words. She directly indicts me of wrongdoing."

He had a good point about why she'd blog under an anonymous name yet accuse him of similar things in a public setting, where anyone could have overheard the conversation. "What about the new technology at Grey Sports Complex? How did that get funded?"

"I don't know all the details going on behind the scenes at Braxton. The Board of Trustees decided. You should touch base with Councilman Stanton. He's on the Board," he replied. "That all?"

Nana D would be a perfect person to grill the councilman. Since I couldn't bring up the mysterious phone call, I jumped to other topics. "Why didn't you tell me that Maggie and Connor were working at Braxton? I was just here in December, and you could have said something. Or picked up the phone."

"I didn't think it was important. You haven't mentioned either in a decade. I'd assumed you lost touch and cared little about what had happened to them. You've never been one to rehash the past."

Ouch. The digs were back in full force. "That's a little unfair, Dad. I may have lost touch, but Mom's having weekly coffee dates with Maggie. Connor works as your director of security."

"I thought you'd be happy I hired your friends. Some might call that nepotism."

Why did he always know what to say to shut me up? And why did I always feel like I was five years old around him? Since throwing a tantrum wasn't an option, I reined in my frustrations and leapt into the big topic. "Who do you think murdered Abby Monroe?"

"That's a matter for Sheriff Montague. I can tell you that neither I nor Lorraine had anything to do with it. What the sheriff does next, I don't know, but hopefully, she listens to me on the topic."

"Which means… what?" Seriously, did everyone have this much trouble with their parents?

"We had a complicated relationship. I liked Abby as a person, but she wasn't qualified for her position. The Board of Trustees was too worried about potential lawsuits if we tried to fire her. Instead, we kept her power in check," he said while crossing his arms and scowling. "I have it on good authority she'd been job hunting before Saturday's incident. The woman made enemies and was going through a nasty divorce. The sheriff plans to investigate those angles and put an end to this entire affair. Can I now discuss what I wanted to talk to you about?"

Abby was the person my father had been talking about failing to terminate on the call I'd overheard. I considered all his news and rationalized he had a solid theory about the investigation. "Yes, go ahead, Dad. I'm listening." I assumed it had something to do with Emma or my mother.

"Abby's death has left a hole in the communications department. There's only one other professor with experience in media studies, but she's covering Abby's administrative responsibilities for Dean Mulligan. We don't have anyone who can teach her classes for a few weeks until we find a suitable replacement." He paused to see if I had any reactions. If I remembered correctly, Dean Mulligan, Abby's boss, oversaw all the academic departments.

I suspected where he was going with the conversation but wanted him to ask me directly, before I put my foot in my mouth. "I imagine it's quite a predicament. You've solved bigger problems before."

"True, I most certainly have. I'm also supposed to announce the new president next week, transition my responsibilities, help the sheriff and Connor minimize the impact of this tragedy on the rest of the campus, and accept all these changes in my life. I'm not getting any younger, Kellan, and although it may seem like I can do everything all at once, I cannot."

Wow. I didn't think I'd ever hear my father admit a potential weakness. "You're strong and persistent."

"While that may be true, it's time to let someone else step into that role for this family. As a starting point, I'd like you to takeover Abby's classes until Dean Mulligan can decide how to handle potential reorganization of the department and hire her replacement."

After a fifteen-second void occupied all notions of life inside my head, I found the courage to respond. "I can appreciate your faith in me, Dad, and I'm honestly touched you would—"

"I'm not done. Just let me get this out," he replied, retreating from the counter toward the back window. "You're tired of everyone asking how long you plan to stay or when you'll move back. You've mentioned missing your friends. Your mother wants to spend more time with Emma. As do I. You've kept yourself distant from this family for a reason, and I've let this go on long enough."

"Dad, please don't say any more. I don't want to have this conversation." I knew where he was going. He'd tried this once before. We had a horrible fight when I left Christmas night two years ago, after accusing him of driving away all his children.

"Kellan, I'm not saying you're right or wrong. I'm saying you've done it your way ever since Francesca died. I wasn't there for you when it happened. I admitted I never cared much for her. But she was your wife, and Emma's mother, and I should have been a better father." He rested his hand on my shoulder. I hadn't even heard him walk toward me in those few confidence-shaking seconds. "All I'm asking from you, is three weeks to a month."

I told my father I needed the rest of the week to think about his proposal and would let him know my decision on the weekend. I abandoned him in the kitchen and raced out to the garage. I didn't know whom to turn to at that moment, but his words hit way too close to my heart.

I spent the rest of the day driving around Braxton and reminiscing about all the great times I had in the past with college friends and family, including when Francesca and Emma came home with me on a few trips. Taking the temporary job meant risking any opportunity I had of getting my own television show, to escape Derek and achieve something I'd been dreaming about for years. I had a lot more thinking to do before I could make any definitive decisions.

No longer interested in worsening my mood by talking to the sheriff, I pushed that task off until the following day. I also needed to let Connor know Coach Oliver had lied to me about how well he knew Abby. Regardless of their relationship, he'd been going through her mail when I was standing in the driveway. If he was lying to me, he was lying to the sheriff too. I first needed to get some sleep, then I'd deal with all the concerns tomorrow.

Chapter 10

When Wednesday descended, I felt stronger and more alive. Going to the fitness center the prior day helped motivate me. I returned in the hopes I could work off some frustration and anger. It was even quieter than it'd been the day before. Only one other person was working on chest exercises, as if the weight amounted to nothing more than a pillow.

I approached the lat machine to his right, adjusted the seat height, and chose the amount of weight I hoped I could handle. I was about to get started when the other guy called out to me.

"Hey, would you mind spotting me on the bench press? No one's been in here all morning." He wore a baseball cap and a long-sleeve college jersey with the number three.

I wasn't sure I could lift the same amount of weight he could, but I'd try. "No problem. Are you on the baseball team?" I took his grunt while lifting for a yes, then asked more questions in between sets.

His dark hair was clipped short, and he hadn't shaved in a few days. "Yep, name's Craig Magee, but everyone calls me Striker. I'm the team's pitcher. You a student here?"

The famous Striker. Did he know who was pitching in the game on Saturday? Coach Oliver said he wouldn't reveal the decision until Friday to the public. "Me? Former student, but thanks for the ego boost, man." I enjoyed knowing I could sometimes still pass for my twenties.

"I'm Kellan. I've heard a bit about you before. What does the three stand for?"

"Number of pitches it takes for me to knock down all the batters. Three strikes in a row and they're always out," he said with a huge grin.

"Clever. Ready for Saturday's game?"

"That's why I'm here today. Final pre-season practice tomorrow and then the coach decides the starting lineup." Additional reps failed to wind him.

"I'm sure all the extra focus will be helpful," I replied as Striker finished his third set, increasing the weight by ten each time. I would soon reach my limit on how much I could spot, but I didn't want to stop his momentum. I could push myself to hold more if necessary.

"Yep. I think I've got this in the bag, but it's not just the upcoming practice. I'm waiting on a few grades to confirm I'll be allowed to play. Dean Mulligan put me on academic probation and threatened to take away my scholarship because my GPA dropped below a 3.0 at the end of last semester."

"How do you plan to fix that?" I asked, recalling the conversation Abby had with someone on her phone in front of Memorial Library. Was she talking about meeting Striker that night at eight thirty?

"I was right on the border, but the dean said I could play as long as I kept up a 'B+' all semester long. Waiting on two grades from my biology class and Professor Monroe."

"Isn't Monroe the professor who had an accident last weekend?" I played dumb to see what else he'd reveal. I hadn't realized my coming to the fitness center would be an enlightening connection this morning. Kudos to me for doing the right thing. Nana D was right—I was brilliant.

"Yep," he replied before wiping himself off with a towel. "I'm confident I did well on a biology paper. I should know this morning. We haven't heard if Professor Monroe turned in the grades before... well, you know." He made a *BOOM* sound and dropped his head to the side.

I was dealing with someone just as mature as I'd once been. "Do you think Professor Monroe gave you a passing grade?"

"Doubt it. She didn't like me very much last semester. She's the one who failed me. That's why I'm back in her Intro to Film class again this semester. It fills one of my elective courses and unfortunately was the only other one that matched my schedule between baseball, my job, and other classes." Striker tagged me in to do my own set of chest presses.

"If you need any help with the class, I could tutor you. I was a communications major here a few years ago, and I'm well-versed in the broadcast curriculum."

"Seriously, you'd help? I barely know you." His friendliness and smile were contagious.

"You seem like a good guy. Besides, I met Coach Oliver yesterday. He's counting on you to take the team to the championship this year, even get you to the majors." I didn't want to inflate Striker's hopes, but he might have the scoop on Coach Oliver and Abby. Or he could have been the person who knocked Abby on her head and pushed her down the stairs.

When we finished working out, I handed him my cell number and advised him I'd be around for a few days. He mentioned he'd let me know after he found out his latest grade.

"Was Coach Oliver friendly with Professor Monroe? I wondered if he tried to talk with her about getting you some help with the class." It seemed unusual that those two had some sort of relationship while one of the star baseball students was stuck in the middle. I also remembered my mother mentioning changes to the policy of fraternization between certain departments, citing a scandal a year ago involving a staff member accused of harassing someone. Was Coach Oliver to blame back then?

"Wouldn't know. I tried to stay away from Professor Monroe as much as possible. Coach Oliver told me he'd help however he could, but I don't know if he did anything once she failed me last semester." Striker drank some water from the fountain, then wiped the bench with a wet towel. "I'm gonna hit the showers. Got class in thirty minutes. Thanks for spotting today."

"No worries. Good luck, Striker."

After he left, I finished my workout and reflected on our conversation. Had Sheriff Montague learned the same information and decided how the Jenga puzzle mysteriously collapsed in murder?

When I pulled out my phone to call her, I saw a new email from Derek with the name of the hotel and a copy of his check-in registration. He'd checked out the day before, which meant he was back in Los Angeles. I dialed the number for registration and pretended to be him inquiring about my final bill. While I listened to a lovely but ironic minute-long version of Michael Jackson's *Smooth Criminal*, I walked to the locker room to change into a towel before showering. The clerk came back on the line and confirmed the purchases I'd made in the room last Saturday and Sunday, as well as the additional damage fee for the state I'd left the room in. She mentioned it was the first time they'd ever had to replace a mattress due to guest misuse. "*Oops, my bad*," I said, trying to sound like Derek but feeling a sense of fake guilt for something he'd done.

Unless Derek had sent someone to Hawaii in his place, enabling him to show up in Braxton, he likely hadn't killed Abby. I felt better knowing I didn't work for a murderer, but I still had to call the creep. After showering and noticing the marked improvement in my muscle definition, I pinged him on *FaceTime*, so I could see if his *tell* gave him away. Just to put the final check mark on his alibi, I asked if he knew any good mattress stores, claiming I was in the market to find a new one.

"Dude, I don't know but call and ask that hotel. Somehow my date and I broke the springs. They had the audacity to charge me an extra fee!" He didn't blink, nor did his lip quiver. He had told the truth.

With the alibi now confirmed and my stomach near revolt, I updated him on Abby's death formally being considered a murder. He responded, "Kel-baby, you've got quite a story. We could reposition season two to focus on her murder. Find out everything. This is your top priority. Do whatever you have to do."

"Yep, I'm on it." This time I hung up on him, feeling a sense of pride and accomplishment. Now I had many compelling reasons to say involved in the case.

I called the precinct to verify Sheriff Montague was in her office, but Officer Flatman told me she'd driven to Braxton to meet with Connor. Perfect, I could talk to them both after I stopped off at The Big Beanery to pick up a bribe—I meant thoughtful and kind gesture.

Twenty minutes later, I parked in the guest lot and dashed to the BCS Office. When I arrived, I saw the frown forming on Sheriff Montague's face from the outside walkway.

"Good afternoon," I announced through the screen door and entered the foyer. "I thought I'd visit my old friend, Connor. Fancy running into you here." I set the three coffees and donuts on the counter. "I have an extra cup if you're interested, sheriff."

"Little Ayrwick, you're pushing me... Flatman already texted that you were looking for me. What do you want?" She had the classic annoyed detective appearance again—hands on her hips, tweed blazer too tight across her back and pushing her shoulders up in the air, lips pursed, and frankly, that same look Nana D got when she'd consumed too many prunes.

"You might want to hear a few things I learned this week. Maybe you could give me an update on access to Abby's office or on anything happening with the case?" I stepped back in case she swung at me, but either she held out for one giant wallop, or she was considering my offer.

"Something tells me you won't go away until I entertain whatever you feel the hernia-popping need to divulge. If you have helpful information to share, maybe I'll feel obliged to return the favor. What's got those purple lacy panties crawling halfway up your—"

Connor spit out his coffee this time. "Dude, she's got your number. You better watch yourself."

His interruption had at least stopped her from finishing her thoughts. As much as her attitude annoyed me, I enjoyed being abused in a humorous sort of way. Little did she know I once had to wear a pair of purple lacy panties after losing a bet with Connor during our junior year. Could April Montague and I be friends in some alternate universe? When I thought about having to look at that dreadful tweed blazer over drinks or at a football game, I had the obvious answer. I stopped myself from retching.

"I went to Abby's house to see if she had a roommate or husband that might let me in to check, but when I got there...." I reiterated everything I'd learned to date. "It might have been a coincidence, or the meeting the night of Abby's murder might have changed times. Just felt it my responsibility to share the news."

Sheriff Montague smirked. "Not bad for an inexperienced, nosy pain in the butt. You discovered a few things my detectives haven't come up with yet. They'll suffer, thanks. We knew about her neighbor and that Abby was seen around with someone, but not about it being Coach Oliver. I appreciate the academic tips, but we're already looking into her cell records. Next time... one, don't dillydally before telling me, and two, stay out of my case. You've been warned not to interfere."

"Wait a minute! I have it on good authority you've nearly completed your search of Abby's office, yet there's been no phone call telling me when and where to show up." What could she do with Connor standing there as a witness?

"All accurate information except I didn't promise you. I said I'd take it under advisement. And I did. I also chose to follow proper protocol. Something with which you have difficulty." She manhandled two of the donuts and the remaining cup of coffee, enabling me to confirm she wore no wedding ring. "Thanks for the snacks, Little Ayrwick. I'll be in touch if I need additional assistance from Seraphina Danby's errand boy and savior, or if I learn which of you two won the award for Braxton's latest interfering washerwoman who likes to gab." She turned to Connor. "I know you have no control over him, and I direct none of this at you. I value your help as Braxton's security director."

I ignored the huge grin on Connor's face. He clearly hadn't picked up on the sheriff's crush. Nana D and I did not deserve that comment about gabbing. "Wait, didn't you say you'd share something as long as I provided useful information? Come on, Connor, you heard it too? How about the murder weapon? Any clues yet?"

I swear little hearts shot out from the sheriff's eyes in Connor's direction. "You kinda said that," he replied. "But I could have heard it wrong."

"Boys, and I mean boys for one of you, this is not a game we're playing. Let me wash, rinse, and repeat for those of you who own stock in all the hair gel companies. Murder is not a game. I can appreciate that you want to do your part. I don't think you have any ill intentions, Little Ayrwick. I need to protect the evidence and paper trails in the case, so we can clearly put our criminal behind bars. Keep your dirty paws to yourself. I'll only ask nicely once."

I nodded since she had a good point. "I'm not looking to receive any special favors this time. Maybe you could keep me in the loop. I'll immediately share anything I learn and stay out of your way. Honest!"

"We're still running tests to identify the shape and size of the murder weapon. I haven't given you access to Abby Monroe's office because I haven't been cleared to do so. I need approval from her next of kin and from Braxton staff. I just finished chatting with your father. I'm meeting momentarily with the other." She saluted us both and headed to the door. "Expect a call tomorrow, Little Ayrwick."

As she left, I turned to hit Connor in the shoulder with as much power as I could muster after having been deflated and emasculated by Sheriff Montague. "You could have stood up for me, dude."

Connor laughed. "I work with that woman all the time. I don't want to be on her nasty side."

"Oh, is there another side of her you want to be on?" I teased, forgetting how diesel he'd gotten and how easily I could end up on the floor from one punch. I'd never learn my lessons, would I?

"I'll ignore that. But I'll also point out you missed a key revelation there, Deputy Clueless. Besides her not liking your hair, pretty boy." The sheriff's comment was obviously meant for me given I had the long and wavy curls. Connor's buzz cut seemed off limits to her.

I shook my head. What clue did I miss? "I'm not sure what you... oooh!" If the sheriff was meeting with Abby's next of kin, then Alton Monroe had been located. "The husband's back in town!"

"Always the first one to figure it out, eh, Kellan? Listen, I need to finish some work before I meet up with Maggie. Take it easy, man," Connor replied while shoving a donut in his mouth.

He disappeared into his office, leaving me standing alone and disgruntled. What was he meeting Maggie for? I reached into the bag to grab a donut, but there were none left. "Bollocks! You got the better of me too many times today, Connor. Don't make me start a war."

I spent the rest of Wednesday working on urgent items that Derek needed me to handle for *Dark Reality*. Promo schedules, contract negotiations with supporting actors, and script edits to introduce Abby Monroe into season two's scope. Although we didn't have a full story, he wanted to show the updated plan to his boss at the network. I quickly pulled together revised outlines and some taglines, feeling a little unnerved about using Abby's death as a marketing ploy.

Chapter 11

With my immediate deadlines addressed, I went for a run Thursday morning and intentionally stopped at the Pick-Me-Up Diner to touch base with Eleanor. As I entered, Eustacia Paddington grabbed my arm and shook her head wildly. "You gotta do something about that wicked grandmother of yours, Kellan. She's outta control!" Wisps of gray hair shot out in all directions underneath a furry blue hat three-sizes too big on her frail and wrinkled head.

Eustacia Paddington had gone to high school with my nana. They'd been frenemies ever since. Whatever Ms. Paddington did, my nana had to go one step further in their quest to annoy one another. On the last count, Nana D rallied six volunteers to rotate weeks for shoveling snow at Willow Trees, a nearby senior citizen's community where Eustacia Paddington resided. Somehow all the volunteers were under the impression they could drop the mounds of shoveled snow on the corner lot. Eustacia's lot. Which Nana D had told everyone was empty for the winter while the tenant was in Florida. But she wasn't away, which meant Ms. Paddington couldn't get out of her home for a week.

I wasn't looking forward to hearing the latest battle. "Good to see you, Ms. Paddington. That color blue makes your eyes shine. How are you doing?"

"I know when I'm being worked. Don't even try the *you-catch-more-with-honey-than-vinegar* game with me. Your nana is the fly in this flaming puddle of hemorrhoid ointment, sonny." She stomped her wooden cane on the ground and caused a picture frame to fall off the wall. "She's trying to steal Lindsey Endicott. Everyone at Willow Trees knows we've been dating for months. You tell her—"

"I don't think she's trying to steal him away from you, Ms. Paddington. Nana D seems hardly interested in dating," I began, but was interrupted before I could finish my thoughts. Could Nana D really be putting herself on the market again? After that last debacle with Eustacia Paddington's brother, Nana D pitched such a fit I thought she was going to take a vow of chastity and join the nunnery.

"That woman is out to get me. You tell her not to start something she won't be able to finish!" As she left, all I could see was the blurry image of her giant pink parka waving in the parking lot like one of those tall, inflatable tube machines people put outside stores when holding sales and trying to capture shopper's attention. She looked like Gumby's ancient grandmother in need of an oxygen boost.

"You know Nana D probably flirted with him." Eleanor pushed the cash drawer shut. "She was in here earlier talking about pulling the wool over someone's eyes."

My sister was right. I didn't doubt it, but I couldn't let Eustacia know I was on to my nana's tricks. "Speaking of sly ones, what's up with you avoiding me yesterday?"

Eleanor lifted the countertop and passed through to the main waiting area. At least she'd swapped out the condiment-stained outfit from two days ago with a clean pair of pants and a brighter top. "Just busy. You take everything so personally sometimes, Kellan. If I didn't know better, I'd think my big brother got his wee feelings hurt." She kissed my cheek and placed two menus back in the cubby on the entrance wall while humming a tune from some psychic medium show.

I rolled my eyes at her. "What do your Tarot cards say?"

"Touché," she teased. "I'm sorry I ran off the other day. It's been a busy few weeks. Everyone's a little jumpy with the professor's death." Eleanor had a habit of shutting down whenever something was bothering her instead of opening up to me or anyone else. I assumed my mother had said or done something to annoy her again. *Twinsies* gone rogue!

"Tell me about it. I've been home for less than a week, and everything's changed." I followed her to the back office. "Hey, have you noticed anything going on between Connor and Maggie? I'm not sure if I picked up a weird vibe or if—"

"No, why?" she replied abruptly.

"I think she's seen him twice already since I've been home. Whenever I notice them together, they're making googly eyes—" I couldn't finish my thoughts again. People enjoyed interrupting me. Did I need to be more assertive?

"I'm sure they're just being friendly since they both work together at Braxton now." As she sat in her office chair, the phone rang, and I listened to her argue with a supplier about a late delivery.

Eleanor had squashed my theory about anything going on between Connor and Maggie. Still, I asked myself, why did I care? I had more pressing things to worry about. I scanned for email on my phone, but nothing from Derek. I was flipping through my calendar when Eleanor hung up.

"There's nothing between them. I'm sure of it," she replied. "Sorry about that, I'm having trouble with a supplier."

Something told me there was more going on than Eleanor was willing to reveal at that point. Since I wasn't ready to get into it with her, I dropped the Maggie and Connor discussion. "Maybe you could swap suppliers. Perhaps the place Mom used to help with Dad's party could provide an alternative option."

"I'm capable of figuring it out on my own, Kellan. Did you need something or were you just swinging by to perform today's good deed?" She rose, giving me the distinct impression it was time for me to leave. All the color had drained from her face.

"Well, I guess I should go," I replied, leaning in to offer a comforting hug. "I love you, Eleanor, and when you want to talk, I'll drop everything for you." I exited her office and headed to the Jeep. Before I started the engine, she texted me.

Eleanor: *I'm sorry. Let's get dinner Saturday, and we'll talk.*

I knew something was up, and now I needed to be patient until she revealed the source of her grief. When I arrived at Diamond Hall, things were no longer cordoned off, yet a sign still indicated classes were held elsewhere. I climbed the stairs, assuming someone might stop me but making it all the way to the second floor with no interruption. I called out on my way to Abby's office. "Hello, anyone there?" Was Sheriff Montague inside? I wasn't prepared for a battle of well-timed quips and her brutal one-liners.

A mid-forties, curly blond with a recent sunburn stood behind the desk. He was dressed casually and didn't appear to be a member of the Braxton police force. "Good afternoon. May I help you?"

"Kellan Ayrwick. I'm reviewing Professor Monroe's classes. I thought I'd drop by to see if…." I should have prepared better. I couldn't waltz into the office and rifle through drawers without questions being asked. Worrying about the sheriff had thrown me off my game.

"Oh, Kellan. I'm supposed to call you this afternoon. It's good to meet you. I'm Alton Monroe." He gestured at me to join him. "Sheriff Montague mentioned you wanted a quick peek at Abby's files."

So, this was the soon-to-be ex-husband and Lorraine's half-brother. I saw a slight resemblance between Lorraine and Alton, in their pinned-back ears, hair color, and narrow jawlines. He didn't look dangerous. I supposed I retained little worry over being alone with him in Abby's office. I was grateful I could finally poke around Abby's things, despite Sheriff Montague failing to notify me herself. I shook his hand and leaned against the doorframe. "I appreciate it. I believe you just got in from out of town, somewhere visiting…?" I paused, hoping he'd fill in the blank.

"A remote village near the border of Alaska and Russia. I go on occasional nature treks for an online magazine to write about animals going extinct." He prattled on about some bird whose population had been slowly declining in the last decade, allowing me a chance to scan the office.

As the department head, Abby had occupied one of the bigger offices on the floor. Two small wooden chairs sat across from an enormous mahogany desk. I idled near one of them, and what I assumed was Alton Monroe's briefcase borrowed the other one. Dozens of bookshelves lined the walls. On the open wall space were Abby's diplomas, confirming the schools I'd seen in her profile during my research. A few scattered papers cluttered the desk, the garbage pail had recently been emptied, and what looked like a grade book sat on the corner table near a reading lamp. Striker would love to get his hands on that. I was curious if he'd found out his grade and would be cleared to play in Saturday's game. The room was organized but devoid of any actual personality other than books. Abby liked a plain workspace.

It suddenly dawned on me Alton had stopped talking. I hoped he hadn't asked me a question as I'd lost interest in his story while scanning the room. Not that I didn't care about the plight of the short-tailed albatross, but I had more immediate problems to solve. "Very interesting. Sounds like a good trip. I heard you didn't have any wireless access. Hearing the news about your wife must have been a shock."

"Soon-to-be ex-wife," he replied smugly. "Although, that's not important anymore. Abby and I were trying to salvage a friendship, but I'm afraid things went south many months ago."

"I wasn't aware. So sorry to hear," I fibbed again. I wasn't in the habit of lying, but if it procured fresh information out of a potential source, I could comfortably blur the lines. Mostly, I was an honest and direct guy. Ask Eleanor. "They'll hold her funeral early next week. I expect I'll see you there?"

"Abby had no other family. I feel obligated to attend, perhaps a final goodbye."

"I imagine so. That's good of you." I paused, hoping he'd volunteer more information. In past interviews, it always seemed people of his nature were uncomfortable with silence, suddenly sharing things they might not normally say until the solitude nudged them over the edge.

"Sheriff Montague mentioned you wanted to look for some papers. I've been here for twenty minutes doing the same thing. She was planning to sign over a few rights, but her death might change the divorce, huh?" It was said too matter-of-factly for my taste. Alton noted that he'd found the grade book trapped between the desk and the wall. I assumed it'd either fallen there accidentally or been knocked down during a struggle at the eight thirty meeting.

"Have you figured out what happens to her assets? Did she leave a will?" I wasn't sure he'd answer, but there weren't any reasons not to inquire.

"Not that I'm aware of. I changed mine a year ago when we separated. As I said, she had no other family. I suppose that means it all comes to me... if she even had anything of value." Alton lifted the papers on her desk, then pointed to the far table. "There are also a few course materials. Your father mentioned you may need those."

Had my father already told strangers that I would take over Abby's classes, even though I hadn't given him a decision? My harried brow must have clued in Alton.

"He and I briefly met when I borrowed the key from his assistant. Your father also expressed his condolences. He mentioned you might stop by for the coursework."

A voice coming up the stairs startled us. When I turned around, Lorraine walked through the hallway toward me. "Kellan, it's wonderful to see you. Did my brother leave already?"

"No, he's right inside." I stepped sideways to allow Lorraine access.

Alton's cheeks reddened when he realized I knew about his connection to Lorraine. I grew curious how solid his alibi was and mentally noted ways to follow up. Abby's sudden death provided too many valuable gains for him.

"Are you about ready to head out?" she asked her brother, then turned to me. "Alton and I have a few things to talk about, Kellan. I'm thinking about getting a lawyer. Sheriff Montague keeps returning with more questions about the night of the accident." She nibbled on her lip in frustration.

"She's covering all her bases. I'm looking into a few angles myself. I gave the sheriff some useful information earlier about Abby's connection to others on campus."

Lorraine attempted to smile. "Oh, that's good news. I hope they figure this out soon. It's draining your father. Poor Alton can't move forward on her estate. I'd like to be out of the line of fire." She shivered and wrapped her arms around herself. "We should get going, Alton."

After Alton and Lorraine trotted off, I searched Abby's office. The book on her corner table was her current grade keeper. Subjecting myself to Dr. Castle's presence to decipher it offered little comfort or warm, fuzzy feelings. *Out damn spot, dearest Lady Macbeth.*

All I found of potential interest in the drawer was an oddly shaped key, the unsigned contract between Derek and Abby, and the folders with *Dark Reality's* research notes. Derek would finally get what he was looking for. I packed them in an empty box I found in the corner, then perused several titles on the bookshelves. Mostly theater, media, and academic books stood out. Abby was also undeniably a fan of reality television shows and the paranormal.

When a large book with a red cover and no title or author captured my interest, I pulled it off the shelf. Though partially hollow, it had something hidden inside. Given the sheer volume of books, checking everything on the shelves couldn't have been part of the sheriff's sweep. Was Sheriff Montague not as skilled as Braxton needed her to be? I enjoyed thinking about how to best use the mistake against her in the future. Would her failure be my win? Time to put that sheriff in checkmate!

A locked, leather-bound journal lurked beneath the fake red book cover. I grabbed the key I'd found in the drawer and matched it up. The lock opened, and I suddenly had access to Abby Monroe's personal thoughts. Could I invade her privacy? I permitted myself to scan the pages for any current entries. When I found a few, I dropped the journal in the storage box, deciding to ponder how comfortable I'd feel crossing such a line. I added her grade book and several printed copies of her current class syllabi to the box too. I had some reading to do that evening. How much would I learn about Abby's secret or not-so-secret life?

Prior to heading home, I connected my phone to the hands-free device in the Jeep and dialed Nana D. She picked up after the second ring. "Where've you been the last few days? I thought you'd have come by for more pie or to talk about Bridget Colton."

So, the elf had a last name. Nana D bringing her up again definitely concerned me this was a setup. "I ran into your bestie this morning. Ms. Paddington had some interesting information to share with me. It's time you and I had afternoon tea." I was sure she could hear the sarcasm dripping from my words, but then again, she'd ignore it even if she had.

"Pish! That woman speaks nonsense. She's worse than her brother, and after what he did to me, I have no time for those Paddingtons anymore. Troublemakers, I'm telling you," she chided. "I can't do tea today… maybe tomorrow? Why don't you come over around three? I should be home from the farmer's market and ready to hear some gossip."

"No, Nana D. I don't have any gossip. It's your turn to share." I had to be stern with her, otherwise she'd cross the line every time.

"What's that? Sorry, fuzzy connection," she replied, squawking loudly. I distinctly heard her making static sounds before she stopped to hack up what sounded like a hairball in the middle of her routine.

"Fine. I'll come by tomorrow." I played along with her charade, then asked if she knew anything about Marcus Stanton's role on the Board of Trustees. "What might you know about the anonymous donations to Braxton and who authorized all the new spending in the athletics department?"

"I'm meeting with Councilman Stanton tomorrow. I'll see what I can find out. We've got a few things to settle, and that man's gonna listen to me this time if it's the last thing I do." She harrumphed in the background before drinking a swig of something that caused her to shout, "That did the trick!"

"What does he need to listen to you about?" I raised the heat in the Jeep.

"Stanton's using Wharton County funds in all the wrong places. I intend to prove he's clueless."

I was surprised at how up to speed Nana D was on things going on with the county's fiduciary decisions. Then again, she always was sharp with insignificant details. "I wonder if Stanton has any kids at Braxton," I asked, suddenly remembering they would probably be about that age. "I didn't know he was on the Board of Trustees until Dad told me."

"Yep, that star pitcher, Craig Magee. You've probably heard of Striker. Can't wait to see the game on Saturday. This town needs a boost."

"Wait, what did you say about Striker? They have different last names." I was confused.

"Striker is his stepson. He married Striker's mother years ago when the kid was young. She died from cancer around the same time Francesca died. Good woman too."

"You need someone to go with you on Saturday?" I wondered whether the councilman had been Abby's eight thirty discussion that night. I'd need to recall when he'd left the party, but it was probably at the same time as my father for that impromptu board meeting.

Nana D and I confirmed our plans for tea the next day. She also noted she'd get back to me on the game as she might attend with someone else, but she wouldn't say whom. I suspected Nana's potential alternative date would not thrill Eustacia if his name was Lindsey Endicott.

I drove the long way to my parents' house and considered my next steps. I needed to go through Abby's papers and journal. Not that it was a fair thing to read her personal thoughts. I could either give them to Sheriff Montague, or I could casually check a few pages to verify whether any reason existed to share them. I wouldn't hide vital clues, but it wasn't fair to waste taxpayer money by forcing the sheriff to read the journal if it amounted to nothing, right?

Chapter 12

After hanging up with Nana D, I scheduled a time for dinner with Eleanor after the big baseball game. She usually took off Saturday nights, so there was at least one weekend evening as an option for potential dates. Unfortunately, the guy she'd hoped would ask her out this Saturday failed to extend an offer, which meant she was looking for company. I spent the rest of the night reading through the *Dark Reality* materials I'd collected from Abby's, so I could get Derek off my back on Abby's research before diving into anything else.

I chatted with Emma before bed, then caught up on some much-needed rest. When I awoke on Friday, I concentrated on reading all the pages of Abby's grade book, which clarified how the late professor documented student records. While the prior semesters had been well organized, as evidenced by Abby's weekly notes, the current semester was mostly empty. The lack of content didn't seem to add up properly at first, but I theorized if she'd been more focused on connecting with Derek for season two of *Dark Reality*, Abby might have let her normal standards slip.

I flipped to the current semester to check the grades and learned the other pitcher, Jordan Ballantine, had earned a 'B+' on the first exam. I turned a few more pages and came across an 'A+' for Carla Grey, wondering if she were related to the ruthless county judge whom I'd crossed paths with once before. I located Striker's page and at first thought he had zero entries, but when I looked closer, he had an 'F' that was partially erased or smudged. I held it up to the light by my bedside table and saw the definite markings of a failing grade. While an 'F' didn't look good for Striker playing in the upcoming game, the fact that it was partially erased made me worry this was why Abby had been killed.

Since Lorraine had run the department this semester while the previous office manager, Siobhan, took maternity leave, she might have some idea what was going on with grading processes. I was also interested in talking with Lorraine about Abby's classes in case I accepted my father's request to assume their responsibility for a few weeks. Lorraine agreed to meet at noon, so I arranged my morning such that I could get in a workout at the fitness center before heading to Diamond Hall.

When I arrived, Lorraine was making copies of class materials. I joined her near the machine and inquired about her brother. "How's Alton handling Abby's death?"

Lorraine shrugged. "He feels bad about it, and although he never would have wished for anything to happen to her, Alton's better off. I don't mean to sound cold, but that woman really made life difficult for the poor man."

"He didn't seem shaken yesterday. Has he been back long from his out-of-town trip?" I was hoping to find out the details of his alibi and return home.

"Just a day or so. When the sheriff finally got a lead on his last credit card receipt, she was able to track down a local officer in Alaska who got word to him." Lorraine turned the photocopier off and walked toward her desk. "You're extremely interested in Alton. You don't think he had anything to do with it, do you? He has an alibi, Kellan."

Alton didn't seem like a killer based on our ten-minute conversation; however, both Nana D and Connor thought this was a spur-of-the-moment crime. "Nah, just trying to pull all the pieces together. I could use your help, Lorraine." Sensing Alton's alibi was airtight, I pulled out the grade book and asked Lorraine if she recognized it.

"Standard issue. We've mostly stopped using them, but some professors keep track manually before uploading any grades to the online system. Where did you find that one?" Lorraine had already sat at the desk to arrange the photocopies in a folder marked *Monday Coursework*.

"Belonged to Abby Monroe. Alton and I found it yesterday. I took it with me to learn more about her classes. You know my father suggested I—"

"Take them over? Yes, he asked what I thought you'd decide." She clasped her hands together. "If you take the job, this folder is for you. What are you going to do?"

Lorraine had thought ahead and prepared materials for me. I'd already decided it was too valuable of an opportunity, given Derek wanted me to stick around longer to find more content for the show. "I'm going to the baseball game tomorrow to observe some students. See if I fit in."

"It's important to your father." Lorraine's eyes were withdrawn and hollowed, and her lips were dry and cracked.

Lorraine wanted to say something, but I wasn't sure how to pull it out. "Is that the only thing on your mind?"

"You've always been so perceptive, Kellan. I seem to be at the center of this crazy situation."

That's when I remembered Coach Oliver's event schedule. Maybe he could prove her alibi. "Didn't you say no one saw you after eight that evening? Coach Oliver mentioned handing you a schedule outside Diamond Hall." I scanned her face for any reactions, curious why she'd failed to mention anything.

"Oh, that's right, I forgot." Lorraine shifted positions, and her gaze bored holes in the floor. "The entire exchange happened so quickly, just a few seconds after I'd left the retirement party. It wouldn't have helped prove much."

"Mention it to Sheriff Montague. My mother saw Coach Oliver. There's a chance he also noticed something or someone without realizing it." I rested my hand on her shoulder.

"Your mother saw the coach? I'll tell the sheriff." She smoothed out wrinkles in her blouse.

I would bet money Lorraine hid something. I'd have to wait until she was comfortable enough to tell me the rest. "You went to get something for me, right? Did you ever find it?" I wasn't worried unless the gift could help prove her alibi.

"No, that's part of what's bothering me. I can't find your present anywhere. I could have sworn I left it on my desk. I meant to wrap it before I left on Friday but got too busy." Lorraine wouldn't give me any details other than mentioning I'd been upset the prior fall, and she wanted to do something special for me.

I couldn't recall the specifics, but I'd find out soon enough. "Where could it be?"

"I wish I knew. That's not the only thing vanishing. A student reported something lost this week. I also can't find the new... ugh, never mind." She threw her hands in the air. "Three different things don't just get up and walk away by themselves, Kellan."

That caused some niggles. "Is Sheriff Montague aware of the thefts?"

"It didn't come up when we spoke."

"Will you inform Connor? Someone should know about them," I said.

"To be honest, I thought maybe with everything going on among the temporary office move, the extra work with Siobhan being out, and the retirement party plans, I must have misplaced your present. I'm still looking around for the other two missing items, but I'm gonna check your father's desk. It might have gotten put in a drawer accidentally before they sent it to storage." She clicked a few keys on her keyboard, then said, "Looks like I have a meeting coming up soon. Anything else I can help you with?"

I couldn't help wondering if the missing items related to Abby's death. With only a few minutes left, I asked Lorraine to describe the grading process. I also mentioned the scratch marks I'd found near Striker's name in Abby's book.

"That's bizarre. When the semester started, I asked each professor how they wanted me to assist with day-to-day operations while Siobhan was on leave. Almost everyone said they'd love it if I could handle all the computer work for them."

"Really, even Abby? What about the last few days, was anything different?" Had I latched on to something potentially important?

"Most professors would grade the papers or exams, then give me the printed documents with their notes to scan and upload before returning to the students. Some professors recorded the grades in their books in case students asked before I loaded the details into the computer. Abby didn't want any help with putting hers online. She told me specifically to stay out of her way. I'd assumed she was old school and didn't like me given everything going on with Alton and the divorce."

"Lorraine, this is helpful. Do you have any idea where I can find the students' exams from Abby's classes this semester?" A picture formulated in my mind. If Abby were somehow involved with Coach Oliver, could she have changed Striker's grades to ensure he played in the upcoming game? That would clarify how those two were connected, but not why Abby was murdered. Unless she changed her mind, and Coach Oliver, Stanton, or Striker killed her in revenge. I needed to focus on Striker's grades and the decision on which pitcher would play in the game. That felt like a place for a motive to lurk.

"No, as I said, Abby kept everything to herself. The only tasks she asked me to do was sort her mail and schedule any student appointments."

Once Lorraine exited the office, I sat at the top of the stairs to process all I'd just learned. I needed to get access to the computer system to find out if Abby had entered grades for any of the students. I decided to ask my father before approaching anyone else about my concerns with the grades. I called his cell when I couldn't reach him at home. No answer. I left a voicemail and followed it up with a text message saying I needed to see him as soon as possible. I took the cable car back to North Campus, excited to stumble on something that could identify Abby's murderer.

On the walk back toward my Jeep, I skimmed the last two months of journal entries. An entry in the week before she was killed expressed her hope that Derek would call soon about the *Dark Reality* contract. There was an entry in early January about an exciting night out with W. A. I flipped a few more pages only to learn things with W. A. had gotten complicated—she had feelings for him even though she knew how wrong it was. Still no full name or obvious clues. Then I read how Abby wanted to get revenge and expose W. A. for what he'd done to her. That must have been the exclusive story she was talking about in the email to Derek and on the call with me.

Stumped over the identity of the mysterious W. A., I was about to give up until a nauseating idea popped into my head. W. A., Wesley Ayrwick. My father had been acting strange lately. He had several nights where he wouldn't mention where he was going or what he was doing. He said his relationship with Abby was complicated. Was my father having an affair? Cheating on my mother with Abby? I sat on the bench for another twenty minutes, trying to convince myself there had to be some other explanation. Why wasn't my father calling me back?

A few students rushed by, yelling they were late for class, which reminded me I needed to get to Danby Landing. I tossed my backpack on the passenger seat and drove across town in a bit of a fog, debating if I should bring up the journal entry. I parked in Nana D's driveway, waved to the farm's operations manager who was unloading a wheelbarrow in the compost pile near the orchard, and entered through the side door into her kitchen. "I'm here, Nana D. What's going on with you this afternoon?"

Nana D hung up the phone. She still had an old-fashioned, buttercup-yellow handset with a curly cord installed next to the refrigerator. I always loved thinking about her standing in the kitchen, twirling it as we chatted on the phone while I was home in Los Angeles. She had cordless extensions in other parts of the home and her cell phone, but she preferred her kitchen have a touch of the past.

"Welcome back, my brilliant grandson. I was just on the phone with your mother. She's gone off the deep end again." Nana D rambled while brewing the tea. "Glad to see you can still read a clock."

"Of course. You didn't think I'd be late, did you? What's Mom's problem?"

"Oh, a little of this and that. That daughter of mine never could handle stress." Nana D uncovered a plate of desserts sitting on the counter. "I made us shortbread with lemon icing and mini pecan pies." She was dressed to the nines in a fitted gray skirt, stylish blouse, and black suit jacket.

The pies looked delicious. I'd enjoy a few of those, most definitely. She'd made at least three dozen bite-sized concoctions small enough to toss between my lips, big enough to force my mouth closed and not to say something I shouldn't. "Mom seems to be doing okay with everything going on as far as I can tell. Just some minor agitation. What happened today?"

"A fight with Eleanor about her job at the diner. Your father seems to have done something she wasn't too happy about last night. I think she had a hangnail too." Nana D shrugged, finished pouring the tea, and carried the tray to the table—a beautiful old slab of oak my Grandpop had cut down from a tree on their farm. He shaped, sanded, and varnished it himself, even leaving some burnt edges scalloped and slanted to lend it an old-world charm. I made Nana D promise not to give it to anyone else in the future. She accused me of wishing her off to an early grave, but I assured her I only meant *if* she no longer had a reason to keep it. I assumed that got me out of hot water, but you never knew with Nana D, Braxton's longest holder of senseless grudges.

"Any idea what Dad did?" I worried my latest theory might be true. I ate my first mini-pecan pie. No one baked better than my nana. The level of gooeyness in the filling and crunch in the crust... to die for! "Eleanor's been a little cranky lately too. I can see that bothering Mom."

"I'm staying out of it. *Twinsies* can solve their own problems. Did you set Eustacia straight about me not trying to date her fella? I ain't going to the baseball game with Lindsey Endicott anymore, so you'll be my escort. The entire town's gone crazy thinking I'm always after them." Nana D plated some desserts for herself and took a seat next to me. "Eat up, I have another meeting shortly."

In between three more pecan pies and two lemon shortbreads, I downed a few cups of tea and inquired about Nana D's meeting with Marcus Stanton. "By the way, how did your discussion go earlier with our fine councilman?" I braced myself for a litany of his latest *crimes* and *misdemeanors*.

"Oh, I'm on to his skullduggery. The con artist claims he has no clue who donated the money. He said the entire board wanted it to benefit the athletic facility. He's hiding something, but I can't figure it out. He also had nothing nice to mention about Abby Monroe," Nana D said as she checked all the notes from her discussion with him. "Stanton thought she purposely failed Striker. Maybe he killed her!"

"I can't imagine the councilman would murder a professor over a disagreement about his stepson's grades." From what I could recall, Marcus only left Stanton Concert Hall the night of the party to attend that board meeting, but I couldn't be certain of his every move. The motive for this crime made little sense based on what I knew so far.

"Have you heard the rumor about a Major League Baseball scout coming to the game?" Nana D shocked me with that one.

"That's a reason someone might be desperate enough to kill!" As much as I loved the place, Braxton wasn't a top-tier school or known for its sports programs. Why would a Major League Baseball scout come here?

Nana D said she'd keep after the councilman to find out anything she could. I updated her on my progression on the Abby Monroe investigation, excluding any fears about my father or the actual initials. She was most intrigued by Lorraine's three missing objects, one of which could be the murder weapon. "It seems to me you need to sit Coach Oliver down, then talk to Sheriff Montague again. I don't like how Coach Oliver acts around women. I wouldn't put it past him to apply some pressure on Abby about the grades. Before I fancy him as the killer, we need to learn more about his little rendezvous at the woman's house. All seems a little too Tanya Harding versus Nancy Kerrigan to me."

Nana D was correct—we didn't know what the relationship was between Coach Oliver and Abby. If Abby were dating W. A., would she also be romantically involved with the coach? "You might be right about Sheriff Montague, although she's none too happy when I try to insert myself in the case."

"You pay her salary, Kellan. She should be happy to get some free help. That woman always had a mean streak to her, especially after—"

"I don't live in Braxton, Nana D. You might pay her salary, but I don't." I realized too late that was exactly the topic of conversation Nana D was bringing up.

"Speaking of where you live, how about you take me up on that offer to come live here at the farm? I could use someone else to talk to during the day." Nana D filled the tray with our empty teacups and dessert plates, then walked to the sink to wash them. "It'll be fun to gab all night!"

Maybe the sheriff was right about Nana D. I packaged the remaining cakes and pies, sneaking two into my pocket for the ride back home, then joined her at the sink. "I might have news to share with you about staying in Braxton when I pick you up for the game. Does twelve sound good?"

"Make it eleven. I need to see some folks before the first pitch. I hope you cleaned up the crumbs you dropped on the floor when those two cakes accidentally fell into your pocket, Kellan." Nana D began singing Kenny Rogers' *The Gambler* as she turned off the faucet, then danced her way across the kitchen. "I would slap your bottom silly if I didn't let you get away with everything, brilliant one."

I shook my head at her. There would be no way to control my nana. I hugged her goodbye and drove back home, wondering whom she was meeting with that evening. Then I realized it was time to plan several interviews of my own to make traction in finding Abby's killer. It'd become a personal quest to solve the case before the sheriff. Perhaps to get Derek off my back too.

As I pulled into the driveway at my parents' house, my father stepped down the path toward his car. "I can't talk now, Kellan. I'm meeting your mother for an early dinner."

I wasn't letting him avoid me anymore. "Nope, we need to chat tonight, Dad," I said through the window, then parked and jogged over to his car, but he'd already slammed the driver's door closed. To his credit, he rolled down the window. "It's close to freezing out here, son. Make it quick."

"Listen, Dad. I think you need to know what I learned about Abby today."

"I understand, but I can't be late to meet your mother. She's not herself these days, ever since I started planning for my retirement. I am trying to do whatever I can to make her happy," he replied before hitting the button to roll up the window.

I grunted. "Breakfast. Tomorrow. Nine o'clock. Don't miss it!"

He smirked and backed out of the driveway. Something strange was going on in my family and at Braxton. The more everyone tried to hide it, the more I wanted to dig deeper.

Next, Derek and I exchanged a brief text conversation.

Kellan: *Got into Abby's office. I found her research notes in the folders. Going through them again this weekend.*
Derek: *Awesome. My boss is reviewing the revised materials you sent over. Didn't have time to tell him they were yours, but I'll be sure he knows how hard you worked.*

Ugh! I needed to call Emma to share the news she'd be coming back to Braxton for a few weeks. I also wanted to map out everything I'd discovered in the investigation. Then I planned to open a bottle of wine. Those were the only three things I thought might improve my night. Plus, the rest of Nana D's baked goods—those were the extent of my only evening plans.

Chapter 13

My mom left for a spa day with her girlfriends early in the morning. I brewed a pot of coffee, defrosted Nana D's blueberry scones, and tossed some turkey sausages in the frying pan. If my father were on time, he'd arrive any moment for the breakfast I'd *suggested* he attend the day before. As I began plating the food, the grandfather clock in the living room confirmed it was nine o'clock. My father pushed open the swinging door into the kitchen. That man had impeccable timing.

"Good day, Kellan. I believe you made a demand for my presence this morning."

Was he attempting to be funny? "We have things to discuss. Are you going to the game today?" I eased into the topic to avoid creating any tension.

"Indeed. I'm still head of the college, and it's the first baseball game. I'm looking forward to Striker kicking off the season." He carried his plate to the corner breakfast nook and sat on the bench closest to the back door. A quick escape route?

"Does that mean Coach Oliver decided the starting lineup?" In all the commotion, I'd forgotten about the pep rally. I joined him at the table and took a bite of Nana D's scone. The blueberry flavoring was so intense I closed my eyes to thoroughly enjoy the experience.

"I guess that answers my question about you taking over some classes. If you were interested in helping, you'd have followed the college's biggest news this week," my father said, savoring his breakfast, which meant I hadn't lost him yet.

"No, that's not exactly true. Is baseball Braxton's biggest news this week?" I shook my head in amazement at how easily he could dismiss a murder just to focus on the Striker-versus-Jordan rivalry. "We'll get to the job offer. First, something came up last night. I didn't check on Coach Oliver's pitching selection. Second, I'm going to today's game with Nana D."

He grunted and dropped his knife. The brash clang of metal against china made our silence more awkward. "I should have known it was Doomsday."

"Really, Dad? You need to stop this war with Nana D. I think you have bigger things to worry about based on our last conversation." I finished two scones and all the sausages during his silent treatment, then changed the topic again. "Any more blog postings?"

"Nothing. The last one was the day after the party."

Myriam was behind it all. I was certain she wanted Abby fired too. What was Myriam achieving with all these crafty illusions and distractions? "I have some questions about Abby for you."

"Go ahead. I'm listening." My father's eyebrow twitched.

"I found a few materials in Abby's office to help me understand the syllabi for her classes. I peeked at her grade book, and a couple of things didn't add up."

The sour expression on my father's face relaxed, but his shoulders still stiffened. "I see this as a good sign if you're researching her classes."

I explained what I'd seen, denoting no specific names. He couldn't offer much background about the process. He'd left the details of how a student's grades were finalized to each department chair and Dean Mulligan. "I rarely take active notice in any specific student's performance unless there's an issue of suspension or a major award. Myriam should help you with the particulars once you decide if you'll come on board."

"I understand. We'll get to that momentarily. Were you getting updates on Striker's grades?" I'd bet money he'd paid attention for a Major League Baseball opportunity.

"Yes." Wesley Ayrwick proved he wasn't a man of many words.

"Would you know what changed to permit Striker to play today? Unless he earned a 'B+' in Abby's class, his suspension from the team's upcoming games would still apply."

"Why the sudden obsession with a baseball player's academic standing, Kellan?" He stood from the breakfast nook to refill our coffee cups.

I was glad to hear Striker could play. I'd liked him when we met at the fitness center, but the 'F' I'd seen in Abby's grade book had set off some alarm bells. It was too coincidental to accept he'd failed the course last semester, and she'd marked an 'F' for his first exam this year. Then suddenly everything was back on track for him to pitch today. "Something fishy is going on with the way Abby graded her students."

"Talk to Myriam. She verified Abby's exam results were loaded into the system earlier this week. It takes a day for them to be approved, then students can check online."

"Okay. To answer your question, I'll stick around to handle Abby's classes for four weeks. I need to clear it with my boss, but he's already given me some signals indicating he'll be happy I'm in Braxton right now," I replied, preparing for my next point. "I have some conditions."

My father's smile brightened over my news. "That's terrific. I'm glad you're keeping an open mind." His bushy eyebrows raised inquisitively.

I explained to him I wanted to keep it quiet—he could only inform those who needed to know I'd be handling Abby's workload for the time being. I could see the news getting out and people thinking I've halfway moved back home already. I also asked him to explain everything he knew about Abby's personal life.

"I'd spent more time with her than I'd have liked. She'd asked for too many days off, been more argumentative with me than usual, and caused some trouble with Lorraine on campus."

"Is that whom you were talking about in your study the night I got home? I overheard your call, and it sounded—"

"Were you eavesdropping? I taught you better than that, Kellan." My father gathered his wallet and keys, mumbling to himself about the downward spiral of society's future.

"No, I came down to use the phone and heard part of the conversation. Who was on the call?"

"None of your business, Kellan." He was very calm and collected, but obviously dismayed.

I couldn't push my luck any further if I still wanted to ask the tough question. "How well did you know Abby? Were you socializing with her after work?"

"What? No, we met at her house a few times, so we could have an honest conversation about her future. That's how I knew she'd intended to leave Braxton in the new term."

He had to be the W. A. in her journal. Alton's initials were A. M. Coach Oliver's initials would've had an 'O' in them. The neighbor had seen a car at her house. Could I ask if he'd been having an affair with her?

"Dad, how are things between you and Mom? She seems worried about you, and Eleanor thought you guys were fighting."

"Your mother is under a lot of stress. You know this is her busiest time of the year." He placed his empty mug in the sink and rinsed his hands. "I appreciate you doing this favor for me. I'll call Myriam shortly to verify you've accepted and to help you get situated. I need to meet up with the guys. Judge Grey's probably on the fourth hole by now."

My father grabbed his jacket from the closet and walked toward the garage. As he pressed the remote to open the door, I stopped him. "Did Mom discover something going on between you and Abby? I don't mean to pry, but I found Abby's journal, and an entry said—"

"How dare you think I'd do something like that to your mother? I thought we were turning a corner with your decision today. Won't you ever grow up?" he shouted before slamming the kitchen door.

My first thought was he didn't answer the question. My second was how would I fix the situation. I didn't mean to aggravate the man, but my father knew something he wasn't telling me. I decided to give him some breathing room for the weekend.

An hour later, I picked up Nana D from Danby Landing. She'd decked herself out in a Braxton Bear's jersey, a pair of dark gray tights, and a baseball cap. The Bears were the team's mascot and most assuredly described the way the team normally played. In the first few innings, they'd always seem sleepy. By the third inning, they'd burst out of hibernation and score. I was optimistic for today's game, but Nana D lacked confidence.

"Striker's a good kid, but he's not prepared. I saw him at the pep rally last night. Definitely psyched to be chosen, but he looked worried about something." Nana D switched the radio station to her favorite country station and forced me to listen to her music.

"He passed Abby's last exam. That should make him happy." I turned into Grey Field's parking lot. We were an hour early, but Nana D wanted to check out the tailgate party. I hadn't been to one in years and guessed she made regular appearances based on her instructions about where to park, what to bring, and who would be in attendance.

"Yep. He was happy, but he mentioned a girl giving him a rough time." Nana D smirked at me. "I assume it was his girlfriend, but he said little. Chicks, sheesh!"

Why would college kids talk to Nana D about their personal lives? "You're everywhere these days."

"I'll be back in thirty minutes. I need to be seen." She gave me the thumbs-up sign as we parked the car, then jumped out quickly before I could ask about the meeting before the pep rally.

She had a more active social life than I did. While Nana D wandered away, I walked to the baseball stadium and watched the pitchers practice. When Striker finished in the bullpen, he crossed by the player's dugout, where Coach Oliver motivated the other team members. "Kellan, that you?"

"Congratulations. It looks like everything worked out with the grade. You must be excited to meet the scout today." I noticed a haze shadowing his eyes and hoped he had nothing to do with Abby's murder. Nana D was right.

"Yes, I passed. Coach Oliver called to tell me. Jordan didn't take it too well, but I think he understood he'd have a turn later this season." Striker tucked his glove under his right arm and fixed the sleeve on his uniform. As he twisted, a large scratch near his elbow appeared.

"Looks like that hurts." I hadn't seen it while working out, but he'd worn a longer shirt that day. Surely, the sheriff would've found his DNA on Abby's body if it had come from a struggle.

"Oh, that, yeah… I don't remember. Wanna meet my girlfriend?" he said as a pretty blue-eyed, blond cheerleader walked in our direction. "This is Carla Grey. She's supporting me today."

Carla smiled and dropped her pompoms on the dugout roof. "Hi. Ready for a great game? Who's your good-looking friend, Striker?" Her bright makeup and a very low-cut uniform with a short skirt stood out.

Striker clarified how we'd met. While I enjoyed compliments, I was distracted trying to recall where I'd seen her before and grew curious about her last name. "Are you related to Judge Grey?"

Carla nodded nervously. "Yeah, ummm… he's my grandfather. Do you know him?"

I did. My father played golf with him all the time. He'd also been the county judge for thirty years. Everyone was afraid of him. I suddenly felt bad for the poor girl. "I've not had the pleasure to directly meet Judge Grey before, but his reputation precedes him."

Carla snatched her pompoms. "I should go. Gotta pump the crowd soon, right? See you around, Kellan." When Striker went to kiss her goodbye, she turned her cheek. "Don't ruin the makeup!"

Carla exited, and Striker's mood worsened. I said, "Everything okay? You seem disconnected. I'd think you'd be thrilled to meet the scout."

"It's cool. Chick problems. Stepdad on my case. I just hope I do well." Striker returned to his warm-up when the coach called him over.

I went back to find Nana D, who was on her second hotdog at that point. She was entertaining several of the ladies from the local chamber of commerce with stories about her and Grandpop's golden days.

As we took our seats, she leaned against me and pointed. "You see that harlot. Eustacia might think she's got one over on me by convincing Lindsey to take her to the game. I'll fix that woman! Can you believe that get-up she's squeezed herself into? Honestly, a woman her age putting on the team's baseball uniform simply to impress a man."

As far as I could tell, Ms. Paddington and my nana were similarly dressed. "Ummm... aren't you and her about the same age, Nana D?"

I felt the pinch on the back of my arm before she'd even begun to verbally assault me. "I am three months younger than that jezebel, and you have no idea what you're talking about. You didn't even wear a single color to support our team today, and if I didn't know better, I'd think you were on Eustacia's side. No grandson of mine would ever do that to me, you little—"

The announcer interrupted her mini tirade to ask everyone to stand for the national anthem. I smiled at Nana D, but it didn't help my case. "No pie for you for two weeks, Kellan."

The rest of the game was a nail-biter like my temporary truce with Nana D, who agreed to forget my comment, claiming she didn't want any tension in the air to interrupt the Braxton Bear's mojo. I was shocked at how much school spirit the woman had. At one point, she tried to high kick with the cheerleaders, but after nearly falling into Dean Terry, Nana D calmed down.

The Braxton Bears led the game four to three when the seventh inning stretch started. Striker had done well, but I could tell he was tiring once he'd given up the last two runs before the break. Coach Oliver warmed up Jordan Ballantine in the bullpen. I worried about both players' chances with the scout.

While Nana D scrounged up a few more hotdogs, I caught up with Fern Terry, the same woman who'd been the dean when I attended

Braxton. Fern was extremely tall with a steel-gray, pixie-style haircut. It hadn't changed since I'd known her, nor had her broad shoulders and puffy face. I'd always thought she'd look better with a longer hairdo, but then again, what did I know? She remembered me and the many times I'd defended my fraternity in her office. "I hear they're close to picking a new Braxton president. Still can't believe my father's retiring this year." I hoped to catch a clue if she was one of the two final candidates.

"Yes, Monday or Tuesday is the big day. I've got it on good authority they'll notify the candidate of the Board's decision," she said with an intimidating tone. When Dean Terry glanced at the dugout, a snarl erased her smile as she zoomed in on Coach Oliver.

"I imagine they picked two people who have served the college faithfully for years and truly know how to make Braxton excel like my father has for the last eight years." I smirked at her as if I were the cat who'd caught a little mouse.

"Most definitely. I'm sure that's the case." Dean Terry nodded, then walked down the bleachers toward the field. "I need to speak with Coach Oliver. Please excuse me."

I thought it odd she was at the game given sports were never something high on her list of interests in the past. Something was brewing between those two, but I was also certain she was one of the two presidential candidates, which meant someone else external was being considered. I racked my brain trying to figure out who could be in the running. Unless it was someone from the Paddington, Stanton, or Grey families, I was clueless.

Nana D returned. "Got you a turkey burger with avocado on an alfalfa sprout bun. Try it."

"Ummm... I've had them before, and since when do they serve health food at a baseball game?" I scrunched my face like the world had ended. I often ate healthy. Not that she realized it.

"When's the last time you went to a baseball game?"

I reflected for a few seconds, which were too long for Nana D. "I thought so. Just eat it, or I won't lift that two-week pie ban." Nana D elbowed me, then laughed. "I ran into Bridget just now."

I knew Nana D was intent on stirring trouble again. "How's my little elf doing?"

Nana D shushed me. "You *are* weird. Just thought you might like to know she was here. You could say hello after the game. Bridget doesn't know many people in town."

I was not dealing with Nana D's romantic set-ups. "Oh, look, the game's starting."

"Yep, seems Striker's out, poor kid. Marcus will grind him over that."

Striker threw his glove at the fence. Councilman Stanton and Coach Oliver argued about something, but I was too far away to guess the crux. Dean Terry walked away with a perplexed expression on her face. "Jordan just took the pitcher's mound. Guess you were right."

"When am I not right?" Nana D tilted her head and lowered her sunglasses. "About Bridget…?"

I shrugged her off, told her to focus on the game, and promised I'd come by the following morning for brunch if she'd leave the topic alone. Nana D was content I'd at least agreed to visit again.

Jordan pitched the remaining innings and only gave up one run when the Woodland Beavers tied the score. Luckily, the Braxton Bears hit a triple in the final inning and won the game seven to four. The crowd went wild when the players took to the parking lot to celebrate, thrilled they'd won the first game of the season. It meant Braxton might have a fighting chance to join this year's championships.

Nana D left as soon as the game concluded, noting she'd bum a ride home with one of her friends. I mingled among the fans and took in the college atmosphere. When I'd attended graduate school and earned my doctorate from the University of Southern California, I didn't live on campus. I'd also worked full time and gotten married, and Emma had been born shortly afterward. It had been a decade since I felt that electrifying school spirit. It was fantastic to see the entire town banding together to support the Braxton Bears.

On the drive home, I confirmed plans to meet with Dr. Castle the following Monday morning. She'd been curt on the phone and didn't want to discuss the classes until we met in person. At least I'd gotten that meeting coordinated, and I could find out more about Braxton's grading process, maybe even see the date and time stamp of when Striker's grades had been uploaded.

Chapter 14

By early evening, I'd gone for my daily run, choosing Millionaire's Mile for viewing pleasure. All the houses were grand and loomed high between Main Street and the Wharton Mountains in the background. The impressive sight for any newcomers to Braxton always encouraged me to recognize my hometown's beauty. I set my alarm and took a catnap before meeting Eleanor for dinner. Watching the game in the chilly, fresh air had tuckered me out.

When I awoke, I remembered failing to share with Connor my news about Abby's journal entries mentioning W. A. Since I was running late, it would have to be a Sunday activity. I found my favorite pair of dark jeans, added a light gray button-down shirt and a black sports jacket to the outfit, and eased my feet into a pair of black boots. A bit of snow had stuck to the ground once the typical evening flurries descended upon us.

I met Eleanor at an Italian restaurant near the Finnulia River waterfront. A few cool places had opened in the last year, but I'd only sampled one when I returned home at Christmas. She'd made the reservations and secured us a table in the back section overlooking the gorgeous, moonlit sandy banks.

"I know the owner. We once trained together at another restaurant." Eleanor had dressed a little more stylish than her normal work outfits, but nowhere near as fancy as the retirement party. I was glad to see she stayed in the warmer color families as her eyes and hair shined best when she wore red and yellow. Just like mine!

"I'm happy you came to your senses the other day and suggested dinner." I wouldn't tiptoe around her chilly attitude earlier in the week. "Thanks for dropping the cold front, *Anna Wintour*."

"I'm sorry about that, *Sherlock Holmes*. I didn't know how to react to something you said." She perused the menu, then recommended shareable appetizers.

I ordered two glasses of champagne to make the night more relaxing. I racked my brain trying to guess what sensitive topic I'd brought up. "Can you clue me in? I'm rubbish at remembering right now."

"Connor."

I hadn't seen that one coming. "He's grated on my nerves lately too. What's he done to you?"

Eleanor tapped her fingers on the white tablecloth and fidgeted with her flatware. "Ummm… well… it's not an easy topic for me to bring up around you."

I'd begun synthesizing what she was about to say before the words came tumbling from her mouth. Connor and my sister? I was torn between rage that he'd considered going out with Eleanor without asking me first and recognizing it also meant there might be nothing going on between him and Maggie. "Has something happened between you two before?"

"Not really."

"That's a crock of dirty rotten horse manure, to quote Nana D. Have you two gone out before?"

"Once. Maybe twice. But nothing's happened, I swear." Eleanor's cheeks flushed brighter than her blouse. "We came here for dinner two months ago."

In between the waitress delivering our cocktails and the appetizers, I learned Connor had stopped by the Pick-Me-Up Diner the prior fall before I'd come home for winter break. Eleanor hadn't seen him in years but was intrigued by his dramatic makeover when they'd run into each other again. They'd met for drinks at the end of her shift, and she thought there was a connection but couldn't be certain. Then he'd asked her to dinner, where they had a fantastic time. A few weeks before Christmas they'd met for lunch, but he'd gone cold in the last six weeks. She was too nervous to ask him what had changed.

"I'd have appreciated someone telling me sooner. Everyone forgets to inform me what's going on." I unleashed an aggravated tone somewhere between a hangry bear and a scorned lover.

"It's not like you've ever asked questions about my dates before. I didn't know what to do, but then you mentioned how close he and Maggie seemed to be, and well...."

I'd pieced together the concern. "You think he dropped you to date Maggie?"

Eleanor nodded. "I don't know what else it could be."

I gave some consideration to the facts. Connor and my sister had gone on several dates. Then he started snuggling up to Maggie, helping her acclimate at Braxton and surrender the memories with her late husband. "By any chance, did you ever talk about me with Connor?" I asked for a specific reason, but I also wanted to know whether he'd been upset about losing our friendship too.

"As if! Why would I chat about you when we were on a date?" Eleanor chided with disdain. "I'm sure I mentioned you were coming home for Christmas, but we didn't actually talk about you."

"How did he react when you said my name?" While Eleanor gave it proper reflection, I chugged my glass of champagne and asked the waitress to bring us more water. I'd already drunk enough liquor during the week, given how my jeans felt at that moment. It couldn't be the desserts.

"Come to think of it, he got quiet. When he dropped me off, it felt very chilly." She cocked her head to the side and wiped her lips with a napkin. "Any thoughts?"

"I was wondering whether he felt a smidge weird about going on a date with you, being my sister and all, right after you'd mentioned me coming home. And then, he probably heard I was coming back again for Dad's retirement party." Connor felt guilty. I knew it.

"He called once, and we talked about getting together again. Nothing ever materialized."

Eleanor and I played three rounds of *Rock, Paper, Scissors* to confirm who had to buckle up and ask them the next time.

"Ha! I always beat you, Kellan." Eleanor jabbed me with her fork. "You're done for the night!"

And she was right. Exhaustion prompted me to beg for the check. While we waited to pay our bill, we talked about everything I'd learned on the murder investigation. Eleanor was certain the W. A. in Abby's journal was not our father. She thought Connor would know other options and encouraged me to ask him about it when I brought up Maggie.

"Don't tell him you know we went on two dates!" she shouted as I closed her car door.

* * *

I slept way later than I intended the following morning and was going to be late to Nana D's. I didn't want to get in trouble or be penalized for any reason, so I exceeded the speed limit on a couple of streets to arrive on time. It was Sunday, and most people would be at church at that hour. As I rounded the corner to reach the dirt pathway to Danby Landing, sirens blasted. If I didn't have bad luck that morning, I wouldn't have had any kind at all.

I pulled to the side of the road and waited for the officer. "And what possessed you to drive fifty in a thirty-mile-per hour zone?" a familiar voice said.

I looked up and noticed my newest good buddy staring back. He must not have any older siblings as I'd never heard of or met anyone in his family before. "Officer Flatman, I'm so sorry. I wasn't thinking. Totally my fault. I didn't want to be late to my nana's place."

"Oh, it's you," he replied with a hint of a smile. His pudgy arms waved around mechanically. "You should know better. How would Mrs. Danby feel about her grandson earning a speeding ticket?"

I studied the crafty look on Officer Flatman's face. He was about to serve me an ironic piece of humble pie, the only pie I didn't like, or he was letting me know he understood my predicament. "I don't suppose you could look the other way."

Officer Flatman asked for my license and registration, then told me to sit tight. While he vanished, I thought about how to ask him if he knew the latest on Abby's murder investigation. He might be so thrilled to give me a ticket, he'd surrender vital information. I organized my approach before he walked back and handed me my paperwork.

"I think we can let this one slide, Mr. Ayrwick. But if I see you as much as a mile over the limit, or failing to come to a full stop, there won't be any second chances. You got me?" he said, holding back a snicker.

"Promise. I'm eternally grateful, Officer Flatman. You must be busy with the investigation. The sheriff speaks highly of your work collecting the evidence. This paperwork shouldn't be anything to get in your way," I replied with grave sincerity. "*Kill 'em with kindness,*" Nana D always preached.

"Did she say that? Wow, I wondered if Sheriff Montague valued my input. Especially when I found the hole in Fern Terry's alibi," he replied with glee as his face brightened.

Oh, it was working. "Definitely. You were such an immense help. And who knew you were such a methodical guy. You'll make detective someday soon, huh?"

"That's my greatest hope. *Detective* Flatman before I turn thirty. I've got a few years left, but—"

I needed to interrupt him if I would catch him off-guard. "Dean Terry's alibi… yeah… heard about that. I hadn't even known she was a suspect." I had no idea how Dean Terry could be connected to Abby's murder. It was a shock to hear her name. "Imagine her being—"

"Fern was seen leaving the retirement party at eight but claimed she left at nine," boasted Officer Flatman. "Eleanor watched the woman leave much earlier right after Myriam left too."

"Did you ever find out what happened?" If Myriam had left before Fern, the Shakespeare fanatic couldn't verify my sister's account of the events. Could anyone else have seen her?

"Nope, I guess Fern must have been wrong about the time. I'm waiting to find out if Sheriff Montague learned what happened between the time she left the party and the time she got home at a quarter to ten." Officer Flatman smiled, then blanched when he realized he said too much.

I couldn't recall seeing her at all, but much of my time had been focused on Maggie in that last hour. "I appreciate you not giving me a tough time today. I should head out to Nana D's."

"Absolutely, Mr. Ayrwick. You have yourself a good day." As he walked away, he giggled hysterically. Odd, given I was the one who got out of the ticket.

Not one to tempt fate, I thanked the powers-that-be for showing mercy on me and ensured the speedometer never passed twenty-nine as I drove down the dirt pathway to Nana D's farm. When I pulled up, she was swinging in a rocking chair on the porch. "Three minutes late, Kellan. You're lucky I had a phone call that kept me from finishing the breakfast preparations on time."

My luck was changing today—two in a row. "So sorry, I ran into a bit of… traffic on the road." She didn't need to know it was just one car standing in my way of arriving here on time. The wind whipped up behind me, reminding me it may have been warmer than usual today, but it was still not decent enough to hang around outside. "Let's head in?"

Nana D continued rocking back and forth. Her braid was pulled apart today, and she looked quite pleased with herself. "Certainly. Aren't you gonna ask me who kept me so long on the phone?"

She was going to bring up Bridget again. "I'm sure it was important. Let's eat that delicious breakfast you've been cooking. What is it, bacon and eggs? Homemade biscuits?" I rubbed my stomach as the hunger pains grew. If she had fresh orange marmalade, I'd kiss the ground at her feet.

"I'll follow you in. I'm grateful Officer Flatman was kind enough to tell me all about your traffic jam." As the door banged shut behind her, she let out a roaring cackle worthy of Fran Drescher.

I turned bright red. It wasn't Bridget on the phone. Flatman had the last laugh. That pig! "You didn't?"

"I did. If there had been any so-called debt between you and me over a past trip to the county jail, it's surely been repaid by now."

All I could do was nod. Repeatedly. Thirty minutes later, I continued to swallow my pride as she chastised me for being late and getting pulled over. "I can't be having people say negative things about my family. We've already got some tarnish because of this murder your father let happen. Don't you follow in his footsteps and add another black eye. It's not gonna help me in the future."

"Help you with what?" I mumbled while shoveling half a biscuit into my mouth.

"Doesn't matter. You know what I mean." She stepped away from the table.

Knowing how much she loved gossip, I traded a few secrets to get myself out of trouble. Nana D wanted to be the one to ask Connor if they'd been dating, but I persuaded her to leave the situation alone.

"Convince Lorraine to report those missing items to Connor. Find out about the grades from Myriam. I'm going around Marcus Stanton and asking a friend on the Board of Trustees. No one's doing much about solving this debacle. I need a crime-free town. This doesn't look good for us right now."

"I'm on it. Why is it so important—" The doorbell interrupted me from finishing. "I'll get it."

"Thank you, Kellan. I'm sure glad you haven't lost your manners."

When I opened the door, I had a case of déjà vu. The elf was back! "What are you doing here?"

Bridget stepped inside and unbuttoned her coat—at least the neon green parka was gone, given the warmer weather. "Didn't we cover this last week? I take lessons from Seraphina on Sunday mornings. Today is Sunday. Any idea why I'm back?"

It appeared my little elfish friend liked to banter. Nana D had well trained her It was then I realized why Nana D was so willing to drop the conversation at the baseball game about finding Bridget at the tailgate party. When I'd volunteered to come for breakfast today, Nana D knew Bridget would be here for clarinet lessons. She was a devil, not an innocent grandmother.

"Music lessons. I'm back in the game, no worries," I replied, feeling glad she'd worn a different outfit this time—an actual normal one. Bridget had chosen a white cable-knit sweater and a pair of skinny jeans that looked modern and chic. "Speaking of games... I hear you were at Grey Field yesterday."

"Yes, I'm a major fan. I support the school teams whenever I can, but I've always had a strong connection with baseball. My pops instilled it in me when I was a young girl," she replied.

"Do you attend Braxton or know any of the guys on the team?" I couldn't remember if she'd said which college last time.

Bridget shrugged. "Yeah, I've met a few of them. I know Craig from stopping by the communications department last semester. I'm in a biology course with him and Carla Grey this year. Everyone else calls him Striker, but I'm not into that whole nickname thing."

While Nana D remained conspicuously absent, I learned Bridget had been orphaned at an early age and raised in foster care. When she'd turned eighteen, she received a scholarship to Braxton and had been there the last four years, which meant she'd graduate in a few months. She was studying to become a teacher with a double focus in English literature and music education. Bridget seemed like a nice girl, but what was my nana doing by setting me up with someone at least ten years younger than me? It may have worked for my parents, but I didn't see it working for me.

It was toward the end of our brief get-to-know-each-other session when I realized she'd mentioned Striker visiting the communications department. "How did you know Craig Magee would go to Diamond Hall so frequently?"

Bridget laughed. "Oh, I work there. I'm one of the student employees. It pays for my supplies and books, so I don't have any extra out-of-pocket expenses."

"Didn't a student overhear Lorraine and Abby fighting? Was that you or a different worker?"

Bridget fidgeted in her seat and unlocked the clarinet case. She looked past me, probably hoping Nana D would enter the room. "It was me, but I didn't mean to get anyone in trouble. That sheriff interviewed me because I worked in the building. She wanted to know if I'd seen anything in the past."

"I'm sorry. I didn't mean to make you uncomfortable. I heard it was a loud argument, and I was curious how it started." I felt guilty she was trying to do the right thing and had probably caused a slight rift in the department. "I'm sure Lorraine knows you only stated what you'd heard. She's an understanding woman."

"Yeah, it's been a little awkward, but I'm sure it will get better. I didn't think Lorraine had it in her, but she was rude to Professor Monroe on a couple of occasions. I saw her grab Professor Monroe's wrist that day and shake her wildly. It had something to do with some legal document. I didn't hear the entire conversation." As Bridget finished speaking, Nana D sauntered into the room as though she hadn't been playing matchmaker in the background.

"I'm so sorry to keep you two waiting. I had to put all that food away. Can I get you anything, Bridget?" Nana D asked sweetly.

"I should go." I cast an unforgiving glare in Nana D's direction. "It was great talking with you, Bridget. Perhaps if my daughter is visiting soon, you could teach her how to play the clarinet. It could be a little extra spending money in your pocket." I had two reasons for making the offer besides genuinely wanting Emma to get more involved with musical instruments. I needed an opportunity to find out how things worked in the communications department. I also wanted Nana D to think her plan to push Bridget and me together was working. Then she'd leave it alone. There might've also been a small part of me that relished in taking away Nana D's opportunity to teach Emma how to play the clarinet. Knowing how much she would love to spend time with her great-granddaughter, I had to engineer small ways to get back at Nana D for always beating me in our little games. We enjoyed teasing each other.

"What a lovely idea," Nana D said. "I'm sure you three would make quite an afternoon out of it."

"Excellent. I hope you'll lend Emma your clarinet, Nana D. I wouldn't want to buy one until I knew if it was something she'd use."

Nana D turned to Bridget. "Did you find your missing clarinet? I'd like to give mine to Kellan."

Bridget shook her head. "Not yet. I found my clarinet case, but the actual clarinet was missing. I'm annoyed about it too. I'm not made of money!"

I learned Bridget had forgotten her clarinet at Diamond Hall the prior weekend, but when she went back to retrieve it, after the cops let her into the building several days later, the case was empty. She reported it, which made sense based on Lorraine telling me there were several items missing. I'd have to ask about the third one. Was the clarinet still missing because someone had used it to hit Abby on the head? I made a note to ask Connor if that could be the murder weapon. I didn't want Bridget to think something of hers had killed Abby when students still thought Abby's fall was an accident. I had to admit it seemed peculiar that a thief would only take the clarinet or that a murderer wouldn't discard both the case and the clarinet used to kill someone.

Chapter 15

Mother Nature blessed Braxton overnight by sending boatloads of powdery white dust to blanket the Saddlebrooke National Forest. The giant fir trees looked gorgeous with their robust green branches covered in bright snowflakes. I pulled into The Big Beanery parking lot to meet Myriam for an early breakfast on Monday morning. After hemming and hawing about what to do, it seemed more appropriate to call her Myriam rather than Dr. Castle since we would be colleagues for the next month.

Myriam had chosen a chestnut brown pantsuit with a vibrant orange, open-collared blouse. Rather than add a tie or broach, she wrapped an elegant silk scarf around her neck. She looked impeccable, and I couldn't argue with her taste in clothes. Her hair, however, hadn't changed since the last time I'd seen her, causing me to wonder if she'd owned a collection of identical wigs. Not a single strand pointed in any different direction than last time. Working in television and research, my mind functioned like a photographic memory—too many nights spent verifying continuity between episodes. I controlled the desire to peel back a section of Myriam's hair to see if it said *Monday* somewhere. She *was* a professor in the theater department.

While Myriam selected a cup of herbal tea and a fruit salad, I ordered a double espresso and a slice of coffee cake, needing the extra boost. "I appreciate you carving out some time for me to get situated with

Abby's classes. I taught some undergrad courses when I was getting my doctorate in—"

"Mr. Ayrwick," she interrupted. "I'm more than glad to do my part for Braxton to ensure the students aren't impacted any further than they've been already. However, your father slipped you in under the radar. He could have told me at the retirement party you were his son. What is it Brutus said in Julius Caesar? '*The abuse of greatness is when it disjoins remorse from power,*' I believe."

Her quote was correct, but she must have also felt guilt over the derogatory remarks about my father. "Perhaps. He has tunnel vision in those circumstances and does the minimum to get—"

"Not that it would have changed anything I said. I stand by my words, and this is another case of Wesley Ayrwick thinking he can play God." Myriam sipped her tea, dabbed a cotton handkerchief from her coat pocket against her lips, and sat taller on the seat.

"Well, rather than get caught up on the past, how about we focus on the classes I'm taking over this morning?" I had finished reading all the materials the previous night and was excited to revisit the introductory content I'd long forgotten.

"I'm willing to assume you can handle this coursework. I reviewed your qualifications, and while I'm appalled at the way your father ushered you into Braxton, I'm pleased you've way more experience than Monroe. Where you lack specific roles as a college professor, you probably make up for it with all you've accomplished in your career." She stuck her fork in a piece of grapefruit I swore winced as it entered her mouth. "And that's not a compliment. Just an observation and comparison. I expect when we hire a full-time professor, we will be more judicious in our candidate search."

This was going to be an uphill battle worthy of Attila the Hun. Myriam and I spent an hour discussing everything she'd known about Abby's current courses and upcoming deliverables from the students. In between discrete barbs and jabs, I mentioned the grading process.

"Monroe didn't upload the grades on that first exam. I did. There was a mix-up in all the commotion when the sheriff was going through things last weekend." Myriam tossed her bowl in the trash bin. "When I received access to the building, I found the folder with all the exams in my office mailbox. The woman had graded everything already, but the marks still needed to be keyed into the system."

"You didn't give the folder to anyone else?" It was odd she found them in the first place.

"I'd normally give them to the office manager, but given the lateness, I entered this round myself to prevent further delay of the results to the students. I approved them on Wednesday evening."

A few Braxton students took seats at nearby tables. I nodded at Connor while he ordered his morning caffeine boost, then turned back to Myriam. "Did you come across Striker's exam?"

Myriam wrinkled her nose. "I'm not familiar with that name."

Was she serious? Everyone knew about the baseball rivalry last week. "Craig Magee struggled in Abby's class last year. This was his second chance."

"Yes, your father specifically asked me to look at that exam. It would seem he's gotten private tutoring or focused on his studies more than his sports career. I don't understand why your father allows that athletic director to pull so much weight around—"

It was my opportunity to interrupt this time. "Do you know Coach Oliver? Was he a regular visitor to the communications department?" I'd been convinced he had something to do with the grade being changed on Striker's exam. I was certain Striker had gotten an 'F' based on the entry in Abby's book. Someone must have swapped his exam to ensure he passed well enough to play for the game.

"I barely know the Neanderthal. As I said, the point of the athletics programs at Braxton is meaningless to me. I'm still shocked at how many donations go their way." Myriam swigged the last of her tea.

"Are you familiar with the blog that's had a lot to say about the allocation of Braxton's donations?" I hoped to make her slightly uncomfortable and to confirm my suspicions.

Myriam huffed and stood from the table. "I've been made aware of it. I rarely read anonymous blogs, but this one has hit the nail on the head, wouldn't you say, Mr. Ayrwick?" She gathered and secured her notes in her briefcase. "I'll stop by later today to see how your first day of classes went. If you need me, I'll be in my office making final stage blocking decisions on our upcoming production of *King Lear*. I thought it was a perfect selection for the change in leadership this year."

As Connor saddled up to the table, Myriam exited. If I had time to respond, I'd have reminded her Lear was a beloved character in the play's conclusion, as well as asked her on which of Lear's daughters she'd modeled herself. I certainly had my vote etched in stone.

"Kellan, today's your first day," Connor stated rather than asked.

I assumed he had to update my campus security clearances, which explained why he knew I was working at Braxton. "Yes. On my way to Diamond Hall now that we have access to use the classrooms again."

He joined me on the walk to the classroom. "I'm sure you'll do well. Sheriff Montague cleared everything last night. She's ready to make an arrest tomorrow."

I was sure they found enough evidence if there was a major break about to occur in the case. "Has she checked the phone records to see whom Abby was meeting? Any chance you know specifically what was used to kill Abby? Perhaps a clarinet?"

"They've completed testing a few objects and have verified the general size and shape of the weapon. The call you overheard came from someone in Grey Sports Complex. I'm working with the technology group for the exact location. Things aren't looking too good for Lorraine." Connor checked his phone and responded to an incoming message he'd be at the security office in ten minutes.

Based on his explanation, Lorraine must have reported the missing items. I also hoped Lorraine had updated Sheriff Montague on meeting Coach Oliver on campus that evening too. "There's no way she could have done it, Connor. I'm certain this has something to do with grades being changed to ensure a certain member of the baseball team could play in the big game. Lorraine has no motive for who pitched last Saturday."

"I think Sheriff Montague is smart enough not to arrest Lorraine without proper evidence. You know Lorraine was angry about Abby's treatment of her brother, Alton."

"What about Dean Terry's lack of an alibi?"

Connor's lips pursed. "Does she have a motive?"

His question was important. Other than a few odd looks at Coach Oliver during the game, I couldn't produce anything peculiar enough. "But she misled the sheriff over her whereabouts."

"Lots of people don't remember their exact movements that night, Kellan. I've had to help interview everyone, and there are still some people who don't have an alibi during the thirty-minute window when Abby was killed." His face squished together tightly with annoyance.

Although he had a point, I wasn't ready to give up. I remembered to ask Connor about the initials from the journal. "That may be true, but Abby was seeing someone named W. A. Might you know anyone on campus with whom she could have been involved?"

Connor gave it a few seconds of thought. "Besides your father?"

"Yes. Anyone else?" I hoped thoughts of Abby and my father together didn't sidetrack him. It'd already made me sick. "Also, do you have access to review the student system's security logs?" I repeated what Myriam told me about the day and time for uploading the grades.

"Kellan, you need to stay out of this investigation. You've got way too many theories going on in your head. The sheriff knows what she's doing. You can't sneak back into Braxton and insert yourself into everything just because you want to." Excessive frustration peaked in his voice.

I began to think his attitude went beyond my interest in Abby Monroe's death. "I appreciate the advice. Fine, I'll let it go for the moment. Seen Maggie lately?" Since he wasn't being open-minded about the investigation, I changed topics. I hadn't meant to be so blunt, though.

Connor halted and grabbed my shoulder. For a second, I worried about his next move, but then he stepped backward and took a deep breath. "Maggie and I have gone out on a few dates. I'm not sure where it's going, but there's chemistry. There's always been chemistry." Connor pivoted away from me and stared at his phone.

"Always been?"

"Yeah. I never told you this before, but it's time you knew."

Twelve years ago, when we were all friends at Braxton in our sophomore year, Connor had a crush on Maggie. He'd asked her out the same day I had, but she told him she needed to think about it. He never understood why until a few days later when I'd announced she and I were a couple.

"Why didn't you say something? I never realized you had such deep feelings for her." A rush of guilt blossomed inside me. "You never seemed upset when we went out without you."

"Trust me, I was angry. But we were all best friends. I didn't want to lose either of you, so I swallowed my pride and focused on school." Connor searched for the car keys in his pocket. "That's why I lost touch after graduation. When you broke up with her, it nearly killed me. I should have fought for her back then, especially if you were gonna ditch her for the first opportunity to leave Braxton."

I noticed the volatile frustration building inside him. Everything became more obvious as I thought back to the last conversation he and I had on campus that day. "So, is that what led to this dramatic change in what you look like?"

Connor nodded. "I needed to forget everything and to focus on my future. I threw myself into working out and the security field... it felt like the best place to concentrate my efforts."

"But when you and Maggie ended up working together at Braxton, you decided to—"

"Give it a chance," he added. "She's an amazing woman. I didn't want to screw up twice."

I had to ask, even if the answer would hurt. "Is that why you stopped calling Eleanor?"

"What? No." Connor looked at his phone again. "I gotta go. Sometimes you can be a real jerk."

As Connor strode toward the BCS vehicle, the jabbing pains in my side eased up, finally accepting there was something between him and Maggie. I wasn't happy about it, but at least it wasn't hidden anymore. Then I worried about how serious it was and whether it meant Eleanor would be in for heartbreak. Unfortunately, I had classes to teach and couldn't wallow in my concerns.

I ascended the back stairs, ignoring the cold sensation overtaking my body as I stepped through the vestibule where we'd found Abby's body. I dropped off my briefcase in her office—my temporary workspace—and shuffled to the main area on the floor to catch Lorraine. She was on the phone but waved and said she'd find me after the first class.

A few students were already hanging out and talking when I slipped back downstairs and sat at the corner desk in the classroom near the front entrance of the building. I said hello and that I'd be with them in a few minutes, then recognized Jordan Ballantine texting on his cell phone. While preparing my introductory remarks, a few stragglers walked in, including Striker and his girlfriend, Carla.

"Couldn't hack it on Saturday, Striker?" When Jordan lifted his head, deep brown eyes focused on his competition. With his shoulders squared and his chest puffed out, he looked menacing. Jordan was confident in his talent and voice and clearly not afraid to stand up for himself.

"What did you say?" Striker replied. "I'm pretty sure Coach Oliver only took me out of the game to give you an opportunity to be seen by the scout. He felt bad for picking me over you."

"That's not how it happened," yelled Jordan. "Your grades magically—"

"Guys, come on. You're supposed to be friends, stop this silliness," added Carla. "Be happy you both had the chance. And we won! That's what counts." Her lips were full and pouty.

It was then I remembered where I'd seen Carla before. She was the girl smiling at Jordan in the fitness center while cycling. I wasn't sure whether the conversation with Connor had impacted my judgment, but it seemed like there was a hidden agenda playing out in the classroom.

"Yep, we won because I saved the game. Striker shouldn't have been playing. He's on academic probation." Jordan shoved the phone into the pocket of his designer jeans and snickered. "I guess something must have changed, huh?"

Carla's face brightened quickly. "Yeah, maybe he studied hard and passed. Leave him alone."

"Exactly," Striker replied. "Coach Oliver wouldn't have let me play if I didn't ace that exam."

"Or something like that," Jordan said. "All seems kinda funny to me how quickly things improved once Professor Monroe died. I was supposed to start!"

When Striker stood and reached a fist in Jordan's direction, I raised my voice. "Welcome back to Diamond Hall, everyone. I'm sure you're curious who I am...."

I delivered my intro speech, which settled the room even if it didn't calm me. If the students gossiped about the peculiarity of Striker's grades changing so quickly, there was substance behind my intuition. I'd return to digging into it once I finished teaching classes for the day.

The first lecture went well. I covered a generic timeline of how the film industry evolved in the late 1800s and the first quarter of the twentieth century. When I dismissed the class, Carla ran out after Striker, followed by a few other students. I introduced myself to Jordan while he packed up to leave.

"Good meeting you, Professor Ayrwick. Would you be related to the president?"

I confirmed, then asked him what had happened before class began. "I noticed a little tension between you and a few other students. Anything I need to worry about?"

Jordan sniffed. "We're all friends, just like giving each other a tough time. Striker and I are cool."

"I saw you pitching last Saturday. You've got a fantastic curveball. I'm sure it impressed the Major League Baseball scout." And it was true, Jordan had definitely saved the season opener.

"Thanks, sir. I appreciate it." He clasped a button on his checkered shirt that had come loose.

Sir? He called me sir. Not even Derek called me sir. "Professor Ayrwick will do. I heard you share some concerns about how the grades were determined. Is there something you'd like to discuss?"

Jordan shifted his weight and tossed his head back and forth. "Nah. If he passed the exam, I'm sure it was legit, I mean, unless maybe Striker did something... never mind, it's just, you know—"

"No, Jordan, I don't know. I'm new here, so if you have information to share, I'd appreciate your candor." I could tell he was nervous, though he seemed to want to say more.

"I'm gonna be late for my next class." He made a mad dash toward the cable car station.

I had an hour before my next class, so I briefly called the sheriff. It had been a few days, and I needed to thank her for letting me obtain access to Abby's office. Officer Flatman answered. "Mr. Ayrwick, how was the visit with your grandmother yesterday?"

"It's always a pleasure to see her. I appreciate you letting me go so easily," I replied, unwilling to let him know I'd known that he'd known he'd gotten the better of me. "She cooked a delicious brunch. Any chance the sheriff is available?"

"Excellent. I'm happy I ran into you yesterday. I can't say for sure why, but my day improved afterward," he spouted before putting me on hold. Was that a southern accent I heard?

A few seconds later, Sheriff Montague picked up the call. "What do you want now?"

"Just to extend my hearty thanks for granting access to Abby Monroe's office. It made teaching her classes today a lot easier." While explaining my new temporary job, I made a list of things to mention about the case should she try to hang up quickly. It'd been a recurring theme in my life lately.

"Seems you wormed your way into things, Little Ayrwick," the sheriff replied. "I've got an arrest to make shortly. Just waiting on the analysis of some fiber samples we found under the deceased's fingernails. Make this quick, please." If there were fibers, it meant there was a struggle before Abby had been hit on the head with the mysterious and missing murder weapon.

"Absolutely. I hear Lorraine Candito notified you about the lost gift she'd intended to give me, as well as the other items stolen from Diamond Hall. Have you found anything? I'm keen to learn what she got me." I crossed the floor toward the staircase.

"We've not located that particular item, but should we stumble across your little trinket, you'll be the first to know. If that's all—" Her caustic tone left little room to debate, but it wasn't stopping me.

"No, actually, sheriff, I have a few other things," I confirmed while worrying she wasn't taking Lorraine's news about the thefts seriously. "I came across Abby's personal journal while sorting through her office."

The childish sarcasm dripping from the sheriff's tone was borderline obnoxious. If it hadn't been directed at me, I might have found her funny in a ridiculous sort of way. "And you called to tell me she had a crush on some movie star? How sweet! But I'm in the middle of a—"

"If only that were the case. Abby mentioned having a relationship with someone. I was curious if you might know the person's identity." I didn't want to reveal the initials yet.

"Nope, I'll send someone to get the journal. I followed up on your lead about Coach Oliver being near the crime scene. Lorraine confirmed his story, but it still leaves time for either to kill Abby during the death window. While I appreciate you letting me know these little pieces of random news—"

"Got it. Unless you want to share the results of Abby's phone call from someone in Grey Sports Complex, I guess we're done here," I replied, realizing she wouldn't be of any help. I'm not sure who hung up first, as I was already thinking about my next move. I received no answer about the phone call.

While ascending the stairs to find Lorraine, I emailed the technology department and asked them to confirm whether there were any logs on the student grading system indicating record changes. Sometimes it wasn't about directly finding the culprit but eliminating all your suspects until left with just one. As I reached the top, Lorraine smiled back at me from behind the desk. I opened my mouth to say hello, but my phone vibrated. Why wouldn't people leave me alone to investigate this crime? I retrieved it and read a text message from Eleanor.

Eleanor: *Talked to Connor yet? This is taking too long.*
Me: *In progress. Will update you soon.*
Eleanor: *Hurry, please. I'd like to know if he's still interested. I'm not very patient lately.*
Me: *Classes today. I'll come to the diner for lunch tomorrow.*
Eleanor: *The position of tonight's moon is not in my favor, but tomorrow looks great.*

Eleanor wouldn't be happy about the news I'd learned. I was hoping to chat with Connor before our lunch the next day, to understand what happened between him and my sister. The stress creeped back in, and I desperately craved one or four of Nana D's double fudge brownies.

Chapter 16

Lorraine and I walked around South Campus. I couldn't wander too far with another class starting in thirty minutes. She looked worn down, almost ready to yield to the pressure swirling around her.

"I'm so sorry you have to go through all this drama. I wish I could convince Sheriff Montague to focus on someone else besides you." I loosely placed my arm around her waist as a show of support. "Maybe you could help me decipher something I came across while reading Abby's journal."

"I'll try," Lorraine said when we stopped at a nearby bench. "I'm pretty useless these days. Alton thinks I should take a vacation, but I've been told not to leave town."

"I'm hoping to find the truth soon," I added, taking a seat next to her. "Do the initials W. A. mean anything to you? Abby mentioned going on a few dates with someone."

While running her fingers through her hair and pulling the bangs away from her forehead, Lorraine considered my question. "There's your father, of course. My mother was a W. A. before she married my daddy, but I doubt that Abby would write about her since she's been long gone."

"Anyone on campus? A faculty member, maybe a student Abby knew? After I saw Coach Oliver at her house, I thought I had the initials confused, but I double-checked."

Lorraine shook her head, then a look of fear materialized. Her eyes opened wide, and she gritted her teeth. She quickly transitioned from loving puppy to vicious beast. "It can't be! That louse."

"What? Do you know the person's identity?" I watched her eyes fill with tears and pulled her in for a hug. "Talk to me, Lorraine. Maybe this will help prove your innocence."

"The coach's full name is W. A. Oliver. His parents weren't very bright and incorrectly filled in the first and middle names on his birth certificate with only his initials, W. A. He was embarrassed as a child that he never had an official name and told everyone to call him Oliver. When he started coaching, it became Coach Oliver, and that's how most people refer to him now."

"How did Abby know? And what do they stand for?" I pondered several guesses.

"I'm not sure. He won't tell anyone what his name was supposed to be. I heard Abby call him W. A. in the cafeteria once," Lorraine replied. "I think he's the person she was referring to in her journal."

"It makes sense given I saw him at her house last week, but how would you know about his nickname?" I noticed Lorraine's expression change from sad to angry, almost enraged. "What's wrong?"

"Oh, Kellan. I've been keeping a secret from everyone, but I can't do it anymore if that scoundrel was two-timing me." Lorraine dried her tears and beat her fists against the bench.

Lorraine explained that she and Coach Oliver had been dating the last few months. He begged her to keep the relationship just between the two of them because it was against school policy for colleagues to date without informing the college. After a lawsuit Coach Oliver had been in the middle of, the chief of staff issued an internal memo notifying everyone if they initiated a relationship with a colleague who met a few of the criteria in the revised policy, there was an obligation to ensure it was formally acknowledged by the school to protect everyone involved. Coach Oliver was insistent no one could know he and Lorraine were dating, fearing he'd be fired on the spot again because of the prior lawsuit. I thought the whole thing was an invasion of privacy, but it would make the situation between Maggie and Connor much more difficult if they'd continued any further in their relationship.

"Lorraine, you can do so much better than Coach Oliver. You're a major catch, and he's just... well, he's not worth your time." I wanted to console her, but if what she'd revealed was true, it would tie a perfect little bow on Sheriff Montague's case against her.

"I need to speak with him right now," she yelled, crunching her fists together. "I'll kill him."

I was alarmed but knew my news had blindsided her. "You best choose your words more carefully. Given everything going on, that's not something others should hear."

"When I get through with him, he'll wish we'd never met. I'm sorry to rush off, but I have to settle this right now." Lorraine thanked me for sharing the info and stomped away.

That's when I realized I'd forgotten to ask about the three missing items she'd shared with the sheriff. I desperately wanted to stop her from doing anything she'd regret, but my next class started shortly. I couldn't afford to annoy both my father and Myriam on my first day. I headed back to Diamond Hall and prepared for Abby's second lecture. I knew none of the students in the History of Television Production class, but it was an easy one to teach. I talked a lot about the recent focus on colorizing older shows like *I Love Lucy*, but when half the class looked at me like I'd just arrived from another planet, my temporary high evaporated.

In need of a boost once the lecture ended, I ordered a double macchiato and butterscotch Rice Krispies treat at The Big Beanery. After leaving and rounding the corner, I noticed Dean Terry talking with Jordan Ballantine outside Paddington's Play House. Although it wouldn't have seemed odd normally, learning Dean Terry had an open alibi and was disgruntled with Coach Oliver, then hearing Jordan complain about Striker still playing despite his previous academic probation, I couldn't help but be suspicious. As I approached, their conversation ended. Both walked off toward the cable car station.

Since following them wasn't an option, I used my break time to update my father. I hadn't heard from him after accusing him of cheating on my mother. I left a voicemail indicating the first two classes had gone effortlessly, and I was about to start the third one. I checked my email and found the location of Abby's funeral service. I texted my mother that I missed her, and she immediately wrote back how proud she was of me for following in her and my father's footsteps by working at Braxton. Seriously, it was only three weeks. She turned every little molehill into a mountain!

When I reached Diamond Hall again, my phone vibrated with two alerts. The package I'd sent Emma had arrived. I couldn't wait to see the gratitude on her face when she found the stuffed Braxton bears I'd mailed her. There were three in the set—a ballerina, a baseball player, and a doctor. She needed as many options as she could find in choosing her future career. I secretly hoped it wasn't the doctor as the thought of her looking after me in my old age or me having to pay for medical school was not appealing. Lorraine also texted that Coach Oliver would be back in his office after his offsite meetings. She she'd confront him at four thirty.

Connor joined me as I scrambled up the pathway back to the classrooms. "Hey, I was looking for you. To apologize for my behavior earlier today."

I tossed out my hand in a friendly gesture. "Apology accepted, but at the risk of ruining the world's shortest truce, can I ask you a question about my sister?"

"That's why I'm here. You deserve an explanation," Connor said.

A few students walked past us. "I only have ten minutes."

"I should have said something to Eleanor sooner. When she mentioned you were coming back for Christmas, I felt foolish about the whole thing and pulled away from her."

"Are you saying you were interested in... ummm... taking her on another... or that you had feelings...." I stumbled with my words. "I'm not sure how to say this. She's my sister."

"Yes. When we ran into one another, I felt some sparks. I thought we had a chance to get to know one another again without you in the middle," he replied.

It was the first time I'd seen Connor hesitant and anxious. It somehow made me feel better about the total mess. "Bottom line, are you still interested in my sister?" I cringed, not wanting to hear the answer but also feeling a need to protect Eleanor. "She's confused about what's going on between you two. And now she's under the impression you're dating Maggie. As am I."

"Ugh! Why couldn't you stay away, Kellan? Then, this whole thing would be ten-thousand times easier!" Connor's body tensed as he leaned against a column holding up the awning.

I worried he might knock the whole thing down. "I don't think that's the question you should be asking. Regardless of whether I came home, you can't date them both, can you? You need to figure out what you want, man."

"I'll give it some thought before I do anything drastic, Kellan. If you're telling me you wouldn't completely hate the idea of me going out with your sister, I'll call her to talk things out."

"I think that's a good first step." Finding out the truth was helpful, but it still meant the four of us were caught up in something complex. I'd only be in town for a few more weeks.

Connor agreed. "By the way, they're trying to match some fibers under Abby's fingernails against a few people and objects from the office. If they find any DNA, they'll move forward against someone."

"Thanks for the status. Can you share what the missing objects were?"

"I only know about the clarinet. Sheriff Montague's not ready to reveal all the details. Sorry," Connor said. "She doesn't tell me everything."

"Okay, thanks. I need to go, but Lorraine told me something I think you should know."

"Sure, what's up?"

I updated him on her revelation about W. A. and how she had been secretly dating Coach Oliver. "I know this makes her seem even guiltier, but if you saw the ire on her face when she realized he was two-timing her with Abby Monroe, she could have—"

"Killed someone?" Connor interrupted with a heavy sigh.

"Well, yeah, but that tells me she didn't know about it beforehand. It's not the reason Abby died. Lorraine is innocent." I felt compelled to stand up for my father's assistant and the woman who'd been so kind to me over the years.

"I'm sure you feel that way, but people can do the strangest of things under difficult circumstances. You understand Sheriff Montague needs to be informed about this, right?" Connor said. When I nodded, he continued. "Let me. The sheriff trusts nothing coming from you right now. I can share the news without her immediately arresting Lorraine. She's a good woman."

"Lorraine or April?" I asked in jest. Then, I realized if Connor recognized the sheriff had a crush on him, the entire Maggie versus my sister problem could go away.

"Both. And check your email. I located the system logs on those grades you mentioned."

"Thanks. Let's catch up later. I need to teach my final class for the day." Connor had come through for me. I felt positive about rebuilding our friendship again.

Connor took off, and I taught three hours on Broadcast Writing. Rather than hold the class for an hour three times per week, Abby had opted for one longer lecture where they could watch various television programs and compare writing styles and format. It was a fun and easy session with mostly creative types looking to polish their communication skills before graduating and searching for jobs.

After the class ended at four thirty, Officer Flatman arrived to bag and tag Abby's journal. When I got back to my office, I jumped online and perused the logs Connor had sent. They confirmed Myriam had uploaded the grades herself last Wednesday evening. There were no previous entries or changes since her upload, which meant if Abby had originally marked Striker's exam as an 'F,' someone had done something to the physical copy between the time Abby had graded the test on the Friday before she was killed and when the exams mysteriously showed up in the folder in Myriam's mailbox. Myriam had found a version with a 'B+' and agreed with the person who'd marked Striker's test with that grade.

I popped my head into Myriam's office, where she mentioned sticking around that evening for a self-defense course at Grey Sports Complex. "I hope you have an exciting time at class. Always good to keep both the mind and the body in a healthy place, eh?"

"*The evil that men do lives after them; the good is oft interred with their bones,*" she replied with a sinister-looking sneer. "Except I much prefer the company of the genuine women at Braxton to that of its weak men who seem so substandard in every sense of the word."

Not having any response other than to ignore her, I left the offices realizing I hadn't eaten lunch. I grabbed a ham and Swiss cheese sandwich from The Big Beanery and headed home to map everything I'd learned about the case to date. I'd just started the drive at five thirty when my cell rang. It was from an exchange used only at the college, but I didn't recognize the number. "You've reached Kellan."

"It's Lorraine. I need to speak with you urgently." Her voice was breathy and panicked.

"Ummm... sure. I just left South Campus and am on the road. Everything okay? I'm worried about you."

"I told Coach Oliver I couldn't be with a cheater, but he swore he never dated Abby."

"Men lie, Lorraine," I said.

"I know, that's why I dumped him. But I need to see you about something else."

"Okay, I can meet you outside Grey Sports Complex." I pulled to the side of the road.

"No, it's fine. I'm coming back to Diamond Hall to finish a few things. I'll grab the cable car in a couple of minutes and meet you at The Big Beanery at six."

"Sure." I wanted to contemplate all my suspicions about the people involved in Abby's death, but this was a higher priority. "Any chance you learned something to find Abby's killer?"

"I might have. When Coach Oliver and I were done, he left his office first. I needed a few minutes to collect myself. I went to the women's locker room in the other hallway to wash my face, but on my way back, I saw someone leaving his office. I thought I recognized the person, but it made little sense. I went back, so I could call you with an update. That's when I found a note on his desk. You need to read it."

"Bring it with you to South Campus. We need to discuss those three missing objects too."

"Okay, I might be able to connect a few dots to several problems on campus."

"Does this have anything to do with Striker's latest grades?" I asked.

"Bingo! I'll give you all the details when I see you in a bit."

I warned Lorraine to be careful, then returned to South Campus, excited to hear her news. By the time I arrived at The Big Beanery at a quarter to six, the daytime crowd had dissipated. Most students were eating dinner in the cafeteria or hanging out with their friends somewhere else on campus. I'd heard something about a mega snowboarding event on the western peak of the Wharton Mountains. I ordered a lemonade as I'd already drunk way too much coffee during the day and grabbed a tall table near the front entrance to catch Lorraine as soon as she came through the door.

I thought back to the crime Abby had mentioned on the phone when we first connected. It made sense that either Coach Oliver was the culprit, or he knew the person's identity. I couldn't figure out why Abby wrote in her journal that her feelings had changed for him, but now that I had confirmation he was W. A., I could ask Coach Oliver myself why he lied to me about his relationship with Abby. What a man is willing to tell his girlfriend versus what he tells another guy were often two vastly different things. If I had any hope of getting Coach Oliver to spill the truth, I'd need to make it sound like I was on his side.

While I waited, my father returned my call. "It went smoothly for most of the day, Dad. I like the students, and Myriam was helpful. She's got a venomous tongue, but if you ignore that part of her, she's somewhat tolerable." I checked my watch and assumed Lorraine would arrive any minute.

"Myriam is keen to share her opinion. I enjoy our discourse most of the time, but occasionally, her words cut deep," my father replied.

For a fleeting moment, I unnaturally thought we were having a normal conversation. "She's annoyed at how you brought me on board to Braxton even though I—"

"Let it go. Just don't annoy her, and you'll succeed in this trial period."

Trial period? What was he talking about? "Ummm... you should be worried about her annoying me and posting those blogs about you. She quoted another line today about *weak men* as I was leaving."

"Let's continue this discussion when you get home tonight, Kellan. Your mother is eager to hear for herself how the day went." After he disconnected the call, I groaned and repeated to myself out loud several times... *I am not a child living at home with my parents again.*

The amber sun slowly set, highlighting the passing of time. My phone said a quarter after six, yet Lorraine was still a no-show. I called and texted but received no responses. I warily rang Connor.

"Did the logs I sent confirm what Dr. Castle told you earlier?" he said.

"Yes, they did. I appreciate it, but that's not why I'm calling."

"What's up? You sound anxious."

I conveyed everything that'd happened. He instructed me to take the cable car back to North Campus to meet him at Grey Sports Complex. He thought I might run into her if I wasn't driving. When I reached North Campus at a quarter to seven, several students were lined up to board the cable car. Carla huddled close to Jordan at the end of the queue. I would've interrupted them, but I needed to get to Grey Sports Complex. While jogging over, I recalled this was the second time I'd seen them together without Striker. Jordan had mentioned they were all friends, but it seemed like those two spent more time together than I'd be comfortable with if she were my girlfriend. Was that what Nana D meant when she'd told me Striker was having girl troubles?

Once arriving at Grey Sports Complex, I entered reception and checked the digital monitors on the walls opposite me. The third-floor fitness center was packed with a large group of students. I tried to locate Lorraine among the crowd, but I only recognized Striker doing intense pull-ups.

After showing my face to the camera, I entered through the middle door in search of Coach Oliver's office. When I arrived, the door was open, and the lights were on, but no one was inside. As I turned to walk down the hallway toward the fitness center, Connor called my name.

"I can't seem to find her anywhere. I checked the entire first floor. Could she be stuck in transit?" Connor's furrowed brow concerned me. "Unless you seriously believe something happened to her."

Lorraine wasn't the type to exaggerate or make someone wait. If she had something important to tell me, she'd have made it to The Big Beanery on time, answered my call, or reached out to explain her delay. "Something's definitely wrong. Let's check the rest of the building, and if we can't find her, then we need to locate Coach Oliver. Lorraine was with him before she contacted me."

Connor sprinted downstairs to check the second floor in case Lorraine was hiding in one of the empty rooms. I remained on the third floor and rushed to the other hallway to check if she was in the fitness center but hidden from the camera's view. No Lorraine. Striker waved to me while preparing for his next set of exercises. Either I was sweating from running around, or the building's heat was too high.

I exited the fitness center and crossed back to the hall housing Coach Oliver's office and the conference room. I doubted Lorraine lingered there, but a window overlooking the front of the building would provide an unobstructed view of the cable car station. Was Lorraine finally boarding the next car to South Campus? It was now seven o'clock.

I opened the door and stepped into a dark conference room, instantly feeling a chilly breeze blowing in my direction. Someone had left the window open, or the heat had stopped functioning. I felt along the wall for the light switch but couldn't find it. Remembering Coach Oliver had said they were installing a new voice-activated system, I shouted, *"Light on."* Two seconds later, the glow from three recessed bulbs flooded the room.

Two shutters banged against the exterior wall near a large open window. When Connor entered the room behind me, I jumped two feet off the floor. He said, "I didn't find Lorraine downstairs. How about you?"

I swiveled around, breathing deeply to regain my wits. "No. But look at all these overturned chairs." I walked to the window, noticing someone had pushed it to the ceiling. The opening was about four feet wide by six feet tall. I stuck my head outside to look in the enclosed front courtyard.

"Anything?" Connor approached my right side. His woodsy cologne overpowered me.

Several students meandered on the ground in front of the building. No Lorraine. It was hard to focus in the darkness. Then I noticed something odd at the base of the statue in the courtyard. "Do you have a flashlight?" When he nodded, I showed him where to shine the beam.

Connor confirmed my suspicions using a cold, matter-of-fact tone they'd taught him in the police academy. "That's a body on the ground near the statue, isn't it?"

Chapter 17

I gulped and closed my eyes, wishing I hadn't seen what I'd seen. We ran out of the conference room toward the nearest stairwell. Connor called Sheriff Montague as we exited on the second floor near the courtyard entrance.

He instructed me to wait while holding me at bay. After I followed his request, he cautiously approached the statue. I watched him kneel to check Lorraine's pulse. When he turned back toward me, a morose expression confirmed the devastating news.

"She's dead?" The weight of my entire body sank quickly.

"Yes, her neck broke when she hit the statue after the fall from the window," Connor replied.

"It's gotta be Coach Oliver. Lorraine surmised he was up to something illegal." My blood boiled as I shuffled toward the statue. My eyes filled with tears. How could this happen?

"Did she use those words? I'm not saying it doesn't look suspicious, but we have to be clear on the facts."

"Not exactly," I replied, calming myself down. "When I asked what she thought was going on, Lorraine confirmed it was connected with Coach Oliver and Striker's grades."

After the sheriff arrived, Connor recapped what I'd already confessed. I waited for them to evaluate the situation. Paramedics arrived and verified there was nothing they could do to help. Sheriff Montague directed her team to bring the coroner onsite while Connor called my father to inform him of tragedy. I wasn't ready to deliver the news, and the sheriff wanted to hear Lorraine's words directly from me.

"Did she sound like she might harm herself?" asked Sheriff Montague.

"What? No, that's crazy! She was frightened and wanted to meet me at The Big Beanery. There's no way she jumped from the window. Lorraine wouldn't do that!" I was irate over the way the sheriff had suggested Lorraine might have lost the will to live. "Plus, she saw someone unexpected. An assailant who killed her just like they killed Abby."

"Relax. I'm trying to ascertain the facts. This will be simpler if you trust me." She commandeered the seat next to me on the bench. "There was a note near Lorraine."

Easier said than done. Sheriff Montague hadn't given me any reason to assume she was on my side in the past. "What did the note say?"

"I can't get to it without moving her arm. I want the team to finish their initial analysis before we touch the body," noted Sheriff Montague, gently resting her hand on my forearm. "We'll find out what happened, I promise. Is there anyone both she and Abby fought with recently?"

I considered whom I'd encountered at Diamond Hall and shared the names. It was a concise list, but there also could have been several people before I'd returned home to Braxton. I wouldn't know their identities. I finished relaying my final account of the entire afternoon as Connor confirmed he'd contacted my father. "President Ayrwick is on his way, sheriff."

I knew how much my father relied on Lorraine, and as standoffish as he could be, her death would devastate him. It had devastated me. Connor and the sheriff stepped away to discuss something. As much as I wanted to pin the crimes on Coach Oliver, it didn't make complete sense. Why would he kill both the women he was dating? Dean Terry's behavior had also been puzzling me. Jordan and Carla's presence together on the cable car queue was suspicious, but any guilt I recognized on their faces might have resulted from someone catching them in a close embrace. Did they have alibis for the night of Abby's murder? Too many clues to follow up on. And it wasn't my job!

My mind had entered overdrive once I doubted if Connor could be responsible. Although I'd found Lorraine's body, the entire setup might have been part of his grand plan to cover up what he'd done. I shook the troubling thoughts from my head, confident my former best friend was not a double killer. I needed to drive home to get sleep and deal with the aftermath.

Sheriff Montague returned to the bench. "Holding up okay? I can't imagine finding two bodies within such a brief period is a normal thing for you."

"No, it's not," I replied, focusing my gaze on the pavement. "I'd like to get out of here."

"You are free to go, but you've figured out the drill by now." Sheriff Montague suggested a time to meet the following day to review a written statement. As I stepped away, she called out my name. "I can't tell you what the note said, but I'll confirm it wasn't a suicide message. I haven't made heads or tails of it yet. We can discuss it tomorrow."

"You mentioned earlier there were fibers under Abby's fingernails. Can you share anything?"

"No DNA. It looks like the fibers match the baseball team's newest jackets. But we haven't finished running all the tests, so please keep this to yourself."

I ambled toward the cable car to access South Campus, find my Jeep, and drive home. I should have stayed to support my father, but I needed to be alone. Lorraine had confronted Coach Oliver because I asked her about the W. A. in Abby's journal. Had I somehow sent Lorraine to her death?

* * *

I must've crashed when I got home because I barely remembered climbing into bed. I tossed and turned most of the night while mourning the loss of Lorraine, but when I woke up on Tuesday, the desire to punish the killer was at the center of my thoughts. I went for a run, then caught up with my mother, who was heading to Braxton at the same time. My father had departed much earlier to talk with the Board of Trustees about last night's incident, so she shared a ride with me to the campus. Sometimes you needed your mother to arrange things in perspective.

"Kellan, we'll all miss her very much," she said as I pulled out of the driveway. "I can't understand why she'd jump to certain death at Grey Sports Complex, but if she suffered from that much pain, I only hope she's in a better place now. Do you suspect she killed Abby?"

My mother knew nothing about Lorraine's relationship with Coach Oliver. While I was certain Lorraine hadn't committed suicide, my mother felt otherwise based on whatever my father had said the previous night. "I think someone pushed her, Mom. Maybe because of something she knew about Abby's death. They must be connected."

"We've never had murders at Braxton. Between those two awful events and this maniacal blogger, your poor father's retirement is causing him so much stress." My mother gripped the small handle on the roof of the Jeep when I took the curve near the river too quickly. My heart breaks for both women's families.

"Has he said anything recently about the blogs? I suspect Myriam," I replied.

"He knows who's behind them. He can't tell me, but we talked about it yesterday. I'm certain Connor is on top of it. There have been no posts since the one after the party."

I dropped off my mom at the admissions building on North Campus, then drove to South Campus to start my day. When I entered Diamond Hall, Lorraine's boxes in the first-floor hallway encouraged the pain to flood my body all over again. She'd have been moving back to the newly renovated executive offices during the upcoming weekend. I slipped to the second floor to steal a few minutes of solitude and map out a plan of attack for the day. Instead, I found a woman with bright red hair dressed in jeans and an oversized Braxton Bears baseball sweatshirt sitting at Lorraine's desk.

"Can I ask what you're doing in here?" Given both murders, I needed to talk to Connor about how well campus security operated if random people wandered into the building and rifled through someone's desk.

When she lifted her head, the wrinkled brow and the volume of makeup she had painted on her face made her look like a clown. "I could ask you the same question. Who are you?"

I wasn't accustomed to being questioned in such a manner when I was clearly in the right. "I'm Kellan Ayrwick. I work here, and this desk belongs to someone else. How about you?"

The woman stepped away and smiled pleasantly. "Oh, it's nice to meet you. I'm sorry I was rude. I didn't expect anyone to come in while I prepared things ready for the department. I'm Siobhan."

I knew the name, but I couldn't place it. "Are you a temp?"

"No, I've been on maternity leave for the last two months. The chief of staff called me last night and asked if I could stop in today to help organize. There was an accident, and Lorraine Candito won't be in the rest of the week." A thick Irish accent accompanied her words.

That's right! Siobhan was the office manager whose responsibilities Lorraine had been covering. "I believe congratulations are in order. Boy or girl?"

"One of each, twins," she replied, retrieving her phone to show tons of pictures of the twins dressed in green outfits. Siobhan and I chatted for several minutes, during which I learned she'd worked at the college for five years and moved to Braxton after visiting a friend who'd attended a semester abroad at a college in Dublin, Siobhan's hometown. She'd undergone in vitro fertilization the year before, never expecting two eggs to be fertilized simultaneously. Being a single mom to twins wasn't as easy as she assumed.

I explained my temporary role teaching Abby's classes. Siobhan had little to say about the late professor, suggesting she preferred not to speak ill of the dead. "Would you know who has access to the student systems. Myriam provided an overview, but I'll need to input the grades for an upcoming paper my students will turn in next week."

"Professors only have access to their own courses. They can't view anything about their students other than contact information, and we keep that at a bare minimum. I have advanced privileges, but I can only enter and update grades for classes if the professor authorizes my access."

I thanked Siobhan for her help and walked toward my office. She followed, querying if I needed anything, but I had little chance to respond. Myriam angrily darted out of her office. "Siobhan, I see you've met Mr. Ayrwick, resident troublemaker."

Me? What had I done? "Good morning. Have I offended you?" I mustered as much of a smile as I could while stepping into Myriam's path. Siobhan retreated across the floor's main area. Either she'd experienced one of Myriam's tongue lashings before, or she didn't want to embarrass me while I received one of my own.

"You mean other than telling Sheriff Montague I'd fought with both Monroe and Lorraine to make *me* look guilty of something? Honestly, the nerve of you spreading gossip after only working here for one day," shouted Myriam as she dropped her bags to the ground. "*One's doubts are traitors and make us lose the good we oft might win by fearing to attempt.*"

Not another weird quote. "The sheriff inquired about whom Abby and Lorraine had spent considerable time with on campus. I mentioned your name, but I didn't accuse you of anything." Disdain for the beleaguering woman percolated inside me. "Unless you count being the author of that nasty blog against my father." I didn't mean to announce the formal accusation aloud. I unquestionably suspected her, and the woman's constant Shakespeare references were getting on my nerves.

"I have nothing to do with it, I assure you. I can see you do not differ from your father, Kellan, and I'll be certain to inform the next president. We can't continue to allow pompous men to work on this campus," she growled while pushing me into the hallway.

"How dare you say something like—" I stopped speaking when I heard another voice.

"Maybe you two could keep it down? Students are arriving for classes below and can hear everything," Connor advised. "Perhaps we could behave like civil human beings and have a rational discussion?" He extended his hand toward Myriam's office, and we all piled inside. "What seems to be the problem here?"

"Mr. Ayrwick is under the impression that I'm a cold-blooded murderer, ruthless blogger, and I can't even imagine what else will come out of his mouth next," Myriam replied. "I'm going to report his behavior to the Board of Trustees, Director Hawkins. You're a witness to this unprovoked instigation on his part."

"I did nothing of the kind, Connor. You were there, you heard everything I said last night." I left out the part about accusing her of being the blogger, but the woman had it out for me. As I reeled in my frustrations, I took notice of Myriam's chosen outfit that day. I couldn't help but admire how polished and poised she looked in her navy-blue, classically tailored pinstripe pantsuit. It was the shiny gold camisole underneath that made the whole ensemble pop to my dismay. *Just let me at the wig to see if it reads Tuesday.*

"Dr. Castle, he's telling the truth. The sheriff asked for anything that came to mind. Kellan didn't throw you under the bus at all, however...." After waiting for Myriam to settle in her chair, Connor added, "Everyone's on high alert after two unexpected deaths on campus. Why don't we agree to let this go?"

"Fine!" Myriam adjusted the tortoise-shell glasses on her hostile face. "I'm willing to accept it wasn't intentional insubordination."

Insubordination? Did I work for her and if so, how had I missed that? I opened my mouth to object, but Connor interrupted. "Let's take a walk, Kellan. I've got a few theories to discuss with you."

Myriam ushered us both out of her office, then shut the door. I followed Connor down the back steps to avoid the crowd assembling on the first floor of Diamond Hall. When we reached the door, I mumbled under my breath, "Never should have come back here."

Connor laughed. "Man, she gets under your skin. Shake it off. I've got some news to share, which might cheer you up a bit. Although, it's not positive on the whole."

His words intrigued me, but I soon learned why the news was a mixed message. Sheriff Montague had authorized him to share a copy of the note under Lorraine's body. It read:

I hope you appreciate how much I've done to help the baseball team reach the championships this year. I understand how important it is to impress the Major League Baseball scout. I'll check next week's exam results too, so there's no chance of the star player missing out.

"That matches what Lorraine told me on the phone before she was killed. She had something to show me. She caught Coach Oliver or someone else writing the note to Striker."

Connor nodded. "This could be the reason she was pushed out the window. The sheriff doesn't think it's suicide anymore either," he replied with a hesitant break in his voice. "But why would Coach Oliver put something like this in writing? Don't you think he'd pull Striker aside and tell him he took care of it? And why would the coach put it in his own office?"

I considered the validity of Connor's input. When I added together everything I'd learned, I conjured another theory. "There's no doubt in my mind Coach Oliver is mixed up in this grade-changing scandal. What if someone is making it look like Striker is part of the scheme? I got the distinct impression from a conversation with Jordan yesterday that he hated Striker."

"So, you think he changed the grades with the hopes it would make Striker look guilty and get him kicked off the team?"

"Perhaps," I said. "I'm concerned Dean Terry is involved too. I saw her and Jordan speaking on campus yesterday in a secluded area."

"And now you suspect a college dean?" Connor huffed as we arrived at Grey Sports Complex. "Hasn't he been training both Jordan and Striker to be star pitchers?"

"You've got a point," I acknowledged. "None of this makes sense, but all of it looks suspicious and ties into what that blogger has been saying. I need to see how upset Coach Oliver is over Lorraine's death. Has Sheriff Montague questioned him yet?"

"Last night after you left. He came back to the building, claimed he'd been watching several practices at Grey Field after Lorraine stopped by his office. He returned only for a few minutes to get his briefcase and go home. He looked quite shaken up over Lorraine's death."

"He's a liar," I argued while preparing to leave. "I'll prove it right after I pay him a visit."

"I admit you were right about Lorraine not being Abby's killer, especially now that she's also dead. The sheriff believes what Lorraine told you about the confrontation with Coach Oliver, but she has no proof." Connor explained he needed to get to a meeting he couldn't skip, but he was working with the technology department to pull all the CCTV tapes and security access logs to Grey Sports Complex.

"I appreciate it. Maybe they'll find out from that know-it-all computer system exactly who was in the athletic facility," I replied, feeling some encouragement from his words.

"Just don't cause any more trouble. You've already annoyed one important member of the college in your attack on Myriam. Try not to get on everyone's bad side, Kellan."

I promised him I'd tread lightly with Coach Oliver. After ignoring the computer voice greeting me in reception, I made my way to the athletic director's office. The coach hung up the phone as I arrived.

"We need to talk," I uttered in my most serene voice, picturing Connor yammering in my head.

"Isn't the news horrible?" Coach Oliver waved me into his office and waited for me to sit in the chair opposite him. "Lorraine was an upstanding employee of this college."

"Don't distract me. Lorraine told me you two were dating for months. I know she confronted you last night." I rattled off my frustrations in list form, failing to tell him specifically what she'd said in the hopes he'd trip up and reveal something.

"Let's not be too hasty in our judgment. I didn't know Lorraine told you about us. We were supposed to inform the college since it'd been more than a few dates. I was protecting her." A harrowing sadness accompanied his voice as he closed his eyes and scratched at his goatee.

While Coach Oliver appeared genuinely upset over Lorraine's death, I wasn't onsite to comfort him, especially when he claimed to be protecting her. He's the one who'd gotten in trouble in the past for harassment. "What exactly was your relationship with Lorraine?"

"I'll tell you, but you have to believe this sounds a lot worse than it is," he replied, fidgeting with a pencil between his fingers. "Three months ago, your father called me to his office to chat about convincing a Major League Baseball scout to check out Braxton. Whenever I stopped by, Lorraine and I flirted a little."

"She mentioned the same thing to me, but that doesn't explain how Abby fits into the picture," I countered, feeling queasy over his confession. "Or why a baseball scout would be interested in Braxton."

"At the end of last semester, Abby and I discussed Striker's inferior performance in her class. She'd asked to meet me for a drink to advise that she would fail him," Coach Oliver said with remorse, shaking off a nervous jitter. "I tried convincing her to give Striker another chance. I wanted to help the kid myself, but I know nothing about communications or television history. I asked Abby to tutor him, but she wouldn't."

"Lorraine said you denied anything happened between you and Abby. I saw you sneaking around her driveway last week." When Coach Oliver looked away, I could tell he'd deceived Lorraine about the extent of his relationship with Abby.

"You know how it is. Things happen. She was an attractive woman," Coach Oliver said. "It was purely professional at first. We met twice to agree to keep Striker on the team. Abby hinted she'd consider going easy on Striker when he took her class again this semester if I, well...." he hesitated, then smiled and bobbed his head a few times. "You know what I mean. I'm sure you've been in that position before, Kellan."

"Yes," I said, lying through my teeth. I'd never been in that position, but I wanted answers and wasn't about to tell the man he was a disgusting fool. "How is it Abby came to write in her journal about her feelings changing for you?" I wasn't sure if he knew about the entries but wanted to catch him off guard. I also didn't want to reveal her plan to expose him.

Coach Oliver stiffened with a shocked gasp. "Huh? It was just a fun time. Nothing serious. I really do like Lorraine," he said after releasing another heavy sigh. "I guess... I mean... *did* like Lorraine."

Although his demeanor grew melancholic, as if he'd finally accepted Lorraine's death, I had to press on. "Was Abby holding something over you?"

"Abby knew I was dating Lorraine. She'd been listening outside my door and heard part of a conversation about Lorraine and I going away together in a couple of weeks. Sometimes she ignored me, other times she put pressure on me to spend more time with her and tell her all about the new technology and perks the athletic facility had received. It was only a few weeks where anything actually happened between us." Coach Oliver kept changing positions and shifting his body weight. I was certain he hid vital information. He'd also avoided any explanation about why the scout selected Braxton.

"When was the last time you spoke to her before she died?"

"The previous Friday," he responded. Something about the way he said the words told me he still wasn't telling the truth. "Abby notified me that Striker failed his first exam again."

That explained why I found the 'F' in her grade book. "But ultimately, she passed him, right?"

"I assumed Abby made good on her promise," Coach Oliver replied with a sly grin.

As much as I wanted to pin both crimes on the pervert, I couldn't connect the dots. He was guilty of something, but it might not be murder. "I appreciate you sharing this version of the story with me. Do you have any idea who could have killed Abby or Lorraine? Could Striker be responsible?"

Coach Oliver shook his head. "No, Striker's a good kid. He may not pass his exams of his own accord, but he's an accomplished pitcher with a future destined for the big leagues. I can't come up with anyone else who had a motive. Maybe two different killers?"

"I doubt that. Neither Braxton nor Wharton County have ever had murders like this before. There's little chance of two deaths happening so close together without some connection. What about Braxton? Why is the scout here?"

"I guess we just got lucky. I'm not sure," he said hesitantly.

I stopped questioning Coach Oliver. My best next step was to dig into Striker's whereabouts when Abby and Lorraine had been murdered. But first it was time to meet my sister for lunch.

Chapter 18

"I'm so shocked," an exasperated Eleanor said while we chatted in her office at the Pick-Me-Up Diner. "Lorraine was such a caring person."

"She was truly a genuine soul. I have to find out who could do something so horrible."

"I understand." Eleanor thanked the server who dropped off two large dishes of a new beef stew recipe the chef was experimenting with for the upcoming weekend. "Does Sheriff Montague have any clue what happened?"

"I haven't talked to her today, but I'll head over to the precinct later. I spoke with Connor earlier. He'll go through all the security tapes and logs this afternoon." I swallowed a spoonful of the stew, then quickly grabbed a glass of water. It was way too hot to eat, but the brief taste I'd gotten before my tongue burned was flavorful. "A little heavy on the red wine, maybe?"

"Chef Manny likes to go the extra mile sometimes." She laughed and gestured like he enjoyed his liquor a little too much. "Speaking of Connor, any chance you talked to him?"

"Yes, Connor was worried about me coming home," I replied cautiously. I had to be honest with Eleanor, but I needed to be careful observing that fine line between revealing everything and saying just enough.

"So, you were right. Is he looking for your approval to go out with me?" asked Eleanor, sampling the stew and letting me know it had cooled off. "You won't stop this, right?"

I wasn't sure I had control. "There's more than me giving you two the all-clear."

Eleanor sank into the chair and pushed the plate away from the edge of her desk. "There's something going on with him and Maggie now. I'm too late, aren't I?" All the normal exuberance disappeared from her angelic face. I wanted to cast some magic spell and make the whole situation go away, but that wasn't likely. "The stars haven't shown me anything lately."

Just thinking about magic made me realize I hadn't talked to Derek about *Dark Reality's* second season. He'd be thrilled to hear about the latest murder. I reached across the desk for Eleanor's hand, but she was too far away. In an awkward moment of silence, we glanced at one another, and I relaxed back into my seat. "He's been out with Maggie a few times, but he has no idea where it's going. Connor wants to do the right thing. He adores you both."

"Really? You don't think he's letting me down easily," she said, perking up from her earlier wane.

I nodded. "Possibly. You're going to have to talk with him yourself, but I wouldn't count yourself out of the game. You're a total package. Who wouldn't want to go on a date with you?" I was in the wrong career. Should I be switching to life coach and matchmaker extraordinaire?

Eleanor's mood improved, and she promised to let the news linger for a few days, then she'd call Connor to suggest meeting for coffee one evening. "I think you should do the same with Maggie."

"I'm not ready to date. Nana D's already setting me up with one of her music students. Know anything about Bridget Colton?" I reminded myself to reach out to Bridget to see if she had anything else to tell me about the inner workings of the communications department. Maybe she saw something strange and didn't realize it was an important piece of the puzzle.

"No, Nana D hasn't mentioned her to me." Eleanor finished devouring the rest of her stew. "Add it to the menu or tell Chef Manny to try again?"

"It's a keeper," I confirmed as I handed the bowl to my sister. When Eleanor disappeared with the dishes, I checked my phone for any new messages.

Nana D had sent a text to find out when I'd come by for dinner. I suggested Thursday evening, which she agreed to as long as it was after seven because she had a meeting with the local miner's union and the head of the civic center. She was up to something, which I hoped wouldn't end in disaster. She was still talking to every member on the Board of Trustees about the anonymous donations.

Upon returning, Eleanor gagged like she was going to vomit. "Were we ever that young?"

"Define young. I thought we still were."

She waved at me to peek out the window in the hallway by the kitchen. "Check the far corner outside at the two lovebirds making out. I understand being in love, but to go at it like that in the parking lot of a decent restaurant. They could shut me down for lewd behavior."

The Pick-Me-Up Diner wouldn't be closed over two people kissing outside. I suspected it was how my sister had felt about anyone sharing a loving moment these days. Jealousy could be a big part of her frustration. When I peeped in the corner, I felt a pang of heartbreak for someone I'd come to know in the last few days. Poor Striker! Carla and Jordan were the two engaged in a passionate embrace. "Wow! Look at those two. I guess she and Striker are no longer dating." I returned to Eleanor's office.

"It's not the first time I've caught them in the act," my sister replied, pulling her hair back and sighing. "They've been sneaking back there a few times late at night."

"Really? I thought she was Striker's girlfriend, but I suspect something might be going on between her and Jordan."

"This has to be tied into Striker's grades and who played in the opening game, right?"

Eleanor and I discussed the different possibilities of how the three students could be involved in the scheme. There was a strong chance Abby had caught one of them and been killed, so she couldn't tell anyone. "All I know is that when Myriam got hold of Striker's exam a few days later, she agreed with the 'B+' before uploading it to the online system. Every student's grade in Abby's book matched except for Striker's. I checked them all myself," I replied, noticing the time. As I stood to leave, another option came to mind, and as much as it seemed silly, I had to mention it. "Unless Myriam is lying and fixed his results, so she could give him a 'B+.' Which I *highly doubt* is the case."

Eleanor laughed. "No chance. Dad says Myriam is a stickler about those things. Maybe the individual changing the grades isn't the same person who killed Abby and Lorraine. It could be unrelated, I suppose. You still don't know specifically what either woman knew about the discrepancies before they died."

Although Eleanor had a point, I was certain the two crimes were connected. I needed to check the exam Myriam graded when I was back on campus to verify that I'd also give it a 'B+' and not an 'F.' It was time to discuss the latest news with my father since it clearly showed something underhanded going on at Braxton. "I'd like to find out who wrote the note Lorraine had with her when she fell out the window. It could be many people based on the vague word choices." I hugged my sister for reminding me about the note and took off for the sheriff's office. "Sheriff Montague needs me to finalize a statement."

Thankfully, Officer Flatman was out on patrol. The sheriff escorted me to her office to cover the final details of last night's events. "How are you holding up, Little Ayrwick?" The tweed coat was back today, but this time she'd paired it with a pair of corduroys and cumbersome hiking boots.

"I'm okay, but I'd be a bit better if you called me, Kellan. I think we're past the formalities, April, and might look to build a friendship." I hoped it would go over well despite her unattractive hairdo.

"Sheriff Montague will do for now," she replied with tentative ease. "I prefer to keep a strict line between business and pleasure, and I don't believe I'd consider us *friends*."

I had no choice but to accept her decision. At least I knew to approach her carefully. I wouldn't get any answers if I pushed too much. "I'd be happy to read and sign the final statement. Any leads you can share? Lorraine Candito was a close family friend."

Sheriff Montague softened at least one level on the friendliness scale. "I'm sure it's been quite a shock. I trust Connor shared the contents of the note?" She continued after I nodded in confirmation. "He's going through the security logs and will update me within the hour. Once he finishes, we'll know more about who was in and out of Grey Sports Complex."

"Do you have an estimate of when someone pushed her out the window?"

"Between five forty and six fifteen," Sheriff Montague replied. "Minutes after your call with her ended. She died instantly after hitting the statue. There was little pain, if that helps."

"It does, thanks." I crossed my legs and relaxed into her office couch. I hoped we were having an open dialog but wasn't sure how much she'd reveal. "Have you given any thought to my grading concerns? I suspect a few students who are conveniently in the middle of what's happened to both women."

"I'm not at liberty to say what I've found out, but I'm learning to appreciate how you've picked up information we wouldn't normally come across." She leaned forward on the table and handed me a prepared statement. "I'm not saying you have any freedom to get involved in the investigation, but having someone like yourself on the inside has come in handy. It's led me to a few other discoveries."

I assumed that meant I could continue poking around in different areas. After glancing over the statement detailing what I'd seen last night—including making a few minor changes to correct Officer Flatman's inaccurate grammar—I signed off. "Thank you. I'm not trying to intervene. It's crystal clear how important it is not to muddy the collection of evidence or risk any issues with apprehending a suspect."

"I'm glad we're on the same page here," she said before standing. "If I learn anything of importance from Connor's security log research, and I believe you can provide further insight, I'll be in touch. For now, be cautious what you say to the students while teaching their classes. We might be dealing with some clever folks." At least she'd chosen to wear a more stylish pair of boots today.

I took her silence as my cue to leave, which I was more than happy to do since we'd brokered a potential understanding with one another. I still wasn't sure how much I believed her desire to separate anything personal from anything professional. Sheriff Montague's refusal to call me *Kellan* yet refer to my former best friend as *Connor* instead of *Director Hawkins* was not a prime example of her so-called strict line. Nor was that comment she'd made at The Big Beanery about *how fine a man* Connor was.

I wanted to hit the fitness center but had no desire to go back to the third floor of Grey Sports Complex given what had last happened there. I changed into a pair of jogging pants and a long-sleeve thermal shirt—it was still a bit chilly—and laced my running shoes. I felt like a kid again as I ducked in the back seat of the Jeep when someone walked by. I didn't need to be caught in my briefs or without a shirt, but I wasn't keen on asking Sheriff Montague if I could use the bathroom in the sheriff's office to change my outfit. As I navigated the roads near the base of the mountains and Crilly Lake, I compiled a list of ways I could check the alibis for Carla, Jordan, and Striker without outright asking them. If they were responsible, any direct questions would give them too much alarm. If they weren't involved in the murders, it would seem creepy for a professor to ask them where they were those nights.

Once the run was done, I pulled into my parents' driveway and slipped inside the house. I showered and dressed while my mother heated dinner, then headed downstairs to offer help. She'd finished following the housekeeper's instructions on how to warm the honey-roasted pork loin, butternut squash, and green beans. Luck was on my side as she'd already set the table. We all sat and talked about our days.

"Looks delicious, Mom. You've excelled in your chef skills tonight."

"It's not that hard to follow a few steps on a piece of paper," she giggled.

"You've totally come so far with this talent," I replied.

"I suppose I could win home cook of the year, eh?"

"Ahem. Are you ready for tomorrow's classes?" inquired my father, disinterested in engaging in our banter on my mother's lack of cooking skills.

"I have a few materials to read over tonight, but yes, everything looks to be in shape." The rosemary garlic sauce on the pork loin tasted phenomenal. I explained everything I'd discovered about Striker's grades to my father. I also told him I'd updated Sheriff Montague about all the students in question.

"It's alarming to think someone at Braxton is responsible for two murders. I don't want to admit we could have a killer lurking on campus," my father said. "I'll ask Myriam to compare Striker's exam results with prior exams and papers to determine if there's a reason to believe it wasn't his work."

"It is frightening, but hopefully Sheriff Montague solves it soon," my mother replied. "Thankfully, Kellan is helping her."

"I wouldn't go that far, Mom."

"I'll also update the Board of Trustees tonight. I think it's appropriate for our attorneys to get involved. Hopefully, Connor has an update to clear any wrongdoing by the college."

"What do you mean, Dad?"

"If there are inconsistencies with our grading processes or someone on our staff has been involved in anything illegal, it will not look good for us. The baseball scout will pick no one from Braxton, nor will we get the final approvals for the plans to… never mind. There's no need to get ahead of myself."

My father's concerns opened my eyes to something I'd missed. This might be larger than getting Striker off the team, so Jordan could play.

What if this was about ensuring Braxton impressed the scout? I asked my father, but he said I'd need to talk with Coach Oliver about that angle—Coach Oliver, who was sketchy about his whereabouts during both murders.

My father added, "Coach Oliver might be a little rough around the edges, but he's not responsible for the murders. Sometimes people can't always tell you the specifics of their alibi."

I wanted to ask what the man had done in the past to cause the sexual harassment policy changes to be put in place, but I wasn't supposed to know about them. My mother interrupted as I cleared the table. "Sit down, Kellan," she said, then sternly looked at my father. "Don't you have something to discuss with our son, Wesley?"

As she left the room with the plates, my father spoke. "I suppose she means telling you where I was the night of Abby's murder." He took a swig of water to allow himself a moment to think.

I wasn't expecting this conversation tonight. "It's important to know where you went."

"You would say that," my father replied. "The Board of Trustees is concerned about me leaving Braxton, especially when they contemplated the development of an entirely new academic program."

"That sounds like a wonderful opportunity. I'm sure they could find someone to make that happen in your absence," I replied, hazarding a guess what new fields they might be considering.

"Did you ask him yet?" my mother said, carrying a peach cobbler to the table. "Nana D dropped this off for you earlier today."

I had the best nana out there, hands down. "Dad's started to tell me something, but I don't know what you mean about asking *me* anything."

"Lord, Violet, would you give me a few minutes? It's not like this is an everyday occurrence." My father pushed his chair back a few inches. "Don't you need to make some coffee?"

"What's going on?" Unwilling to wait any longer, I sliced a giant slice of pie.

"We've been completing a study and working with generous donors in the background about the possibility of Braxton adding graduate courses. The Board of Trustees has given the final go-ahead to obtain approval to convert Braxton College into Braxton University. We'll be starting with three key fields of study, but the plan is to expand our academic offerings to include several MBA options and an extensive Ph.D. program within the medical fields. The third will be a complete rearchitecture of the communications department, enabling us to become the primary school of choice for students looking to build careers in the television industry."

My mother caught the look of surprise on my face. "That's not all. Tell him now, Wesley."

"You can't keep quiet, can you, Violet?" My father turned to me with a huge surprise about to burst from his lips. "I tentatively agreed to take leadership of the entire rebranding campaign and build-out of the new university while my successor runs the existing college. In time, I'll turn over the expanded curriculum to the new president, but it's too much for one person to handle all at once."

I knew he wouldn't retire. My father couldn't sit still if his life depended on it. "I guess congratulations are in order?"

"Well, I had one condition." My father glanced at my mother and covered her hand with his. "It involves you, Kellan."

I didn't like the sound of where things were going. "I see."

"I'll only take on this role if you agree to return home and accept an assistant professor position under the new department chair and president, as well as a role on the committee to assemble the new communications department within Braxton University. I'm talking about developing relationships with all the major television stations, the elite production teams in Hollywood, these digital or cable subscription services like Netflixy or whatever you call them."

I stuffed my mouth full of a massive chunk of pie and closed my eyes. *This can't be happening...*

Chapter 19

After the bombshell my parents had dropped on me at dinner, I excused myself to consider their news. Not only would it be a major life change, but my father needed an answer by the end of Friday, so he could work with the Board of Trustees to structure the announcement they'd make at Braxton about the new president. I went to sleep early and tried to forget all the drama and concerns. Early Wednesday morning, I pushed aside those gnawing fears, skipped my normal run, and showed up in time for classes.

I dumped my briefcase on the desk, retrieved the pop quiz I'd created to verify how well the students had paid attention to the previous lecture, and placed a copy face down on twenty desks. For a moment, I thought a little part of Myriam Castle's personality had invaded me for tossing the surprise quiz on the class, but it was only fleeting. I couldn't be that mean. When students assembled in the room, I asked them not to turn over the papers. Striker and Carla entered and sat together. I looked around the room and saw only two people missing. One student had informed me in advance that she wasn't feeling well, but the other absence belonged to Jordan.

I gave the students thirty minutes to complete the quiz. If they finished early, they were free to leave but had to turn in their overviews of an upcoming term paper due in two weeks, or they could stick around to write it during the remaining lecture time. Although most students dropped off their overviews and depart, Carla turned in her quiz and went back to her desk. I assumed she was writing her overview but couldn't see that far away. Maybe I needed new glasses. Age had nothing to do with it.

A few minutes later, Striker left his seat and handed me his quiz. "Could you look at it now? I'm curious how I did." A few drops of sweat pooled at his temples.

I told him to take a seat while I read his responses. It was a combination of multiple-choice questions and a few open-ended sections, giving the students a chance to dazzle me with whatever they remembered from Monday's lecture. Although he missed a few easy ones, he earned another 'B+' with this quiz. When I looked up, only Striker and Carla remained in the room.

I delivered the good news, happy there wouldn't be any worry over the grades on today's exam. "You should be proud. Look at what you can achieve if you focus."

Carla winked at me. "Maybe you're a more talented teacher."

"Flattery will get you everywhere, Miss Grey, but I was being serious. It's a shame what happened to Professor Monroe. Were you not a fan of hers?"

"I'd rather not say. She was... difficult," Carla noted before turning to Striker. "You ready?"

Striker stood. "Yeah, pretty awful she died, though. You found her, right, Professor Ayrwick?"

"It isn't one of my more favorable memories." I'd unearthed my route to ascertain their alibis. While Striker loaded his backpack, I seized my opportunity. "You know, they always say you remember exactly where you were when something bad happened. How about you both?"

Carla awkwardly smiled at Striker. "We were together. Hanging out at my dorm. Right, babe?"

He nodded. "I had a lot of homework, and Carla was helping me study for a few classes."

"On a Saturday?" Somehow, I didn't believe they studied in the dorms. "That's a different way of spending the weekend than I did when I was a student here."

Carla coughed, then shrugged. "Ugh! Yeah, I guess you got us. We were in his dorm, just the two of us, but there might have been a few drinks and less studying involved, ya know?"

"Sounds closer to my memory," I said.

"I guess we should've been honest from the beginning. I don't turn twenty-one for a few more weeks," Carla added. "But you'll keep our secret, right, professor?"

"We should run. I've got that appointment with Dean Mulligan." Striker grabbed Carla's hand and led her out of Diamond Hall. They were bunched together, whispering something as I watched through the window. When they reached the end of the walkway, Carla yanked her hand away and took off in the opposite direction of Striker.

With them gone, I looked up Jordan's contact information and called his dorm room. He picked up on the first ring.

"Yo, who's this?"

"Jordan? It's Professor Ayrwick," I replied, suddenly feeling ancient. Was I turning into that mean professor who called out his students for missing one class? "I was following up with everyone to see if they had questions on the upcoming term paper."

"Sorry, I missed class. I was with Coach Oliver talking about the Major League Baseball scout. Looks like I'll be pitching this Saturday." Jordan excitedly shared his news.

"Oh, well, that's fantastic. Things come up, no worries. Missing one or two classes each semester is acceptable. You can make up the quiz anytime between now and Friday." Then I stalled, unable to produce a simple way to ask him about his alibis.

We agreed to a time for the redo and hung up. What had changed Coach Oliver's mind to lead with Jordan instead of Striker? I'd have to ask him when I saw him again. I pondered whether he would show up at Abby's funeral service that afternoon.

I peeked at my notes for my second lecture of the day, then had a bite to eat. Just as I finished, Connor called. "Kellan, I wanted to update you on what I learned from the security logs."

"Hit me with it. Is Coach Oliver guilty?"

"There are only a few cameras installed in Grey Sports Complex, but we had an excellent view of the fitness center entrance on the third floor." The sound of his flipping pages in the background filled the empty air. "Keep in mind there aren't any cameras near the conference room, so we can only tell who was spotted somewhere on the floor or in the building."

I pictured the layout as best I could from memory, recognizing this wouldn't be an exact confirmation of who had access. "There were a dozen people in the fitness center when we arrived."

"Yes, but Officer Flatman and I watched the video recording from four thirty to seven, which covers the full period for someone to leave, push Lorraine out the window to her death, and escape without being caught. Only two people I couldn't account for elsewhere entered or exited the fitness center. It doesn't mean someone else couldn't have hovered in the outside hall or approached the conference room, but at least we can eliminate those still inside the fitness center when it happened."

"Got it. Who slipped out?"

"Jordan Ballantine left about ten after five, but I don't see him anywhere else on the camera. Then there's Striker Magee. He showed at five, argued with Jordan, and exited five minutes later. He returned at six."

"Do you know where he was during that time?" I asked, curious why he'd leave in the middle of a workout. I'd seen him doing pull-ups when I got to the fitness center just before seven.

"I checked the other cameras in the building but didn't see him. He might have used the restroom or made a phone call between his workouts."

"Or he might have killed Lorraine. What about the self-defense class?"

"We don't have a camera view where the instructor was teaching it, but he provided the list of staff and confirmed there was only one no-show. No one left early, and he doesn't accept late arrivals. The class ran from five thirty to six thirty. I saw everyone leaving the building when I arrived."

"Who was the no-show?"

"Dean Terry, but she was seen on camera entering the building during the window Lorraine was killed. I'm going to speak with her today to find out why she skipped the self-defense course," Connor replied. "Looks suspicious."

"That's interesting. So where does that leave us?"

"I'm cross-checking the list of people captured by the front camera entering or exiting with anyone we can eliminate based on other camera angles or being in the fitness center or self-defense class. It'll leave us with about twenty people whose time we can't account for inside the building between four thirty when Lorraine showed up to confront Coach Oliver and seven thirty when the sheriff began a sweep for anyone still onsite. We'll document alibis over the weekend."

"That's helpful. Anything else you can add right now?" I asked.

"We can't verify Coach Oliver's whereabouts during the latter part of the period. He says he was at Grey Field for a practice volleyball game, but we have minimal camera coverage in that area. Jordan and Carla were also in Grey Sports Complex during that time, but you saw them at a quarter to seven when the cable car arrived at North Campus. Oddly enough, Alton Monroe met with his sister right outside the building before Lorraine confronted Coach Oliver at four thirty."

"Excellent progress. Thank you for letting me know." A sense of relief filled the empty space inside me. I still grieved for Lorraine, but at least we'd know soon. I was curious why her brother had shown up.

I disconnected and contacted Cecilia, Emma's grandmother. I needed an update on my baby girl, and hearing about her day at school would help me feel better. Then I delivered the news I wouldn't be back for a few weeks as I was doing a favor for my father. Cecilia was unhappy when I instructed her to put Emma on a plane to Braxton. She agreed to only when I accepted she'd be coming with my daughter too. Luckily, she'd only intended to stay long enough to drop her off, as she planned to visit New York City for a shopping trip with some friends.

I called Derek and left a message about the second murder. It was strange he didn't answer my call, but I had a wake to attend. After arriving at the funeral home, I switched off my cell and exited the Jeep. The last time I'd been in one was for Francesca's services. I hadn't wanted to attend today, but it was a necessary evil.

As I approached the front entrance, I almost collided with two women heading down the stairs. "Oh, I'm so sorry. My head's not quite right at these kinds of places." When I looked up, I felt even worse.

"I wondered whether you'd show," Myriam replied. "How did your second day of classes go?"

I nodded at my dreaded colleague. Even in mourning, she was as elegant as possible. It was also the first time I'd seen her in anything but a pantsuit. Her slate-gray winter coat hung open and revealed a floor-length black dress beneath its heavy fabric. A string of diamonds around her neck beamed at me rather than a smile. I supposed it was a funeral, but I recognized in the four or five times I'd met the woman, she always carried a bitter expression.

"Fine, thanks. I'm feeling well integrated and connecting with several of the students." I studied her companion, knowing I'd recognized her somewhere but not how or why. She was taller than Myriam and in her four-inch heels easily matched my height. Whereas Myriam had a sour expression and stark features, this woman projected an ethereal composure—that was the only description coming to mind. Her wavy, golden hair flowed endlessly down her back, and her almond-shaped green eyes sparkled. I thought she was a model, and I'd seen her on the cover of a magazine, but my brain wasn't capable of recalling details right now.

"This is Ursula Power." Myriam cocked her head in the other woman's direction. "She met Monroe a few times last semester during some on-campus events and wanted to pay her respects."

"Pleased to meet you, Kellan. Did you know Abby well?" the goddess replied.

The woman's stunning appearance mesmerized me, but it then occurred to me Myriam hadn't revealed my name when introducing us. How did she know me? "I hadn't met her in person. I was supposed to interview her the day she unfortunately died, but well—"

"*He that dies pays all debts,*" Myriam replied before I could finish. A self-righteous grimace waned as she said the words.

I might have been distracted and not interpreted her body language in the fairest manner, given my less-than-welcoming feelings toward the woman. I also had no idea what her quote meant, but I was more focused on how Ursula knew my identity. "Pardon me, but have we met before?"

"I don't believe so, but I've heard a lot about you."

What had Myriam told her? I had little time to ask any further questions once Coach Oliver interrupted us. Myriam glared at him.

"Hello. Such a tragic reason to bring us together," he noted before introducing himself to Ursula.

Myriam responded, "I suppose you received notice that I've asked Dean Mulligan and Dean Terry to suspend Craig Magee until the investigation into his grades from earlier this semester has concluded. After reviewing the last exam he took for Monroe, there's no way those were his test results. Someone else completed that test or switched his results with a different student's."

"Yes, that's exactly why I stopped to see you right now. Who do you think you are interfering in my baseball team's success? Professor Monroe gave him that 'B+' and you verified it was a passing grade. Striker was ready to lead the game this week. Jordan was only going to relieve him if needed. Now I've got to start the other way around and all because you've stuck your nose where it shouldn't be." Coach Oliver angrily shook his finger in Myriam's face. As his nostrils flared, I could barely contain my glee at two of my least favorite people arguing right before my eyes.

It suddenly made sense why Jordan told me he would be starting pitcher in the upcoming game. I watched Coach Oliver and Myriam go at each other until Ursula inserted herself into the conversation. "This isn't the time or place for you two to have this debate. Regardless of how either of you felt about Abby Monroe or who should pitch on Saturday, this is a memorial service for a woman who was murdered in cold blood," she replied with sheer, impressive elegance. "I'd suggest saving your personal feelings for tomorrow when you can have a civilized conversation about the investigation into the student's grades."

Myriam stepped backward and calmed herself down. Ursula had certainly made an impression on Coach Oliver too. I added my two cents, not to feel left out of the conversation, but also to continue the theme of behaving in public. "I concur, Miss Power. This is definitely not the time or place." I looked sternly at Myriam, as it might have been the first opportunity I could push back on her with no retaliation.

"I think it's time to leave. Shall we, Ursula...." Myriam replied, trudging away. I was unsure if it was a question or a statement. Ursula indicated she looked forward to seeing me around. Both women dashed toward the parking lot. Then a dark-colored BMW angrily tore away from the funeral home. Myriam had been the driver.

"Ain't that Ursula one fine specimen!" Coach Oliver whistled and entered the building with the smug look of a man who needed the expression quickly wiped off his face.

Although I had more questions for Braxton's seedy athletic director, they'd have to wait. I followed him into the funeral home to pay my respects for Abby Monroe. After the customary nods and weak, uncomfortable half-smiles with a few students and faculty members I'd previously met, I searched for any member of my family or Alton Monroe, so I could use my time at the funeral parlor wisely. I set my sights on Alton when he stepped away from the casket and toward a few of the flower arrangements.

"Kellan, is it?" asked Alton, extending a hand in my direction. His expression clearly showed he wanted to escape the room full of people he barely knew. "It's kind of you to come when you never met Abby."

"Of course, it felt like the right thing to do. I'm deeply sorry for Lorraine's death." Despite his tenuous relationship with Abby, the grief on his face was apparent. Losing both his sister and his soon-to-be ex-wife had taken its toll. While I didn't think he could be responsible for the murders, I wasn't ready to cross him off my list and worried what I mistook for grief was guilt. Why he was at Grey Sports Complex at the same moment someone had pushed Lorraine through the window?

"I almost didn't come, but your father thought it would be beneficial to have a representative from Abby's family," he replied as we walked toward a quieter corner of the room.

My parents were embroiled in a conversation with Dean Terry and Dean Mulligan that looked way too uncomfortable. My mother quietly nodded at the deans while my father smirked. I'd have to ask him what it was about when I had a moment. I noticed Connor and Sheriff Montague step into the room as Alton began talking again.

"Braxton's finest," he quipped. "I spent a fair part of my morning with her discussing my whereabouts during my sister's unfortunate death. They are quite persistent about specific dates, times, and places, aren't they?"

Alton's words intensified my curiosity and opened the opportunity I'd been looking for. "I take it they questioned why you were on campus the day Lorraine was killed?"

"Exactly. I told them she called me to help calm her down about some louse cheating on her. I met up with her near the athletic facility to give her the courage she needed to dump him. I asked if she wanted me to stick around, but she told me she needed to confront the man herself. Why anyone would think I could hurt my sister is beyond me. It's appalling the way they interrogate you over the littlest things."

"I'm sure someone can verify your whereabouts, right? That should clarify your alibi."

He shook his head. "Lorraine and I talked for thirty minutes, but I left right at four thirty. I had spent little time on campus before, so I walked through the sports fields, then I got in my car at six thirty.

Unfortunately, nothing will confirm where I was during the time in between."

Alton had an airtight alibi during Abby's murder. "What motive would they have to suspect you?"

"My sister invested in several stocks throughout her lifetime and made a windfall in last year's upturn. I was notified this morning she left two hundred thousand dollars to me," Alton replied, seemingly calm about the inheritance, which made me think he was even less guilty than I'd considered earlier.

"I would never have guessed by the way Lorraine acted or lived her life," I said. Although she always dressed well and drove a nice car, she had no air of wealth or attitude about her. "She was a wonderful friend to me over the years."

Alton nodded and indicated he concurred with me about Lorraine's generosity. "That sheriff seems convinced Abby's death is connected to something on campus, but she wouldn't give me a lot of details. Did you ever find what you were looking for in those files?"

"Yes, it wasn't a lot, but we have the last of her research for the television show. I also came across a few odd things in her grade book, which is why I agree with the sheriff that her death might be related to something underhanded at Braxton."

When Alton seemed interested, I explained the basics of Striker's grades and what Coach Oliver had said about Abby offering to change them if he agreed to give in to her demands. I unexpectedly learned a new piece of information from Alton.

"Abby might have bent the less important rules in life to access a story, but she would do nothing unethical or immoral with students' grades. She also had a severe distaste for college athletics usurping a student's time while preparing for future careers."

"I'm glad to know, but I can't figure out why Coach Oliver would lie."

"I might be able to explain now that you've filled in some blanks. Abby and I'd met up a few evenings to close on the divorce settlement. I don't know whether it was the wine or a momentary truce, but on those nights, it felt like old times. Abby had started dating someone and was glad she and I could settle things. She was ready to finalize our divorce. Then everything came crashing down. Abby realized the guy had only been taking her on dates in the hopes she'd change her mind about a student's grades. She'd caught an incorrect grade once before and originally thought she'd made a mistake, but when it happened again, she knew there was something sinister transpiring. She was going to expose something fraudulent."

Coach Oliver was looking much guiltier. Maybe Sheriff Montague was here to finally arrest him. "Abby mentioned something about a crime happening in Wharton County. Do you know what it was?"

"Regrettably, no. She and I had spoken little afterward. Besides taking out her anger on the guy, she also put the screws to me by reneging on the deal we'd made to sign the divorce papers." That news explained Abby's fight with Lorraine the day before she died.

Alton excused himself and offered his goodbyes to my father. I was on my way to see Connor and Sheriff Montague when Nana D called out my name. Somehow, this wouldn't end well.

Chapter 20

"What are you doing here, Nana D?" I crossed to the funeral parlor's Entrance.

"I had a few stops to make downtown today. Just thought since I was in the area, I should put in an appearance." Nana D wore her standard funeral outfit—a stylish, vintage dress cut just below the knees with a bit of white trim on the hem. "I also needed to talk to you about Bridget."

I couldn't believe her persistence about setting me up with the girl. It was fine to keep inventing ways to bring us together, but it was unacceptable to be so pushy at a funeral service. "Nana D, I think you—"

"Oh, slow your roll. I thought you should hear something she told me earlier today when I called to change the time for our lessons on Sunday."

She ceased talking to me as if I understood what she was implying. "Keep going, Nana D."

"Don't rush me." After helping herself to a few cookies and a cup of tea, she glared at me with a satisfied expression. "Okay, now I can finish my train of thought. I must be doing too much. Feeling like I'm getting a little more mature lately."

"Rest a minute if you need. I'm not going anywhere."

"But I am. I've got to see Marcus Stanton in twenty minutes. That man owes me his final decision, and if he doesn't back down, he won't know what hit him." Nana D slammed her fist on the arm of the chair, sending the tray of cookies way too close to the edge of the table. "Where were we?"

I stopped the tray from falling and waved off my mother when she looked ready to rush over. "What did you need to share?"

"Bridget had some interesting news. Apparently, she overheard a scandalous conversation on campus between someone and that baseball scout."

My imagination overloaded with curiosity. "What did she learn?"

"That scout said that he was doing his best and couldn't be stuck in the middle anymore. The decision was out of his hands."

"To whom did Bridget see the scout talking?"

"Pish! I didn't say she saw them. She overheard them," Nana D contradicted.

"Okay. Did Bridget know to whom he was talking?"

"One, what's with the formal speak? Two, would you let me finish telling the story, brilliant one?"

I kept my mouth shut and let Nana D relay her conversation. While Bridget had been eating lunch in the student union building, the scout sat at a nearby table talking on his phone. She recognized him from last week's pep rally and baseball game, but she wasn't sure who was on the other end of the device. The scout said he'd already made the recommendation for the position and that if all went well, there'd be a place in the Major League Baseball organization after the semester ended at Braxton. The scout also said he couldn't do anything else to help, then hung up.

"What do you think it's about?" I couldn't think of who else would be on the call but Coach Oliver. Was he looking for a job outside Braxton? Was that why he was so adamant about an optimal baseball season?

"Bridget didn't understand what the scout meant, but she thought it was peculiar. That's why she mentioned it to me. I might have inquired about what the students thought of Abby's and Lorraine's deaths."

"Why are you sticking yourself in the middle of this investigation?"

"Listen, pot. This kettle already told you I'm worried about the county. Since that school keeps this town running, it's important I pay attention." Nana D stood, insisting it was time to leave.

I couldn't argue with her since I'd also inserted myself into the search for the killer or killers. Nana D said she had one more meeting to uncover the anonymous donor's identity, then left. As I walked to the foyer, Connor approached me. "That grandmother of yours sure likes to make an entrance and exit. I think she might have pinched my bum as she walked by."

I felt my skin flush at the thought of Nana D doing that to Connor. I was going to ask how long she pinched him but thought better of it. "It must have been an accident. She was in a rush."

"Somehow I'm not sure I agree. I know she's not the sheriff's biggest fan, but that wouldn't win her any points," he replied with a smirk. "April is waiting on some test results. They picked up a few fibers under Lorraine's fingernails. She's hoping they might match the samples they found under Abby's too. I can't tell you anything else yet."

I temporarily ignored the fact that he called the sheriff by her first name. Connor was taking advantage of his admirers these days. I told myself I wasn't jealous, but the jury was still deliberating on that one. "That's good to hear. Hopefully, it will give them a big lead." I updated him on the news Alton and Nana D had shared with me earlier.

"Are you going to tell Sheriff Montague what you've learned?"

"I thought I might get a chance to speak with her here, but she left while I was talking to Nana D. I could stop by the sheriff's office on my way home." I considered my options yet found myself reluctant to be the guy always delivering the latest news. Both pieces of information had fallen into my lap. I never went in search of the clues. Didn't the responsibility belong to Alton and Bridget to tell Sheriff Montague? After all, *April* told me I was merely a private citizen and warned me to stay out of it.

After Connor headed back to Braxton to finish interviewing the people whom he'd seen on the CCTV tapes, I updated Derek. When I wrapped up, he mentioned relaying the details to the network executive the following morning. They'd called an impromptu meeting to talk about *Dark Reality*, but he wasn't sure why. He asked for my advice on how to handle the meeting, explaining he didn't have a good feeling. It was the first time I'd ever heard or seen him act nervous and ask for my opinion as opposed to instructing me to do something for him. Part of me wanted to assuage his worries, but just like sharing the updates with the sheriff wasn't Kel-baby's responsibility, I needed to let things happen without my interference in Derek's world too. I'd stood up for myself with my boss. Letting that twenty-four-year-old know-it-all learn a lesson on his own was a step in the right direction.

* * *

Thursday morning passed quickly given most of my time was focused on convincing Emma's first-grade teacher and school administrators why I had to pull her out of classes for three weeks. Then I struggled with my former mother-in-law to defend my position on why Emma needed to be with me until I finished my temporary teaching assignment. Once that was settled, we coordinated the flight arrangements for Cecilia and Emma to arrive in Braxton when my last class ended on Monday. Eleanor would meet Cecilia at our parents' house, ensuring my delay wouldn't interrupt her driver's schedule to arrive in Manhattan that evening for dinner with her best friends at a Michelin-starred restaurant. Oh, to be a Castigliano and have the world drop everything to impress you. Or ensure they didn't wipe your existence off the face of the earth.

After a run and a simple lunch, I set off for Braxton to prepare for the next day's classes and to administer both students' makeup exams. The first one showed up on time and finished the pop quiz in less than twenty minutes. When Jordan arrived, I got to know him better before making him complete the quiz.

"Getting ready for Saturday's game?"

"Yep. I spent most of my morning perfecting my curveball with Coach Oliver. The scout watched us for a few minutes too. I didn't know he was Coach Oliver's best friend."

While Jordan searched through his bag for a pen, I contained my shock about his news. No wonder Coach Oliver was so focused on ensuring the team looked good. I filed that under a list of things to analyze later in the day when I had more time.

"How are you handling Tuesday's incident at Grey Sports Complex?" I asked, remembering that Jordan was on the building list when Lorraine had been pushed from the third-story window.

"Two accidents in the same month. That's scary, huh?" He slunk further into his seat and uncapped a pen. "I can't believe I'd just seen Mrs. Candito a few minutes before it happened."

"Really, I didn't know. You must have been one of the last people to see her alive." I was surprised he volunteered the information, but he must have been questioned by the sheriff or campus security. "Did you already talk to Director Hawkins?"

"Yeah, he grilled me a little while ago."

I removed the test from my folder and leaned against the main desk in the classroom. I didn't want Jordan to start, so I continued asking more questions. "Where did you see Mrs. Candito?"

"I wanted to talk about an issue that'd occurred during a workout with Striker, but Coach Oliver wasn't in his office. Mrs. Candito was on the phone talking to someone. I felt awful. I wish I'd stopped her from jumping out the window."

It seemed like news hadn't gotten out that it was murder. "What time was this?" Could he have seen the killer? Or was it him?

"Had to be just before a quarter to six. I was in a rush to meet my study group. I mentioned it to Director Hawkins, but I didn't actually speak with Mrs. Candito. She never saw me."

"What was the issue with Striker?" I assumed Jordan had almost interrupted Lorraine talking to me on the phone.

"Ummm... Striker had been working out while I was at the fitness center. We had some words. I didn't want to cause any more problems." Jordan wrinkled his brow and groaned loudly, then confirmed he'd shown up at four fifteen and worked out until five when Striker came in. After their disagreement, Striker left. Jordan finished his workout, then went to the locker room by five fifteen to shower and change.

"But I thought you mentioned you and Striker were friends the other day in class. What happened?"

"After class, Carla told Striker she wasn't sure about dating him anymore. He was angry and confronted me about it. I wanted to give him some breathing room, I guess," Jordan said.

"Why would he confront you?" While he was nattering, I took advantage of the opportunity to learn as much as I could about the three of them.

"I think Carla finally told him something occurred between her and me the night Professor Monroe fell down the stairs. Striker accused me of moving in on his girl, but that's not how it happened. Honest." Jordan sat back up and placed his hands on the desk. "Can I take my quiz now?"

I was about to hand Jordan the paper when I remembered that Striker and Carla previously told me they'd spent that night together drinking in the dorms. Someone was lying. "Sure, in a minute. I don't mean to pry, but I've seen you and Carla together a few times. It looked little to me like you were completely innocent, Jordan."

"We went to the movies that night just as friends. Carla needed a break from all the work and drama with Striker and his stepfather freaking out over who would be the starting pitcher in the opening game. Halfway through the movie, she grabbed my hand, then asked if I wanted to leave early. On the walk home, she kissed me. I told her I wanted to see her again, but not until she broke up with Striker. I know what it looks like, but she came onto me, Professor Ayrwick."

"What time did you end up leaving the movies? Did you meet up with other friends or see anyone else?" I needed to find out if he had a legitimate alibi for the night of Abby's murder.

"I dropped off Carla at her dorm. She promised to think about what I said, then I went home. I guess it was somewhere between eight fifteen and nine. I hung out in my room by myself and caught the end of the

Phillies first spring training game. Oh yeah, and my aunt stopped by to chat."

"What about Carla? Did you hear from her again?" If he spoke with his aunt, that could cement his alibi. I knew it was the Phillies first spring training day too. I'd caught a few news clips the next day. Either he was telling the truth, or he'd seriously rehearsed his explanation should anyone ask for his whereabouts.

"Striker called her while we were walking home. I guess she went to meet him. I didn't talk to either of them again until Monday in class. You've got a lot of questions, Professor Ayrwick. What's up with that?" Jordan was becoming irritated with my rapid-fire technique. His perceptive manner meant the inquisition needed to slow down.

"Oh, I'm just worried about this getting too far out of hand. I've been in your shoes before. It's hard when you have feelings for your buddy's girlfriend. I guess that was the only time something happened between you two, huh?" I remembered Eleanor also mentioned seeing them hooking up in the parking lot of the Pick-Me-Up Diner recently.

"No, we met a few times to talk about the chemistry between us. We kissed and well, you know how things happen." Jordan shrugged and reached his hand toward the quiz.

He sounded like a younger Coach Oliver. I couldn't keep harassing him without some pushback. I let him take his quiz and thought through everything he'd revealed. Carla and Striker's alibi didn't match Jordan's confession. Jordan also put himself on the suspect list by stating he was alone after eight fifteen unless his aunt could prove part of his alibi. Connor had to have security records from that night for all students entering the dorm room unless there were no cameras there either. Jordan finished the quiz and exited in a rush without asking to know the results. As I scooped up his exam to head back to my office, I fortuitously encountered another person with whom I needed to speak.

"Good afternoon, Myriam." I blocked her from heading downstairs. "I'm glad we ran into one another. Do you have a minute?"

"I have to teach a class. What can I do for you now?" Myriam seemed to forget I'd witnessed her unseemly argument with Coach Oliver at the funeral parlor, but it was crucial for me to bring it up.

"I'm curious about your decision to push for Craig Magee's suspension from the baseball team over his grades. Can you give me any background on what happened?"

"Why is it any of your business, Mr. Ayrwick?"

"The student is in a class I'm teaching. If there was an issue with past exam performance, I think it's important for me to know about it now. Don't you agree?"

Myriam hesitantly nodded, then took off her glasses. "After you expressed concerns about grading processes within the department, I studied copies of Magee's past exams. Not only was the handwriting different, but his sentence structure and word choices were dissimilar. There's little chance he actually took Monroe's last test, and I intend to find out what happened. In the meantime, until we know the truth, he shouldn't represent Braxton on the baseball team, nor should we have lifted his suspension."

"I agree with assuming something funny happened on that last exam." I suspected it would be one of the few things Myriam Castle and I would ever concur on. "Would you mind sharing with me who's looking into it right now?"

"Based on discussion with your father, Magee has been placed on suspension for one week while Dean Terry, Dean Mulligan, and I investigate other student papers and exams to see if this is an isolated incident or happening with multiple students in Abby's classes or others in the communications department." Myriam looked quite angry over the situation as she wandered away.

"I'd be happy to help in any way I can." On my walk toward the cable car station, I ran into Dean Terry. "What brings you to South Campus? It's rare I see you here."

"I'm meeting with your father, Kellan. We have a few issues to work out before Monday's announcement about the new president. He asked if I could join him this afternoon for a discussion with the Board of Trustees in the executive offices. And he's the *current* president, right?" she said with a curious smile and a slight bit of nervousness.

"I suppose there will be tremendous changes coming soon."

Dean Terry shook her head and sighed heavily. "You're telling me. At least we can take pride in the positive impacts the baseball players have brought to Braxton this year. We should all be thankful for whatever stroke of luck has blessed the team and the scout's presence on campus this year. The sports program has been a major source of comfort and excitement for the community despite the students' concerns over the two shocking deaths we've had recently."

Dean Terry excused herself for the meeting with my father while I hopped on the cable car toward North Campus. I'd never known her to be so interested in the school's athletics program. When I'd been a student, Dean Terry focused on the honor societies and student government rather than sports, sororities, and fraternities.

Since I'd remembered to bring gym clothes with me, I stopped by the fitness center to get in a workout before going home. Upon arriving, I averted my eyes from the second floor as it would bring too many memories of Lorraine lying helpless at the statue's feet. After stretching my muscles, I focused on strengthening my back and legs since the bed at my parents' house was destroying my posture. An hour later, I overheard a conversation between two students who'd just entered the fitness center and sat side by side on the rowing machines.

"Totes. My boss just came back from the executive building and kicked everyone out. She was royally pissed off."

"What did Dean Terry say?"

"She was angry about the selection of the new president."

"Yeah, weird. The cops were onsite interviewing students who were at Grey Sports Complex on Monday. I told you something funny happened to that professor and the president's assistant who bit the dust."

"Seriously, I thought they both fell."

"Don't be so dense. Two people falling and dying so close together can't be a coincidence. Even your boss was trying to cover it up when I asked her for a quote for the school's newspaper. I got the distinct impression she was hiding something. After I pushed her more, she warned me that people sometimes get hurt by asking too many questions."

When my cell phone rang, the girls looked in my direction. Since I didn't want them to know I'd been eavesdropping, nor did I want to interrupt anyone's workout, I stepped into the hallway to answer the call. I had little time left to get Emma's input on our possible permanent move to the East Coast.

Chapter 21

Emma had just gotten home from school and was excited to visit Braxton the following Monday. I promised her a trip to a local farm to see a few horses, sheep, and goats. By the time I finished explaining the potential job change I was considering, Emma's pure excitement became contagious. She astutely admitted while she would miss Nonna Cecilia, she hardly ever got to see my parents. Emma had reasoned out we should come back to Pennsylvania for six years since she'd lived six years in Los Angeles.

"That's fair, Daddy, right? Splitting my time between both sets of grandparents?" Emma asked with the assured confidence of a much older girl.

"Yes, honey. You're looking at things the proper way." When I hung up, I thanked the powers-that-be for blessing me with the most amazing daughter. Now that I had her opinion, I was ready to make my decision.

While showering and changing before the trip back to my parents' house, I processed the conversation I'd overheard in the fitness center. What had gotten Dean Terry so irate she kicked everyone out and threatened a student for asking so many questions? I was certain she'd gone to see my father about the presidency, but given the reaction, that didn't seem logical anymore. I tried to connect all the dots, but it was time to visit Nana D.

Between the new paella recipe she was testing out and the scrumptious coconut cream pie, I was in a food coma for most of the evening. "Nana D, I might need to crash here tonight. I don't think I'm capable of driving home the way I feel," I mentioned while rubbing my stomach and curling up with a blanket on her couch. As I wrapped myself in it, I fondly remembered spending cozy afternoons in the summer with her and Grandpop while they'd babysat us as young children.

"I've been telling you it's about time you came home and moved in with me. I'm not getting any younger, and that daughter of yours needs my guidance." She dropped off a cup of tea on the end table next to me. "And this four-week teaching gig you committed to your father ain't gonna cut it, brilliant one."

"I know what you mean. There's something going on at Braxton that might be a reason for me to stick around longer. Dad doesn't want me to talk about it. I respect his need to keep the information quiet, but it's a hard decision, Nana D."

"You must be talking about those plans to expand the college, huh? Don't think I haven't already heard about them." Nana D sank into the recliner across from me. "Not that your parents ever thought to mention it to me. I've got my own ways to keep in the loo."

"I think you mean in the loop." It hurt to laugh at her confusion, but I pushed through it. "I should've assumed you picked up clues somewhere. I won't even ask how this time."

Nana D sipped from her teacup, exorbitantly satisfied with herself. "Good boy. What do you think you're gonna do about the new university? Is the offer big enough to convince you to stay?"

"I'm excited about the opportunity to build an entire college program that could put our town on the map one day. Then again, I'm not keen on working for my father. We've struggled to get along too much in the past." I'd been considering it in between all the activities keeping me focused on the murder investigation, but I consistently arrived at this causing a huge family rift.

"Set some ground rules with the man. Tell him what you will and will not do. If he doesn't agree to abide by 'em, then you know it won't work out. But if he says he will, you've got an opportunity most people never see fall into their lap. Tis could help launch your own career and get one of them television shows too," Nana D said.

I agreed with Nana D about the new role putting me in the spotlight with Hollywood. I could use those connections to find support and funding for my own true crime show. Maybe even center the first episode around what was happening at Braxton this semester. "I should sleep on it. I promised Dad I'd let him know tomorrow since the big announcement is next Monday about both the new college president and the expansion plans."

"In that case, tell me what's going on with the investigation. Figure out who murdered those two ladies yet? I asked the sheriff yesterday, but that woman's lips are sealed tighter than this new denture cream I'm trying out." Nana D clicked her jaw, then proved she couldn't easily remove them. She was on a roll this evening.

I said, "Sheriff Montague doesn't like to take risks. I can understand that, but I'm planning to see her tomorrow. Connor mentioned they'd have the results of the analysis on what they found under Lorraine's and Abby's fingernails."

"I finally got the lowdown from someone else on the Board of Trustees. She's confident that anonymous donation came from Marcus Stanton himself—that's why he's been so secretive. If he's the one pushing for all the improvements to the athletic facility and team, then he's the person the blogger has it out for. Not your father as much as I love seeing him get roasted," Nana D said.

Nana D and I chatted for another hour despite not coming to any specific conclusions. When we couldn't come up with any reason Marcus would want to hide his donation, we called it a night. Nana D had already made up one of the guest rooms, and I crashed within minutes of hitting the mattress. Her offer to live at Danby Landing made the whole prospect of moving home a lot more tolerable. Giving the same sort of experience I had as a child to Emma was a comforting thought.

* * *

After a solid night's sleep, I hightailed it to the office early on Friday to accomplish as much as possible. Once the quizzes were graded, I dropped them off with Siobhan, who'd stopped into the office for a few hours. She planned to scan and enter them into the student system for me, then return them to my desk, so I could deliver them to the class the following week.

Although I tried to talk to Striker after class, he was one of the first students out the door. I was stuck answering questions from a more talkative kid who wanted to tell me she'd watched *Dark Reality* reruns the night before and loved my episodes. I appreciated the compliments, but between my desire to corner Jordan and Carla and the need to avoid brown-nosers, I ended the conversation as soon as possible. By lunchtime, I desperately needed a break and something to eat. I'd only had a small piece of cake at Nana D's and was starving.

Maggie was in a staff meeting again. My mother was knee-deep in reviewing profiles of all the students to whom they'd finally settled on offering acceptance. She planned to verify all the state's guidelines had been met, so there was a fair balance of diversity among the prospective class. With no one else around, I visited Grey Sports Complex in case Coach Oliver hadn't eaten. I didn't relish the idea of sitting down to a meal with him, but it'd be an opportunity to elicit some facts. As I strolled down the hall on the third floor, I heard loud voices in Coach Oliver's office.

"I didn't do it. I swear. Believe me." Coach Oliver was adamantly defending himself from something, but I couldn't tell who was with him.

"If you won't cooperate with me, I'm happy to make a formal arrest in a more public setting. I am giving you a chance to willingly come downtown with me, but if you insist on screaming at me, I will detain you right here and now," Sheriff Montague calmly replied.

I turned the corner and found Officer Flatman and Connor standing outside the door. In the office, Coach Oliver pointed his finger at the sheriff and refused to leave. Everyone turned and looked at me.

"Just what we needed. An audience with a penchant for being the second coming of Miss Marple," said Sheriff Montague.

"I'd prefer to think of myself as Hercule Poirot if I need to be compared to a literary character from nearly a hundred years ago, *April*." When she frowned at me, I shrugged and turned to Coach Oliver. "What's going on here?"

"Tell her I'm innocent, Kellan. I didn't kill Lorraine and Abby. I'm being framed."

Connor pulled me aside while Officer Flatman and the sheriff applied more pressure on Coach Oliver to stop resisting them. He explained the results of the fingernail analysis and a second test they'd run on Coach Oliver's car. I hadn't known about the last one. Then again, I suspected Sheriff Montague didn't feel compelled to tell me anything about the case. After the sheriff revealed what she'd learned from Abby's journal, validated Abby's call discussing an eight thirty meeting had come from Coach Oliver's office, considered Lorraine's call to me accusing Coach Oliver of something, and discovered the suspicious note in Lorraine's hands when she was killed, Coach Oliver admitted he'd been dating both women. He claimed that when Lorraine had confronted him, they argued, and she left. When the test results on the red fibers under Abby's fingernails definitively matched the baseball team's jackets, Sheriff Montague convinced Judge Grey to issue a warrant to search Coach Oliver's house and car given his connection to both women and potential presence at the scene of both crimes. That's when the sheriff found stronger evidence she couldn't ignore.

A few drops of blood on the passenger seat in Coach Oliver's blue sedan matched Abby's DNA. I had suspected Coach Oliver all along, yet while I wanted to pin the crime on him, I wasn't feeling confident we had the whole story—especially with the news about Marcus Stanton being the anonymous donor. Coach Oliver was assuredly part of the grade-changing scheme, but there was more going on than anyone knew at this point. I had to prove it.

"What about Lorraine? Any evidence he pushed her out the window?"

Connor smiled, then breathed loudly. "There were also fibers found under Lorraine's fingernails. I suspect both women tried to stop him and grabbed onto his jacket. Maybe there was a brief struggle in Abby's office where she grabbed the killer's jacket, then ran away toward the stairs. In Lorraine's case, she probably reached for the killer before he pushed her out the window. In the process, it transferred fibers. The sheriff also found fragments of skin under Lorraine's fingernails. If they turn out to be Coach Oliver's, the sheriff will arrest him tonight."

"Can't anyone buy those jackets in the school store?" They were mostly for the baseball team, but it wasn't as if they'd been custom or specially given to select individuals. I thought it might have been the gift Lorraine was searching for.

"That wasn't the gift, Kellan, but it was the third supposedly missing item from Diamond Hall. Coach Oliver swears he dropped off a new jacket for Lorraine the day of the party after he'd received the shipment, but she never saw it. These were the new ones just issued for the upcoming baseball season. Very few had been sold or given out," explained Connor. "Only Coach Oliver had possession of them, except for the players and cheerleaders. The sheriff is checking with anyone who received a jacket to see if those have a rip or any damage."

"So now what happens?" As I posed the question, Sheriff Montague led Coach Oliver away in handcuffs.

"I'm taking him into custody, so we can convince him to tell us everything. When I know more, I'll share it with you, Little Ayrwick. For now, I'd appreciate you keeping this quiet. I trust you can handle these instructions," the sheriff said with a pointed stare that gave me the chills.

"Yep, I understand," I replied to the sheriff, then turned to Connor and shared the details of the conversation Bridget had overheard with the scout.

"It lends more credence to why it was so important for the baseball team to do well this year. If Coach Oliver was holding out for a job at the Major League Baseball organization, he needed to look good when his best friend, the scout, was onsite. Coach Oliver was probably doing anything he could to keep Striker on the team, all the while working with Jordan as a backup." Connor stepped further into the office and checked on Officer Flatman's progress. "I will need a list of everything you find and take from the office. This might be a murder investigation, but this is still college property. There could be confidential information in here."

Officer Flatman acknowledged Connor's request. "We can start with this note I found under his desk."

I poked my head inside to hear what they were talking about. "A note?"

"Yes, Coach Oliver was holding it when I walked in, but when the sheriff placed the handcuffs on him, it fell to the floor. He kicked it under the desk."

When Connor asked to see the note, Officer Flatman handed it to him. He read it aloud.

You're an amazing baseball player who deserves to be the starting pitcher at this Saturday's game. I hope I can make this happen for you. I'm behind you all the way and won't let you down again. I believe in you and will do whatever it takes to help you take the lead spot.

Connor and I turned to one another. I was certain he had the same thoughts. "It's identical handwriting, isn't it?"

Connor pulled up the image he'd shown me on his phone earlier in the week. We compared the two notes and smiled. "Exactly the same."

"But what does it mean?" It made no sense why Coach Oliver had this note in his possession. It would be stupid of him to write a message to a student in such an open manner, which meant he was probably not the author. It also could have been about Striker or Jordan. Maybe the person who wrote the note was hoping to fix Striker's grades to get him permission to play again or to help Jordan by having Striker forced off the team permanently for cheating.

Connor instructed Officer Flatman to deliver the note to the sheriff as soon as possible. He turned to me and said, "Other than Striker himself, who's been angry about him not getting to play?"

"My first guess would be Marcus Stanton, but he was busy at the retirement party or board meeting when Abby was killed. Nana D confirmed he was in a council meeting when Lorraine was pushed out the window. Carla Grey has some explaining to do regarding her waffling support between Jordan and Striker," I replied. It was time I got to the bottom of whatever game she was playing.

"While we wait for the sheriff's team to catalog any additional evidence, do you have a sample of Carla's handwriting?" asked Connor.

"I might." I tried to remember what was in my possession. After recalling I'd left all my class materials in Diamond Hall, I told Connor I would check my office. We agreed to touch base later that evening to outline a game plan.

I took off on foot back to Diamond Hall. I shuffled through all the papers on my desk but couldn't find the recent pop quiz. Then I remembered dropping them off with Siobhan to photocopy, enter into the grading system, and return to me before classes next Monday. I thought it was odd and quickly scanned my email to see if she'd messaged me about them. And she had. Siobhan had taken the papers home with her to get the work finished on the weekend while the babies were sleeping. Since I didn't have her phone number, I replied to Siobhan's email asking her to upload Carla's quiz as soon as possible and to send me a copy. I also left an urgent message for Myriam to provide Siobhan's home number.

Two hours later, I was fully caught up for my classes but still had no updates from Siobhan or Myriam. Before leaving, I texted Connor with my current status. He was just departing Braxton for the night after the sheriff's crew had finished their search of Grey Sports Complex. The sheriff mentioned she wouldn't arrest Coach Oliver until they could review all the evidence over the weekend. Coach Oliver would be free to leave the precinct later that evening.

When I arrived home, I offered to cook dinner since my mother was running behind from visiting Eleanor. I made garlic bread and threw together a pasta dish with zucchini, tomatoes, orange peppers, and a white cream sauce. It was already getting late, and I didn't want to have a full stomach when I went to sleep. It would be important to get enough rest to prepare for tomorrow's game and hopeful discovery of the killer.

I mentioned the concerns to my father about what I'd overheard in the fitness center regarding students' fears over the recent deaths. He was grateful and understanding at the same time. After recalling I had heard nothing about the mysterious blogger, I said, "I haven't seen any new blog posts about you. I guess Dr. Castle is behaving herself?"

"As I mentioned previously, the blogger is not Myriam. In fact, we've solved the situation." My father reached for another piece of garlic bread and sampled a glass of the wine I'd poured with dinner. "There won't be any more blogs being written about me."

"Can you tell me who wrote them?" If it wasn't Myriam, I had no other suspects in mind unless that was the reason he'd called Dean Terry to his office. Was she lying through her teeth to me about supporting the athletic program? Or tossing out confusion in various places?

"Not yet. After Monday, I can share the name with you. Sheriff Montague is convinced it has something to do with both deaths and has asked me not to discuss the person's identity with anyone."

"This is all getting too frightening," added my mother. "I'm wondering if Nana D has a point about this crime taking too long to solve."

"Your mother is a gossip, Violet. She's not content unless there's someone or something to complain about. This is just more fodder for her to sink her teeth into," my father replied.

"Nana D is right, Dad. Tomorrow is two weeks, and the sheriff hasn't made a lot of progress. Just today she dragged Coach Oliver back in for questions, but I've been telling her all along to dig deeper into his alibis for both nights."

"Kellan's right, Wesley. He's more on top of this than Sheriff Montague," my mother said.

"Let's agree to let this go for now. Murder's no topic for dinnertime," my father announced, pushing his plate away and changing subjects. "I'm able to move back into my regular office after tomorrow's baseball game. The movers will have my desk and belongings returned to the executive building. Things will finally be back to normal again."

"I'm sure moving back and forth was difficult, Dad." It's always about his inconveniences.

"Speaking of moving, I believe you owe me an answer."

"I believe you are correct. And I believe you gave me until the end of today, right?"

He nodded.

"Then I've got a few hours left."

My father stood, raised his finger as if he wanted to chastise me but thought better of it, and left the room mumbling to himself.

"Do you really think that's how to solve your problems, Kellan?" asked my mother while scraping food from his plate onto hers to carry them to the kitchen. "I don't see how you two will ever work together if you're both so similar and intent on aggravating one another all the time."

Similar? What was she talking about? I was in no way, shape, or form like my father. Was I? After retreating to my room, I stewed like a child who'd been reprimanded by his mommy for doing something bad. But I had done nothing wrong. They'd given me until the end of the day. It was only dinner time. I knew I needed to make my decision. When it was approaching midnight, and I still hadn't come to any conclusion, I admitted she was right.

Chapter 22

I continued to second-guess my decision regarding acceptance of the new role, despite tacking a note to the door on my father's study at precisely one minute before midnight. I spent most of the night listening to the wind rustle through the trees while I laid awake staring at the ceiling. After a quick breakfast, I verified my decision was no longer fastened to the door, which meant he'd read my pronouncement. I should've told him in person, but he'd been sleeping when I'd come to my conclusion, and I didn't want to talk about it anymore last night. I packed my gym bag and drove to Grey Sports Complex.

Upon arriving, I proceeded to Coach Oliver's office to determine if he'd returned from the precinct and was prepping for the afternoon game. With his head on the desk, the disgruntled man snarled at me. "Some help you were yesterday. I just got done a few minutes ago. Now I have to figure out how to motivate the team when I feel like I've been hit by an eighteen-wheeler." The dark circles under his eyes convinced me he'd been telling the truth about being up all night.

"It's time you leveled with me, Coach Oliver. There's something you've been hiding. Why not get it out in the open? You'll feel better." I had to go with my instincts. The sheriff wouldn't have released the man if he was the murderer. I felt safe alone in his office. "Let's start with why they didn't arrest you."

"My attorney has advised me not to discuss it with anyone." He shrugged and squarely set his jaw, then relented. "Fine, I guess I can tell you if you promise to help me." Coach Oliver waited for me to agree, which I did, knowing I could back out if it involved anything illegal. "My DNA wasn't a match against whatever they found under Lorraine's fingernails. The blood they discovered in my car was a match with Abby's, but her nosy neighbor verified she'd watched Abby cut herself in my car weeks ago. There wasn't enough to hold me any longer."

"I guess that's a good thing for your case, but you still don't have valid alibis for either murder, do you? I don't believe you about dropping the schedules off for my father the night Abby died. You were at Diamond Hall to see her, weren't you?"

"All right, yes. She agreed to chat at eight thirty to discuss Striker's grades." Coach Oliver explained he'd been about to enter the back of the building to meet Abby when Lorraine whispered his name. After Lorraine led him to a nearby bench, he handed her the schedule and talked for ten minutes. Once she walked back to the building, Coach Oliver took off and contacted Abby, but she never picked up the phone. He went to the retirement party, assuming Abby would call him back at some point, then ran into Eleanor at nine when it was about to end. My mother had seen him after Lorraine left him. "That sheriff has no clue what's going on and wants to close the case, so she doesn't look foolish," Coach Oliver noted.

I agreed with him, but taking a stance on Sheriff Montague's intelligence wouldn't help me. "I'm sure they're looking at other suspects besides you. What about the note under your desk?"

Coach Oliver's head jerked back in alarm. I'd caught him off guard and temporarily speechless. "Ah, I'm not exactly sure. I won't deny it. That cop saw me hide it."

"It's illegal to conceal evidence. I'm sure you're aware they could charge you with something for that," I added, hoping to scare him into talking more. "You must have told the sheriff something about it."

Coach Oliver explained how he'd been finding notes since the semester started from someone claiming Striker should be the starting pitcher. The person had previously left one for Striker, indicating they had ensured Striker's grades were good enough to lift the suspension. Coach Oliver had stolen the notes as he didn't want his star to worry or get in trouble. He hoped it was someone messing around. He grew alarmed when he got a second note and Striker's grades didn't match what Abby had earlier told him about an 'F.' He knew they'd been changed, but not how or why.

"I don't get it. Why was it so important for Striker to pitch?" I inquired while shaking my head. I went out on a limb to test a theory I'd been considering ever since Nana D conveyed the conversation Bridget overheard. "Does this have anything to do with the rumor about the scout helping somebody at Braxton get a job at the Major League Baseball organization? And that you happen to be the scout's best friend?"

Coach Oliver turned as white as a ghost. "How do you know about that?"

Bullseye! "Were you hoping that by ensuring Striker played in the game, you'd have a better chance of getting that job? Was it some sweet executive position? Access to all the major league teams?"

"No, you've got it all wrong," shouted Coach Oliver as he paced the room. "From the beginning, I wanted both Striker and Jordan to play. I care about the guys and want them to land a contract with one of the Major League Baseball teams after graduating from Braxton. That's why I privately coached both last semester and encouraged the competition between them. I needed my buddy to see how well they both played and draft them into the leagues."

"So, you're saying the league job isn't for you? This is entirely for the players?"

"Right, I don't want to leave Braxton. I love working here, but I was being blackmailed."

"I don't understand what you're saying." I pushed him to explain the complete story.

"Last fall, Marcus Stanton approached me, suggesting he knew I needed improvements in the athletic department. He offered to buy new gym equipment, returf the baseball field, and fund our technology."

"Isn't that a good thing?" I asked, suddenly arranging things together. It was Marcus Stanton threatening my father on that call I'd overheard. He didn't want anyone to know he'd made the anonymous donation, but I couldn't figure out why. It might've looked a little self-centered if he were donating money that helped his stepson, but that wasn't enough reason to be so secretive.

Coach Oliver explained how Marcus made an anonymous donation indicating a majority needed to be allocated to whatever Coach Oliver said was a priority for Grey Sports Complex. Marcus had only one condition. He wanted his stepson to be the only star—Coach Oliver had to convince his best friend, the Major League Baseball scout, to recommend Striker join a team after graduation. When Coach Oliver said he couldn't do that, Marcus Stanton revealed his knowledge of the secret relationship with Lorraine Candito. He planned to expose Coach Oliver if he didn't agree to the deal. Blackmail was a much better reason to remain anonymous with his donation, so it looked like two vastly different transactions.

"I cared so much for Lorraine and didn't want her to get hurt, plus I didn't want to get in trouble again. They'd fire me, and I'd be out of a job with no chance of being hired ever again. That stupid policy was put in place because of me, and I wasn't supposed to be dating anyone from the college at all. I finally agreed to force my buddy to recommend Striker to a major league team."

Coach Oliver explained once Striker failed his class last semester, Marcus demanded he fix Striker's grades. Coach Oliver tried to convince Abby not to fail him, but it didn't work. He later tried to wine and dine her, which started changing her mind. She considered being easier on Striker by using an academic Bell Curve grading style to help him pass, but when Abby found out about Lorraine and Coach Oliver, she realized he was just using her. When she threatened to report him to the Board of Trustees and my father, he revealed Councilman Stanton's blackmail scheme. Coach Oliver wanted to meet with Abby the night she died, to pass Striker and prevent her from exposing the entire situation.

I recognized the similarities between Coach Oliver's explanation and Alton's conversation with Abby before she died. She'd stumbled upon all this happening and thought she could write an exposé about small-town sports and politics. "I'm still not sure why he was so worried about donating in his name. He's also got alibis for both murders unless he hired someone else."

"Marcus didn't want to interfere with Judge Grey. He'd been the primary person to fund the athletic facility in the past, hence why it's named after his family. Stanton is also running for mayor in the next election. He wanted everything to look squeaky clean. He's not a killer. If people thought he was bribing the scout to get his stepson onto a Major League Baseball team, they'd never vote him into office," Coach Oliver said.

"They'd probably strip away his role as a councilman too. Is this absolutely everything you know? You've lied several times before." I scowled. As slippery as he'd been before, I believed him this time.

"Yes, Marcus can't hurt me anymore now that Abby and Lorraine are gone. I've got nothing to lose. He won't reveal anything as it would hurt him too." Coach Oliver ushered me toward the door. "I need to get ready. My buddy is coming by to watch Jordan play, since Myriam won't release Striker from his academic probation. At least I can give one of the players a chance. Maybe with Jordan finally earning his opportunity, Dean Terry won't give me any nasty glowers and interfere in today's game."

I stopped short in the hallway. "Wait! What did you say?"

"Dean Terry's been attending all the games this past year. She's always looked dismayed over my interactions with Jordan," Coach Oliver replied. "It's like she wants me to show favoritism because she's his aunt. I'm so tired of the games women play." When he finally closed the door, I stood in the hallway, more stunned than when I'd arrived.

If Dean Terry's nephew had a chance to be the team's starting pitcher and get noticed by the scout, how much would she manipulate behind the scenes to ensure no one took that opportunity away? Was Dean Terry trying to make it look like Striker was cheating or changing his grades, so he would get put on probation? I left Grey Sports Complex and shuffled to the BCS Office in search of Connor. I wanted him to be with me when I called Sheriff Montague, but he wasn't around. A student employee radioed Connor, who indicated he'd be done with his security checks on the field in an hour. I planned to meet him near the hotdog stand on the west side of the bleachers at eleven thirty.

I dashed to the cafeteria to buy a cup of coffee and logged into the student system to retrieve Carla's and Striker's contact information. I needed to meet with them both before the game started, to learn as much as I could about their actual activities the night of Abby's murder. Striker picked up my call and told me he was leaving his dorm room and on his way to the field to meet with Coach Oliver. Although he still wasn't allowed to play in the game, Striker had to support his teammates and warm up in the bullpen in case anything changed with his probation. I asked him to meet me at a quarter after eleven before his practice began. When he agreed and hung up, I tried to reach Carla, but she didn't pick up her dorm phone. I'd have to try again after I met Connor and Striker at the field.

I scrolled through my email but had nothing from Myriam or Siobhan, which meant I couldn't yet check Carla's handwriting against the note we'd found in Coach Oliver's office. I left the cafeteria and began my hike across North Campus toward the baseball field. I took the longer route as I had several minutes before it was time to meet Striker. After passing the last set of academic buildings, I heard my name being called. I turned and saw from a distance Dean Terry jogging toward me. I stood on the far side of the campus, not remotely near any other buildings. It was a half-mile walk to reach the parking lot for the sports field, which meant I would be alone with Dean Terry for too long. Although I could defend myself, two women had already been killed.

"Dean Terry, what brings you along this path? It's a little out of the way to get to Grey Field." I stepped several feet away. Everything I'd learned could be a coincidence, I reminded myself.

"Oh, I was getting ready to attend the game. It's gonna be an important one." Dean Terry was a bit winded from trying to catch up with me. She wrinkled her brow and pulled her bottom lip into her mouth. "Then I saw you walking by, and well, I had to follow you."

"Yes, big game. I would never have pegged you for an enthusiastic sports fan. Back when I was a student, that didn't seem to be one of your focal points." I danced around the topic to gauge her state of mind before asking any direct questions.

"I know, me neither," she said, then reached a hand to grab my elbow. "I think you and I should talk. Do you have a few minutes to come back to my office?"

"Ummm… not really. I told several people I'd meet them at Grey Field. I wouldn't want to cause them to wait unnecessarily for me." I tried stepping away, but her grip was too tight.

Dean Terry breathed deeply. "I know you're aware, Kellan. I need a few minutes of your time."

Was she about to confess? Or get me alone to silence me too? "I'm not sure what you're talking about. Maybe we could chat at the field once I'm done? Connor Hawkins is expecting me any minute." I thought mentioning his name would keep her at bay if she was going to try anything. I didn't like the annoyed and distant look she was giving me.

"We can chat more later, but there's no pussyfooting around it, Kellan. The Board of Trustees didn't choose me as your father's successor. Your father insisted I couldn't talk to anyone about it until after the announcement on Monday, except for the Board and you. I guess that means you're aware of the expansion plans too. They told me I should feel honored over being asked to take a larger role in the new Braxton University. Some consolation prize, huh?"

It was then I realized Dean Terry wasn't stopping me to discuss her role in the grade-changing scheme or either of the murders. "I didn't know they gave the presidency to the other candidate. I thought they would choose you." I wasn't exactly sure what had transpired, yet I felt like it was better to stay on her good side. "I'm so sorry. Do you know whom they selected?"

"I don't. They wouldn't tell me. Thanks for your understanding. Once I found out I was their second choice the other day, it annoyed me. When I ran into you, I genuinely thought they were going to offer me the job. I was a real witch when I got back to my office afterward. I have to apologize next week to everyone who saw me get heated."

The conversation I'd overheard with the students made sense now. I felt like I could ask some questions about Jordan without causing too much suspicion. "I heard your nephew will pitch today. You must be excited."

Dean Terry nodded. "I'm proud of how well he's done. I feel bad Striker is still on probation. I even tried convincing Myriam there was no proof Striker was involved in the grade changes. While we suspect his exam isn't his own work, Braxton doesn't have enough evidence to suspend him. She wouldn't budge. That woman is a piece of work."

"Are you saying you didn't want to put Striker on academic probation? I assumed you agreed with Myriam." I was glad she openly admitted Jordan was her nephew, but her support of Striker confused me.

"No, I urged the need to complete an investigation and thorough analysis, but this has gone on long enough," she replied. "Without Striker on the team, Coach Oliver is much harder on Jordan. I prefer when he can split his focus between them. The coach is trying to strengthen their confidence, but he's a monster with motivating and training them."

"That's why you've been issuing dirty scowls at Coach Oliver?"

Dean Terry explained she'd never thought Jordan could break into the big leagues when he was in high school. He was a cocky kid who had little discipline. In the last few years, she finally saw him prove his pitching prowess. That's when she took a bigger interest in his baseball career and changed her tune about the sports program at Braxton.

Coach Oliver didn't like her getting involved on his turf and had misread her intentions for getting tangled in his department's operations. "Wow, I wish I knew this sooner. I never realized you were his aunt. By the way… did you visit Jordan the night of my father's party? Jordan mentioned you'd stopped by."

"Yes, I'd forgotten I left the party to give him some encouragement. He'd only gotten home a few minutes before I showed up at nine. He'd been out on a date and just left the girl's dorm room," she replied. If that were true, then Carla and Dean Terry corroborated his alibi. Dean Terry might have had time to leave the party, kill Abby, then visit Jordan, but it seemed unlikely.

"How did your self-defense class go?" She wouldn't understand why I asked, but it might finalize the open issues with her alibi.

"Never made it. I got pulled into an urgent call with your father and showed up tardy. There was a sign on the door indicating no late arrivals, so I went back to the office." Knowing that cleared up the confusion and meant Dean Terry wasn't a murderer, I wished her success in her expanded role at Braxton. I sidestepped the conversation about why I'd known anything about the plans for the new university since she didn't need to know whether I was going to join the project. While her explanations left minor doubt over her guilt, casting her as the murderer had too many holes. I was missing something but couldn't prompt a breakthrough.

As I took off in the direction of the baseball field, breathing a sigh of relief I hadn't been a third victim, my phone rang. It was Myriam. "I'm not used to being summoned on a Saturday with another crucial college issue, Mr. Ayrwick. I'd have thought with your father identifying the blogger this morning, you would be busy figuring out what that was all about. Surely, you have a good reason to disturb me?" Myriam knew the blogger's identity.

"My father has mentioned no names yet. I will ask him again soon."

"It was Monroe. Apparently, she'd been pressuring him about the donations, but he hadn't put it all together until you started asking questions about who installed the new technology systems at Grey

Sports Complex. She was a classic fool worthy of Shakespeare's court jesters."

"How did Abby post that last article after she died?" It didn't add up.

"It was the very last thing she did. She'd been writing the blog while walking around the retirement party, set it to post the following day, and then went back to her office. I checked the date and time stamps and validated it was last saved at eight o'clock."

"How do you know this?"

"When I received the materials from her office, I found her username and password for the blog. I tried to log on, and it worked. Once I confirmed it was her account, I saw all the posts. That's when I updated your father, Connor, and the sheriff." Myriam sounded too smug in her explanation.

Myriam's news timely explained why my father was so busy this morning. "I apologize. I only contacted you because of an urgent police matter. I need a copy of some exams that Siobhan took home to upload into the grading system."

"You're quite obsessed with grades. Were you a poor student when you attended Braxton? Is it a self-confidence booster to point out when someone has tampered with a student's grades?"

Given she brought up the subject, I requested a status on the analysis she held up. "Dean Terry said she's recommended closing the investigation and allowing Striker to play today."

"Mr. Ayrwick, I've turned over everything to Dean Mulligan. Everyone on the committee has weighed in as of an hour ago. There will be a decision on Monday. I'm sorry this means your little friend, Craig Magee, cannot play today. There's more to life than tossing a ball around for a few hours."

"I appreciate your candor. I'll keep it in mind," I said politely. "And Siobhan's number?"

"*All the infections that the sun sucks up. From bogs, fens, flats, on Prosper fall, and make him. By inch-meal a disease!*" Myriam growled in disgust.

"Surely you're not comparing me to an insect or an illness. Is that the most appropriate quote you could summon, Myriam?"

She rattled off the phone number and hung up without a goodbye.

Chapter 23

On the walk to the field, Siobhan returned my call. "I'm sorry I missed your email, Kellan. I've been so busy with the twins and scanning all the exams, I hadn't checked my account."

"No worries, I understand. If it weren't important, I wouldn't bother you over the weekend."

Siobhan confirmed she would log online when she got home that evening to email me a copy of her exam. When I asked what her schedule was for the next few weeks, she mentioned they'd hired a temp to fill in while everything was sorted out with the new chair of the department. "I'll be onsite three mornings a week to transition everything in the meantime. I'm also asking the student employees to work a few extra hours. I'm sure they can use the money since your father cleared the expense for the short term." Siobhan put me on hold when a baby cried.

I'd forgotten about the student workers in the communications department until Siobhan mentioned them. When she returned, I said, "I met one worker, Bridget. I don't believe I know the other one."

"Yes, I'm not surprised. Bridget's fantastic, very enthusiastic. I was none too pleased when they assigned the other girl to me last semester. She's always late and barely did any work."

"Why wouldn't you ask for a reassignment? Or fire her?" It seemed logical to me. I'd rather not have to deal with someone incompetent for the next few weeks while I taught Abby's classes.

"There's no firing Carla. Can you imagine Judge Grey's fury if I gave his granddaughter the heave-ho? That might cost me my job, Kellan." Siobhan laughed loudly before adding, "And with two little ones at home, that's not an option."

Wow! How did I miss that fact? I hung up with Siobhan, checked my watch, and rushed off to meet Striker. He was leaning against the dugout wall when I arrived at Grey Field's baseball stadium. Given he was dressed in his uniform, I didn't have the heart to tell him based on Myriam's latest status that he had no chance of playing in today's game. I felt awful holding that information from him, but knowing his current or former girlfriend might be the person who killed Abby and Lorraine seemed far worse.

"Hey Striker, how are warm-ups going?"

Striker tried to smile despite his face's refusal to comply. "I'm in decent shape. Part of me wants to head home, but the coach won't let me leave. He says I need to show the scout I'm a contender."

"He's right. The scout's seen students deal with academic probation before. He cares about your pitching consistency and attitude on the field. Not what the dean says about the results of one exam," I added, feeling the soft spot I had for the kid, reminding me to give him a boost. I hoped he wasn't the murderer.

"I don't understand what happened with that test. They won't show me the paper, but Dr. Castle says she believes the version she graded wasn't mine. How does that occur?"

I asked Striker to clarify exactly what he remembered transpiring around the time of the exam. He explained that Profess Monroe had promised to grade it over the weekend and let him know the following week before the next practice. Then he heard she'd fallen down the steps, and everyone was searching for the exams. Coach Oliver had called Striker last Friday afternoon to say he'd gotten a 'B+' which meant he could play in the game. At the pep rally, everyone was excited he could still play. Then Dean Mulligan called a meeting and told him there was suspicion over whether it was actually his test results.

I had no reason to suspect Dean Mulligan, but I should check his alibis. "Now what happens?"

"I meet with the dean again on Monday to review the exam they're saying isn't mine. My stepfather's gonna kill me if I don't make it to the major leagues."

"I'm sure they'll figure it out soon. I'll see if I can attend the meeting. Would that help?"

Striker nodded. "You've been really cool about this. I wish you'd been my professor all along."

Everyone wanted me at Braxton these days. "Striker, I have to ask you a sensitive question. I wouldn't ask if I didn't have a good reason, but I need to share something confidential with you. Can I trust you not to talk to anyone else about it?"

"Yep. You're the only person on my side. Of course, I'll answer anything you want."

I asked Striker why he'd left and returned to the fitness center on the day Lorraine died. He explained he didn't want to be around Jordan, then mentioned a few people saw him in the sauna and could confirm he was present until he finished working out. I'd verify it later. "Have you ever been given or found any notes about helping you pass your classes so you could play on the baseball team? Or has Coach Oliver ever told you about them?" I hesitated in revealing something the sheriff wouldn't want to be shared, but it might yield me valuable insight.

Striker jerked back with a shocked expression. "Notes? Like emails or text messages?"

"Not exactly. A piece of paper taped to your locker at Grey Sports Complex? Or something through the mail?"

"Nope. Got no clue what you're talking about, man. Did someone say I did?"

"Nobody's said you did anything, Striker. I'm trying to piece together a very peculiar puzzle. So, you do not know of anyone tampering with your grades, telling you they did anything, or sharing any sort of communication about you deserving to play in the baseball games?"

"Seriously, I'm clueless. This is turning out to be a horrible senior year. First, I can't play baseball. Then Carla dumps me. I just want to go home."

"What are you implying, Striker?" Alarm bells were going off, but I couldn't figure out why.

"I might as well tell you. She's the one who looks bad, not me." When Striker kicked the dirt, clouds of dust wafted by us. "Carla was just interested in me because of the scout. When she thought I had a chance of getting into the major leagues, she threw herself at me last semester. She and my stepfather kept pushing me to do better, so I could get a lucrative contract. But as soon as I got put on academic probation and the scout looked elsewhere, Carla distanced herself."

"I'm not surprised. I must admit I didn't get a positive vibe from her when I saw you two together at last week's game or in the classroom this week. She's very flirtatious with other guys."

"I was too distracted by everything. I didn't notice it. That's why I lied to you last week about where she and I were the night Professor Monroe died. Carla and I had a few drinks in the dorms, but it was much later than I said. I was at the fitness center most of the night. We met up at nine thirty."

"I don't understand why you couldn't say that when I asked," I complained, recognizing Carla was looking increasingly suspicious.

"I didn't want to contradict her in front of you since we were already fighting all the time. I figured if I agreed with her, she wouldn't start something again. She said we were together because everyone assumed the professor's death wasn't an accident. She didn't want anyone to think I killed the woman over my poor grades. I guess Carla was covering up that she was cheating on me with Jordan that night," Striker said.

"I think you're partially right. When did she break up with you?"

"When I was put on probation again and couldn't play for the scout, Carla told me she needed space to think about whether she could be involved with someone who was suspected of cheating."

Based on Striker's news, neither he nor Carla had a complete alibi during the window of time when Abby was killed. Striker explained that the scratch on his arm was from Carla when they had a fight about his return to academic probation. He was glad not to deal with Carla's frequent physical attacks whenever she didn't get her way. Once he left for the dugout, I walked to the hotdog stand near the west bleachers and located Connor. "Able to give the all-clear for today's game?"

"Yes, we're in solid shape. With two murders on campus, I'm more cautious than normal."

"I have to admit, security seems to be lacking around here. I don't mean any offense, but anyone can walk in and out of the academic buildings. Grey Sports Complex only has security cameras and card readers in a handful of places. Grades or exam results are being changed." I took the risk of antagonizing Connor, but it had to be said.

"You're absolutely right. That's part of the reason your father hired me. The previous director had gotten lax about protocols. There have also been significant changes in the national security requirements around colleges and universities given all the school shootings. We've got a two-year plan to bring everything up to standards."

"You've got your work cut out for you."

"I'm glad to have your help, Kellan. Just be careful how integrally involved you get. I've been in the middle of some nasty wars in the past. What did you need to talk to me about?"

I updated Connor on all my conversations. While he put a call into the sheriff, I scanned the stadium. Bridget was talking with Dean Terry in the stands on the third base line. She had on the giant green parka again today, but in her defense, the temperature had dropped quickly. The latest weather report mentioned another blizzard from the north in the coming days. I studied the crowd for anyone else I knew. Nana D hovered a few rows behind them, near Marcus Stanton. I watched them interact for a few minutes, and as the time passed, their discussion grew increasingly animated. By the time the game started, the councilman had thrown his tray of fries on the ground and stormed up the steps to the exit.

Then Derek called to tell me the results of his big meeting with the executives. They weren't happy with his season two plans. Instead of giving him another chance, they fired him. While Derek had already found himself another gig, he advised me to be ready for news from the network about my future.

Jordan pitched for all the innings while I forced myself to ignore Derek's news. Since we were the home team and ahead going into the ninth inning, when the Millner Coyotes failed to pick up any additional runs during the top half, the game was over. The Bears had won both of their games so far this season, and the crowd was intense with excitement. Dean Terry was cheering, Nana D was performing some a mock Moon Dance, and Jordan's teammates carried him off the pitching mound. It was exactly what the campus needed to keep its mind off the murder investigation.

With the event concluding and the fans heading back to the parking lot for post-game parties, Connor and I called the sheriff to reveal our latest news. We searched for a quiet area in the stadium and found a table under a covered awning.

"I appreciate your help, Connor. We spent another round here at the precinct going through the alibis for everyone who was recorded entering or leaving Grey Sports Complex. Officer Flatman will drop off a copy at your office tonight to do a final compare to see what doesn't add up."

"How about Carla Grey? Any chance you remember if she was included? Now that we know she was lying about her whereabouts the night Abby died, she's clearly at the top of the list," I said, unable to help myself. Connor had asked me not to speak, but I couldn't keep my mouth shut.

"Yes, she was on that list, Little Ayrwick, as were at least six other people who might not have alibis the night of Abby's murder. Cross-referencing everything is not as easy as it sounds. Nor do I intend to incur the wrath of Judge Grey or Councilman Stanton if we don't have an airtight case against either student."

Connor chimed in. "So, April, how do you want to handle talking to the suspect?"

"I think our best chance is to get Carla to meet with me. If she thinks it's about her last exam or something to do with class, she might slip when I ask questions about the nights of the murders." She was hiding something. I could feel it. Nana D would say it's a sixth sense unique to the Danbys, but I wasn't so certain. I was skilled at reading people who had something to conceal.

"I agree asking Carla about her dating life or what she does while working in the communications department would come across better from you. And she wouldn't run to her granddaddy because you asked to meet," Sheriff Montague replied.

"Exactly, which is why—"

"But," she continued, "verifying her alibi for both nights is something my office should handle. I'm willing to concede it's also something Director Hawkins could ask as part of a campus review on access control. I will make you a deal. While you two are talking to her, I want to be present. I will be sitting nearby listening in, so I can stop you if you're doing anything to ruin my case."

Connor attempted to speak, but I interrupted him. "Connor used to be a police officer. I'm sure he's qualified to keep my conversation with Carla from causing any detriment to your case."

"That's not my point. It's my butt on the line here. If anything goes wrong, I'll be held responsible for allowing you to do this," the sheriff argued. "I don't want to be accused of setting up a witness and then not being able to arrest her."

"Are you saying you don't trust me?"

"I wouldn't trust you if you were the last person on the planet and I needed your help to survive. I'd rather let the zombies eat my flesh alive than turn to you as a savior. I'm only giving this a chance because Connor will be present."

I distinctly heard the obnoxious guffaw of Officer Flatman in the background. Connor had the decency to stifle his outburst. I'd caught her referring to him as *Connor* again. That professionalism sure came and went like my aunt Deirdre's fake British accent. She'd moved to the UK years ago and was notorious for using it whenever it worked to her advantage, but it was sure gone when she drank.

After we all made our concessions, the plan was to invite Carla to The Big Beanery the following morning. While I was dialing her number, Connor received another call and stepped away. After Carla picked up, I mentioned I wanted to meet with her about the upcoming term paper. "My schedule is packed next week, and I know it's last-minute notice, Carla. I was hoping maybe you wouldn't mind getting together tomorrow."

"Sure, would ten work? I can only stay for thirty minutes. I usually meet my grandfather for brunch on Sundays, but he lives on Millionaire's Mile, which isn't too far away."

"That's fantastic. Bring any handwritten notes. It'll help us complete the full outline for your paper. I appreciate it."

"You're welcome. It's always hard to say no to a cute guy," she replied in a kittenish tone.

I'd only talked to her the one time outside of class, but I'd never picked up this type of direct flirtation with me before. Was she really acting that way toward her professor? I assumed I'd read into it and let it go for the moment.

"Excellent, Miss Grey. See you tomorrow." I hung up, eager to tell Connor about the call. When he returned to the table, I noticed his puzzled expression. "What's up?"

"You'll never believe who contacted me."

"Well, don't keep me in suspense. Out with it." If it were Nana D playing another game or my father trying to cause trouble, I would scream in frustration.

"The facilities crew was moving your father's desk out of storage. Since everyone was at the game today, they finished the relocation, so he could have his office back on Monday."

"Wow, scintillating. Who would have thought an office move would get you so worked up?"

"Cut the sarcasm, man. They accidentally bumped the desk into the handrail while walking up the steps. They couldn't hold on, and it went sliding down the staircase."

"Oh, no. Not his antique mahogany desk. The one he found at the historical auction years ago?"

"Yes." Connor shook his head back and forth, then reminded me that my father had asked for his desk to be moved to storage once the sheriff had placed a lockdown on access to Diamond Hall's upper floors. After the sheriff had done a quick check on the desk the next day, she cleared Braxton's facilities department to store the furniture. Today was the final move back to his post-renovation office.

"Ummm... okay... what's got you so unnerved?"

"Does your father play the clarinet as one of his hobbies, Kellan?"

I knew the answer was no. But I also remembered that Bridget's clarinet had gone missing two weeks ago. "Did it have blood on it?"

"That's what I'm about to go check out," Connor said.

Chapter 24

After Connor took off to meet the facilities crew, I returned to Diamond Hall to retrieve my briefcase and download Siobhan's emails. When I compared the photo of the note we'd found in Coach Oliver's office to the handwriting on Carla's pop quiz, some letters were almost identical. A couple on Carla's paper were much loopier and grander. I needed Connor's advanced security system to be certain, but he was busy checking out the potential murder weapon discovery. He sent me a text that while the clarinet had some damage, it could've been from the fall and not from hitting Abby. The sheriff's team had confiscated the instrument and would run tests overnight. He'd update me the next day before we met with Carla Grey.

I went home only to find my father locked in his study and not in a position to talk. Sheriff Montague was already in there. I didn't dare interrupt that conversation, no matter how much I wanted to be a fly on the wall. While I believed there had to be a reasonable explanation for the missing clarinet's presence in his desk, I knew my father was in no condition to be questioned once his beloved antique piece of furniture had been destroyed. Once I heard the sheriff leaving, I checked with my mother. She begged me to let it simmer overnight. I agreed and proceeded with other important tasks.

Cecilia verified that Emma was excitedly packing for her trip. I called Nana D to let her know the latest news and made plans to stop by the next day. We agreed on a late brunch, as she had something important to tell me about a decision she'd made. Was she going to finally retire from Danby Landing altogether? While most of the staff handled the day-to-day tasks, she still went to the daily farmer's market, decided on what to grow each year, and found ways to reuse and recycle everything she could on the land to help protect the earth. Her latest focus had been a study in composting, and while I applauded her efforts, the last time I'd been there I recommended she move the pile further away from the back door. It was not the most pleasant of odors, and no matter the deliciousness of her baking, it couldn't overpower overly sweet or rotten fruit.

I also found time to research and select a restaurant. I thought Simply Stoddard near the riverfront would be a perfect backdrop, so Maggie and I could have dinner on Tuesday evening. I confirmed a time with her and scheduled a reservation, still contemplating whether it should be for two or three. If I brought Emma, it might make the conversation much easier and lighter, but it would also mean Maggie and I would spend the time getting to know one another again rather than discussing Connor. As I pulled up the bedcovers, I closed my eyes and prepared for my conversation with Carla the following morning.

* * *

"Livid. That's the only word I can come up with right now," my father said while slamming his fists on something inside the kitchen on Sunday morning. "I will have to find a specialist to repair that desk, and it will take weeks if not months. Now what am I supposed to do, Violet?"

I'd been standing outside the door in the hallway listening to their increasingly tense disagreement for the last few minutes, debating whether to wander in and surprise them or make a decent amount of noise, so they knew I was about to enter.

I pretended to stub my toe on the kitchen door and made a splashy entrance as if I were in pain. It would make me feel better about interrupting their conversation and let them quickly cool down, so there was no embarrassment over their argument. As near as I could tell, my mother wanted my father to hire a lawyer, but he was insistent he had nothing to hide.

"Ouch! I can't do anything without coffee. Why am I always walking into things?" I whined and winced while entering the kitchen. The room was overly chilly when I hobbled to the counter to pour myself a cup.

"You need to be more careful, honey," my mother said, standing near the back door and staring into the backyard. "And wear some shoes. Then you won't hurt yourself."

I nodded. "How was everyone's night?"

"I'm leaving for Braxton. I need to see the damage myself and find out if there's any hope for a repair," my father said while exiting the room.

"He's a bit grumpy, huh?" I poked around the cupboard and looked for something to eat.

"Your father refuses to acknowledge Sheriff Montague is out to get him. And he doesn't want to cooperate with her on the investigation." My mother settled into the breakfast nook and sighed.

"What happened?" I spread Nana D's raspberry jam on a corn muffin and took a huge bite.

"Your father was tired of moving offices back and forth between the renovations and the eventual move when he retires from the presidency. He told them to put his desk in storage until he made a final decision. He was worried that something might happen to it once it became apparent how easy it was for a murderer to sneak around campus. Nothing sinister."

"And the clarinet?" I asked curtly. "I'm assuming few people knew about that secret panel?"

"Lorraine knew, but his best guess is someone playing games by hiding things. He doesn't know how they found out about it," my mother replied with increasing desperation. "This has to end, Kellan."

"I know, Mom. It's been a rough two weeks. I've got a little experiment prepared. It might help bring this to a close soon. I'm sure Dad's telling the truth. The sheriff will figure it out before long." I knew this morning's discussion with Carla would be fruitful, and I hoped every-thing would come together by the end of the day.

"I appreciate it. I've got to get ready for church." My mother kissed my cheek and shuffled out the kitchen with a heaviness that tweaked my heart.

An hour later, after a quick run and shower, I pulled into the parking lot at The Big Beanery. I located Connor, so we could compare notes.

"There wasn't any blood on the clarinet." The anguish in Connor's voice was concerning.

"I don't understand. Does it mean that's not the murder weapon? Is this all a coincidence?" There had to be a logical explanation, but it wasn't obvious to me.

"It could be many reasons. Maybe the killer wiped it clean and hid it there, thinking someone would discover the lost clarinet and assume it was a practical joke." Connor shook his head and inhaled deeply. "The sheriff hasn't told me everything yet."

"There were those thefts too. I suppose it could be unrelated to the murders," I added, then checked my watch. "Carla will be here in ten minutes. Where's April?"

"A slight change of plans. *Sheriff Montague* came across some ad-ditional evidence this morning and wanted to check it out. She's as-signed Officer Flatman to monitor us." Connor pointed to the corner where a man with a snow hat and giant fuzzy sweater sat. "See him?"

It took a minute, but I finally recognized him in his disguise. Officer Flatman looked like an ordinary patron of The Big Beanery, enjoying a cup of coffee and reading the paper on a Sunday morning. "Okay. I guess it's a good sign she has confidence in us."

"She has confidence in me. I have specific instructions to shut you up if you cross any lines with Carla," Connor said authoritatively. "Don't make me use force on you if I have to."

I acknowledged his sarcasm and ushered Connor out of the café, so he could reenter after Carla arrived. I ordered a cup of coffee at the counter, then walked to the table near the corner behind Officer Flatman. "How's that article on cross-stitching?" I whispered as I sat.

"Shut it, Mr. Ayrwick. The suspect just walked in," he replied.

Carla waved hello and came by. As she peeled off a heavy winter coat, I told her to place an order at the register, and they'd deliver it with mine in a few minutes. While waiting, I assumed her conservative skirt and long-sleeve baby-blue sweater were par for the course when meeting her grandfather for brunch. The pearls gently bouncing around her neck as she walked back to the table were an even nicer touch. Maybe I didn't have it so bad in the Ayrwick family.

"Thanks for buying my coffee, Professor Ayrwick."

"It's the least I could do for asking you to meet on a Sunday morning," I replied as she sat across from me. "What did you think of yesterday's game? You must have been upset Striker wasn't pitching."

A hesitant smile formed on her lips. "Nah, Striker had his chance, but he screwed that up. I'm with Jordan now. He was awesome yesterday. I'm sure that scout's gonna find a place for him in the major leagues."

A trail of steam rose from her cup. As it dissipated near her cheek, I considered how to keep her talking about the baseball team until Connor arrived. She seemed relaxed for someone who might have committed two murders. "Oh, I misunderstood. I didn't realize things ended between you two. I'm sorry."

"Don't be. He wasn't the right guy for me. I want to be with someone who has a future. Someone who can impress my grandfather." Carla's hand reached part way across the table and closer to my coffee cup.

"I guess that explains why I saw you and Jordan together a few times this week at the... ummm... diner." It was an awkward way for a professor to mention noticing his students making out. Nor was it any of my business, but it would get her to tell me more. As I grabbed hold of my cup, Carla rested her hand on top of mine.

"Oh, that... yeah, we just started dating. You know how it is. Sometimes I think I should be with someone older, more established." Carla smiled at me and squeezed my hand.

I quickly pulled back and faked a yawn, so she wasn't touching me. She was clearly flirting with me at the same time as telling me she'd dumped Striker for Jordan. "You're so young. I imagine there are lots of things you want to explore one day. It must have been a shock when Striker was put on probation again. I'm helping him next week when he meets with Dean Mulligan."

My phone vibrated. When I looked at the screen, it was Nana D. I couldn't take the call and sent it to voicemail. I'd feel the wrath later, but this was more important. She'd eventually understand.

"Someone needs to help him. I tried studying with him, but school-work's not his thing, ya know?" she said, tapping a finger against her temple. "But I can tell you are into—"

Luckily, Connor interrupted. "Kellan, Miss Grey, two of the people I've been searching for."

"Hi, Connor. What can we do for you?" I asked. Carla turned in his direction and smiled.

"I'm trying to complete the remaining interviews with anyone who was near Grey Sports Complex the day of Lorraine Candito's accident. Could I ask you both a few questions? Should only take a few minutes." Connor was exceptionally smooth, making it obvious why he'd gone into the security field.

"Sure, we don't have a lot of time. Carla and I are going over her term paper, and she's meeting Judge Grey in a few minutes."

After he pulled up a chair, Connor studied Carla first. "I'll make it quick. So, you entered the building around a quarter to five from what the security camera recorded. Do you remember seeing Mrs. Candito? I'm trying to figure out if anyone knows what kind of mood she was in. Perhaps she was sad or upset, and it led to her drastic decision to jump."

Carla shook her head and widened her eyes. "It's so awful, but I heard it may not have been suicide. Is there any truth to that rumor?"

"I'm not sure what the sheriff thinks. I'm trying to confirm a time-line in case there was anything Braxton could've done. Can you clarify the times you were onsite? I take it you didn't see her?"

"Nope. Let's see... I ran the indoor track for an hour from five to six. Freshened up and went to the student union building to check my mail about six thirty, then met up with my boyfriend, Jordan. Didn't we see you at the cable car station around a quarter to seven, Professor Ayrwick?" Carla replied, sipping from her cup and sitting back in the chair.

"Yes, I thought I saw you. Couldn't stop since I'd been on my way to meet Lorraine. I guess you never saw her, huh?"

"I would have said hello and helped her if she was upset. I worked with her at Diamond Hall," Carla said, saddened by Lorraine's death and unlike someone who could have killed her.

My phone vibrated with another call from Nana D. I sent it to voicemail again. Hopefully, she would remember I had an important meeting this morning and stop calling soon. If not, I'd turn off the device until we finished.

Connor pretended to ask me a few questions, then said, "I appreciate it. That addresses two more people on my list. Anything else you might share, Miss Grey?"

"I don't think so. I should finish talking to Professor Ayrwick about my term paper." She pulled out a new copy from her bag and placed it on the table. "There are a few changes to discuss regarding Hitchcock's early movies."

It contained a bunch of handwritten notes in the margins. I looked up at a smiling Connor. "Oh, that's great. I had some ideas for you too."

Connor interjected. "Can I look? I'm a huge Hitchcock fan. What's your paper about?"

As Carla explained her theory, Connor pretended to check something on his phone. I knew he was bringing up the images of the notes we'd found. He looked at me and shook his head quickly. I couldn't be sure what he'd meant and lifted my eyes in confusion.

"It looks like you've got a great outline here," Connor advised, pocketing his phone. "I don't think it matched my expectations of what I thought you'd write about, but I'm sure you'll do well."

He was trying to tell me the handwriting didn't match. I worried she was clever enough to disguise her penmanship on the notes. "Well, I guess you've got everything you need, Connor? Anything else I can do to help you?"

My phone vibrated again. This time it was a text message from Nana D.

Please call me as soon as possible, or I'll slap you silly later. I found something. Crucial.

Nana D's urgency could be anything from a secret episode of *Myth Busters* to a new recipe for German chocolate cake. I would call her back as soon as I finished with Carla.

Since Connor was leaving, I could offer Carla a few tips on the paper and end this charade. We'd learned absolutely nothing except she wasn't guilty of murder. Probably guilty of leading Striker on and dumping him for a potentially better opportunity. Possibly guilty of flirting with every available man. But there was little reason for her to be involved in changing grades. She simply wanted to find a guy to impress her grandfather and was even considering me. Not that there was any chance of it happening.

"No, I'm going to let everyone know what I've found out today and head back to my office. I'll be in touch if I need anything else," Connor said before walking out the door.

Officer Flatman departed thirty seconds later to compare notes before they updated Sheriff Montague. I turned to Carla. "Well, that was weird. What were we talking about before he stopped by?"

"I was saying someone needed to help Striker learn how to study. And that I was glad to have your help on my paper." Carla reached for my hand again. Luckily, I was too quick and grabbed my coffee cup.

"I imagine Striker didn't take the news well about the break-up, huh?" I needed to stop her from flirting with me. If she talked about Striker, maybe she'd eventually feel guilty for what she'd done.

"He's a big boy. He can handle himself. I'm sure the girls will be lining up for him. Speaking of girls lining up for someone—"

If I didn't nip this in the bud, I was going to have a big problem. "Miss Grey, I need to make you aware that your attempt to flirt with me today is not something I can reciprocate. You are one of my students, and I make it a policy *never* to get involved in any personal relationships with them. It is also against Braxton's rules of conduct—"

"Oh, lighten up, Professor Ayrwick. I'm just playing. Girls flirt all the time. If you knew how often dozens of them tried to seduce Striker in the past. The obsession one of them had! So ridiculous."

"What do you mean?" I feared Connor and Officer Flatman had left too early.

"Ugh! This one girl has been in love with him forever. She goes to his games and stares at him all the time. It's creepy if you ask me." Carla shoved the term paper into her bag. "She came on to him at the game yesterday and didn't look happy with Striker's response. I saw them talking during the seventh inning stretch. He practically had to shake her away to get her to leave him alone."

"Do you know the girl's name?" I asked, desperate to find out what she knew. This was going to be the major break in the case I needed.

"Yeah, I work with her. She always acts like I don't exist and purposely forgets to tell me things to do for the professors. Listen, I need to meet my grandfather. Maybe we could chat again?"

"Hold up. You're not talking about Siobhan, are you?"

"No way! Bridget Colton is the fruit loop in love with Striker."

Chapter 25

My brain entered overdrive to assemble all the information I'd learned in the last few days. I couldn't believe how obvious it had been. "Tell me everything you know."

"She's always sneaking into his dorm to talk to him. She almost caught Jordan and me together when we got back from the movies the night Professor Monroe died."

"What do you mean? Where did you see her?" My heart raced as everything plunged into place.

"Jordan escorted me to my dorm and was about to kiss me goodbye. Bridget came running onto the floor, all freaked out. I thought she saw us as she dropped her clarinet case. I remember laughing when I noticed she was wearing one of the new baseball jackets. They wouldn't be put out for sale in the school bookstore until the following week for the new season, and already she'd bought one. That's one obsessed nutjob!"

Nana D rang my phone again and out of sheer shock, I hit the accept button. "I can't talk—"

"Kellan, I've been trying to reach you. Why didn't you pick up?" Nana D sounded exasperated.

"I'm with a student. Can I call you back?" I tried to stop Carla from putting on her coat.

"No. This is important. I found something," yelled Nana D.

Carla tossed her bookbag over her shoulder and waved to me. "Professor Ayrwick, I need to go. I'm gonna be late, and my grandfather will get angry."

"No, wait," I whispered to Carla.

"Nana D, hold on, please."

"Kellan, I was cleaning out the compost pile after you read me the riot act about the smell. I think I found the weapon used to kill Abby," said Nana D in a hushed voice. "Please get here as soon as possible."

Knowing it must have been Bridget all along, my stomach sank. She worked in the communications department. She had a crush on Striker. She claimed someone had stolen her clarinet. "Okay, Nana D, give me a few minutes. Don't hang up yet."

I turned to Carla. "I might call you in a little while. Will you answer the phone, please? I need to know if there's anything else you can remember about Bridget."

"That's all I can think of, but sure." As Carla scribbled her cell number on my free hand, my mind exploded with new connections.

After Carla left, Nana D rambled on before a gigantic crash occurred. "Bridget, what are you—"

"What's going on?" I shrieked in a panic.

A few seconds later, Nana D said, "Let's not be hasty, dear. We can talk this out."

Then a dial tone blasted through the phone. Bridget must have walked in and had seen what Nana D found in the compost pile.

I grabbed my jacket and dialed Connor to tell him what I'd learned. He would call the sheriff and meet us at Danby Landing. I drove as quickly as I could to save my nana. If anything happened to her, I wouldn't know what to do with myself. I loved my parents, but the bond and connection I'd built with Nana D would always be the one I felt the most. She'd showed up in Los Angeles a few weeks after Francesca's funeral, setting up camp in my small three-bedroom house to look out for Emma and me until we were ready to start a new life on our own. For the first few days, Nana D had entertained Emma and taught her how to cook. There were days I couldn't even leave the bedroom. The thought of Nana D being caught in Bridget's web of lies was too much to bear.

I slammed on my brakes and turned off the ignition in the Jeep. I didn't even bother to close the door and instead raced into Nana D's house. Upon arriving, I heard them arguing in the kitchen. I stopped short in the doorway when I noticed Bridget holding a knife on Nana D near the back counter.

"Please don't hurt her, Bridget. We can figure this out," I muttered with little remaining breath.

"I'm so sorry. I don't want to hurt her." Tears streamed down Bridget's cheeks, highlighting a genuine fear and concern for what she was doing. She must have known she was losing control.

"Why don't you tell us what happened? Nana D's a superb listener. She's always helped me figure things out." I needed to keep her talking until Connor or the sheriff arrived. The more people to stop her, the better.

"It just happened. I never meant to kill her. Believe me." Bridget tightened her grip around my grandmother's waist with one hand while her other pressed the knife against Nana D's throat.

"Are you talking about Professor Monroe or Lorraine?" I asked.

Bridget closed her eyes and bit her lip. "Professor Monroe caught me changing Striker's test results in her grade book. I was trying to help him. I loved him. I wanted him to play in the game, so the Major League Baseball scout would choose him."

"Tell us what happened, Bridget. Walk me through what you were thinking." I watched Nana D struggle a little, but she looked relatively calm for being held hostage.

"I was so angry when she failed him last semester. I'd changed his grade once before, but somehow Professor Monroe caught it and assumed she'd made the mistake. I thought if I could change his grade just one more time for that first exam, he'd be allowed to play in the opening game. I didn't think anyone would discover the switch until much later. By then, Striker would have impressed the scout, and it would all blow over." Bridget pulled Nana D closer, and the tip of the blade landed against the small indentation near my grandmother's windpipe.

"I saw the original 'F' in the grade book. What were you doing to make the changes?"

Bridget explained she'd stopped by on the evening of the retirement party to change the exam's grade but had gotten distracted by the jacket Coach Oliver had dropped off for Lorraine. She put it on, pretending Striker had given it to her as though she was his girlfriend. "I had a blank copy of the exam and copied over some of his answers, then I altered a few to ensure it looked like he had a 'B+' instead of the 'F.' I had already put the updated version back into the folder for Lorraine to enter into the student system. I was changing the mark in Professor Monroe's grade book when she found me in her office." Bridget swallowed deeply, internalizing the pain over reliving her crime.

She hadn't fully thought the scenario through. Even if Abby hadn't caught her that night, Abby would've eventually realized it when she entered the grades into the student system. Bridget didn't know Abby let no one else access her class materials or students' exams and papers.

"It's okay, honey," soothed Nana D. "You wanted to help your friend, Striker. Is that all?"

"Yes, he was always so nice to me in the beginning. I hated the way Carla Grey treated him. She's a mean girl. I thought he would realize it one day and dump her. Be happy I was helping him. I left him all those notes, but he told me yesterday he never got them."

Coach Oliver had purposely kept a couple of notes from Striker, so the kid couldn't ever be accused of knowing what was going on. I applauded the coach's efforts to protect the players, but if he'd told someone, none of this would have gotten out of hand. "What happened when Professor Monroe found you in her office?" As I stepped closer, Bridget gripped Nana D tighter around the waist.

"She was furious and accused me of working with Coach Oliver and Councilman Stanton to bribe the scout. I had no idea what she was talking about. Professor Monroe picked up the phone to call campus security. I freaked out. I didn't want to get in trouble and told her I wouldn't do it anymore. But she wouldn't listen to me. She said I needed to be punished, and that she would see to it."

"Is that when you did something to her?" I noticed out of the corner of my eye Sheriff Montague approaching the back door. She held her finger to her lips and nodded to the side. I assumed that meant she'd brought backup with her.

"Professor Monroe started dialing BCS. I pushed her away to stop. We struggled for a few minutes, and that's when she ripped the jacket I'd stolen from Lorraine. She must have been scared and tried to leave. I followed her to the hallway and begged her to give me another chance, but she wouldn't listen. As she was rushing down the back steps, something came over me," cried Bridget. "I don't have anyone else, and she was going to take the only thing I had left."

"What do you mean?" Nana D stretched for something behind her on the counter.

"My parents are dead. I have no real friends. I just had Striker and school. Professor Monroe would've blabbed about what I'd done. I'd be kicked out. I grabbed that stupid award from Lorraine's desk and ran after her. I hit her on the head, thinking I had to stop her. Then she fell down the stairs."

As Bridget broke down crying, Sheriff Montague snuck through the door. Nana D was able to reach a cherry pie she had cooled off on the counter. By the time Bridget realized what was happening, Nana D smashed the pie into her face. Sheriff Montague tackled them. I grabbed the knife from Bridget's hand during the commotion and backed away.

Officer Flatman sprinted through the front door and placed handcuffs on Bridget. Connor hurried through the back door. I hugged Nana D, finally able to breathe again.

Sheriff Montague said, "We have a full confession to Abby Monroe's murder. We just need to find out what occurred with Lorraine Candito."

"What happens next?" I felt bad knowing Bridget was desperate and had no one to support her. I was furious she'd killed someone I cared for very much, but it wouldn't bring Lorraine back.

"I'm going to take her in. She may not talk until her lawyer arrives. If she can't afford one, the county will appoint a public defender," the sheriff replied.

"There's no hope for me now. I thought Striker would give me a chance now that he and Carla are over. But he rejected me at the game yesterday. I might as well tell you everything," whispered Bridget. Officer Flatman had been leading her out the back door to read her Miranda rights when she stopped him.

"You should wait for an attorney," Nana D replied, still wanting to protect someone she'd grown fond of the last few weeks. "I'm disappointed in you, but don't get yourself into worse trouble, dear."

Bridget refused to wait for her lawyer to explain the details. Everything made sense once I heard the entire saga. After Abby fell down the stairs, Bridget panicked. She overheard Lorraine and Coach Oliver talking outside the door and rushed back up the stairs to hide the weapon. The first thing she could find was her clarinet case. She remembered seeing Lorraine hide a bottle of whiskey for my father behind a secret panel in his desk, so she went to the third floor and put her clarinet in its place. Then she put the award, which was similar in size and shape to the clarinet, inside the case and hid upstairs.

When Lorraine ran out after first discovering Abby's dead body, Bridget left with her clarinet case, assuming she could come back for the actual clarinet the next morning. She rushed across campus and back to her dorm room where she convinced herself everything would be okay and that everyone would think Professor Monroe had fallen down the steps and hit her head. She hadn't thought the award would leave a gash and pieces of metal on the body. The next morning, she went back to get her clarinet but saw all the police tape and couldn't access the building. She transferred the award to her backpack and went to her music lesson with Nana D, where she asked to borrow Nana D's clarinet. When lessons were done, she tossed the award at the bottom of the compost pile, thinking no one would find it, and if they ever did, it couldn't be linked back to her.

"And when you went back to retrieve the clarinet, you reported it lost?"

"I thought everyone would just assume someone had played a practical joke on me, or there was a thief taking a bunch of things from the building," noted Bridget.

After the sheriff had publicly deemed Professor Monroe's death an accident, Bridget thought she'd gotten away with it. Although she felt awful, there was nothing she could do but eventually find the clarinet and say someone had returned it to her.

Bridget then explained what had transpired with Lorraine. When Striker was put on academic probation after we discovered his exam was a fake, Bridget went to Grey Sports Complex to leave another note for him and Coach Oliver, confirming she'd fix it again. While Lorraine was in the locker room, Bridget placed the note on the desk and left his office. She was walking down the hallway when suddenly Lorraine had come back to the office.

"You hid in the conference room and overheard my conversation with Lorraine?" I realized Jordan had missed seeing Bridget by only a minute or two.

"I thought I'd been caught. It was so hot in there, I needed to open the window. I couldn't get the lights to turn on. That's when I bumped into the table and chairs. Lorraine must have heard the noises after she hung up with you and came into the room," Bridget said.

"Did you push her out the window?" I asked, hoping Bridget wasn't that cruel.

"No, it was an accident. Lorraine approached me while I was near the window. We struggled in the dark. When I shoved her to get away, she fell through the window. I didn't mean to kill her." Bridget wailed and tried to dry her tears, but Officer Flatman had her hands held tightly.

"Bridget was one of the last names on my list to investigate. I made a connection between the missing jacket, Bridget entering Grey Sports

Complex just before the murder window, and her job in Diamond Hall. Then everything came together, especially after I spoke with Dr. Castle this morning. That's why I couldn't meet you at The Big Beanery," Sheriff Montague said.

"Myriam knew about Bridget's responsibility for both murders?"

"No, Bridget's name kept popping up in different conversations after Dr. Castle shared the fraudulent exam. Dr. Castle pulled some other papers from students in different classes and thought she'd found a match to the manipulated one. I don't think she suspected Bridget of anything more than changing a few grades from time to time."

Once most of her team left, Sheriff Montague approached me. "You did a fine job, Little Ayrwick. Officer Flatman let me know you followed all my rules earlier this morning. Thank you."

"You're welcome. I never expected Carla to reveal anything about Bridget flirting with Striker. Once Connor and Officer Flatman left, I thought we'd finish talking about her exam. I got lucky."

"What do you mean by that?" asked the sheriff.

"Carla started flirting with me. I called her out, and she made a comment about girls flirting all the time," I said, thinking about how Sheriff Montague had spoken to Connor recently.

"Not all girls behave like Carla Grey, Little Ayrwick. Some are much subtler when they're interested in a man." Sheriff Montague glanced at Connor, then turned back to me.

I don't think Connor picked up on it. If he did, he wasn't letting on. "I'd like to think so. When she mentioned a girl flirting with Striker, I asked more questions, and that's when it all fell into place."

"It's a good thing you were at the top of your game, Little Ayrwick. The Wharton County Sheriff's Office is grateful for your unsolicited help, but I'll remind you in the future to stay out of my investigations. As you can tell, I am more than capable of solving things on my own." Sheriff Montague asked Connor to walk her out, so they could cover a few things.

While the sheriff might have figured out it was Bridget in the same twenty-four hours I did, it wouldn't have been possible had I not pushed for alternative suspects and discovered the issue with the grades. But I'd never get credit for it again. I would have to be happy with her minor concession when stating the Wharton County Sheriff's Office was grateful for my services.

When I saw the murder weapon being bagged and tagged, my chest twanged. I recalled the conversation Lorraine had referred to earlier in the week. I'd forgotten how much I'd told Lorraine on the phone the day after I lost the award for my work on the first season of *Dark Reality*. I had called my father to reveal Derek won, figuring it would be easier to hear from me than anyone else. He wasn't available, and I'd vented to Lorraine about the whole thing around Thanksgiving. I'm usually not myself around that holiday and have a challenging time balancing my emotions. Lorraine was overly sweet on the phone. She told me I was the only reason she watched the show and deserved to beat that nasty Derek what's-his-name. It looked like she had a replica of the award custom-made, complete with my name. I appreciated the sentiment, knowing how much I'd miss the woman.

Nana D was fine, just a little shook up. She'd been brewing tea and defrosting cinnamon buns while the sheriff and I talked. "I guess we won't be able to eat the cherry pie I baked!" She laughed, knowing there would be more in my future. After everyone else walked out, Nana D said, "Flirting with college girls doesn't suit you, Kellan. I thought I brought you up better than that."

"What? You were the one trying to set me up with Bridget. Last time it was a two-time bigamist, now it's a two-time murderer," I whined. What leg did she have to stand on?

"Pish! I never once did that. I knew all along Bridget was trouble, and that's why I pushed you together. I thought you'd figure it out eventually, but you're still a little slow on the uptake there, brilliant one. Maybe next time." Nana D checked her cinnamon buns and deemed them ready.

I rolled my eyes at her. "For the record, I would never be interested in someone like Carla Grey."

"I sure hope not, Kellan. Things are already about to get ugly enough for our family." A devious smile formed on Nana D's face. "No more shady connections, please. We've got things to accomplish."

"What did you do now?"

"I heard a rumor Councilman Stanton is planning to announce he's running for mayor of Wharton County in the upcoming election," she replied. "His role in this crime was the final straw."

"Yeah, and what about it?" I could feel my insides trembling. She wouldn't.

"He's no good. Someone needs to stand up to that man."

"What exactly does that mean, Nana D?" She couldn't possibly.

"I've been polling a few folks around town, and well—"

"Nana D, you can't!"

"Oh, but I can. I've got a press conference scheduled one hour earlier than his tomorrow." She slapped her hip and started dancing. "Let's go. Come help me pick out something to wear for my big news! Mayor Seraphina Danby has a magnificent ring to it, doesn't it?"

Chapter 26

I spent the rest of Sunday afternoon answering questions for the sheriff, rehashing the entire experience with Eleanor, and preparing for the week's classes. We needed to tell everyone on campus the truth, but it would have to wait until the public relations department sorted all the details for their press release. I fell asleep early thinking I'd received enough shocking news since discovering Bridget was the killer and learning about Nana D's decision to run for mayor of Wharton County. Little had I known, Monday would be the day when the shocking revelations pushed me over the edge.

I finished teaching my first broadcasting course in the morning. I only agreed to a one-year contract with the potential to renegotiate again. I still couldn't be sure how well my father and I would do working together, but I was comfortable enough to give it a shot given the school wouldn't allow someone to work directly for their spouse or family member. I could only work for my father on the conversion to Braxton University because there would be someone between us once they hired more staff. And I desperately needed that middleman until I heard about my future on *Dark Reality* from the television network. The LA honchos said to wait two weeks while they decided my fate.

In between classes, I spoke with Alton Monroe to confirm the details for Lorraine's funeral later that week. We'd partnered together to assemble a special remembrance service for a woman we both would miss. Lorraine had been like an aunt to me, which made me realize how much I'd lost touch with my family in the last few years. I promised myself to do a better job and stay in frequent contact with everyone, even pull together a family reunion that summer.

The last time I checked, the Board of Trustees was meeting with the new president to determine whether there would be any formal action taken against Coach Oliver for his role in hiding information and misleading Braxton during discussions with the Major League Baseball scout. Unfortunately for Striker and Jordan, the unethical aspects of how the scout ended up on campus prevented them from being offered any contracts to join a team through the Major League Baseball organization. Carla dumped Jordan when that happened and was already in search of her next victim. Striker and Jordan both told me they were focusing on finishing the semester with their heads held high and a prayer to get accepted into the minor leagues.

Nana D's press conference revealed to the entire county her candidacy for Wharton County mayor. I noticed several people including Eustacia Paddington hooting and hollering on the television. I hoped that meant their war over Lindsey Endicott was on hold, or at the very least, they planned to behave like two civilized senior citizens competing for the man's attention. Nana D promised everyone if they elected her, there would be substantial changes. More jobs. Less red tape. No more shady business deals behind the scenes. And free ice cream in Wellington Park on Sundays. I couldn't for the life of me understand why, but her last promise got everyone the most excited.

I checked in with Connor to find out what was going to happen with Bridget Colton after her unique perspective on how to implement an academic curve within Braxton's student grading system.

"Sheriff Montague's charged her with both murders. Based on all the evidence and her public defender's request, Bridget will be detained in the psychiatric ward of Wharton County General Hospital for further analysis," he replied while the call was on speakerphone. Sheriff Montague was talking in the background, which meant she'd stopped by BCS to visit him.

"Thanks, Connor. I wouldn't have solved this without you," I replied loudly, hoping the sheriff would hear too. I couldn't help myself. Somehow, I would win over that sheriff with unequivocally adorable sarcasm. "It's a good thing we kept the Wharton Country Sheriff's Office in line, huh?"

"Listen, Little Ayrwick, one more comment like that, and I'll arrest you for—"

"For what, sheriff? Speaking the truth?" I replied with a rowdy laugh as I teased the woman.

"Try indecent exposure. Connor shared the story of a certain pair of purple lacy panties—"

"Okay, truce. I'm done!" I waved a white flag in defeat. No need to get into that conversation. I'd give Connor a piece of my mind for sharing with her the truth of that embarrassment.

After we hung up, I walked over to the Pick-Me-Up Diner to enjoy lunch with my sister. When I arrived, a big sign out front read *Now Under New Management*. A moment of worry crept inside me, wondering whether it meant Eleanor would be out of a job.

As I shut the door, the bell clanged above me, and she came running over. "We're closed for a few days this week... oh, it's you," shouted my sister.

If she was still there, it was a positive sign that Eleanor hadn't lost her job. "What's going on?"

Eleanor smiled at me. "Well, my former boss no longer wanted to be in the diner-running business after thirty years. He and his wife retired to Florida."

"Have you met the new owners?" Why hadn't she told me anything about it the last few times we'd chatted? The place was empty, and there was construction going on near the kitchen.

Maggie walked out of the kitchen wearing denim overalls and a bright yellow construction hat. A decent amount of sheetrock dusted her left arm and leg. "Kellan, what are you doing here?"

A flood of excitement surged inside me upon seeing Maggie dressed that way. It was the first physical reaction I had about another woman since Francesca was killed in the car accident.

"I guess there's no keeping it a secret anymore, Eleanor," Maggie replied.

After they finished laughing, my sister explained Maggie had stopped by the diner earlier that week to grab a bite to eat. One thing led to another, and they'd made two deals that afternoon. The owners had asked Eleanor if she wanted to buy the diner, but she couldn't afford to do it on her own. Maggie had always been fond of the place and thought it might be a fun adventure to take a risk on. Both had saved enough money to split the costs, talked to a local bank about a loan, and opted to go into business together. Eleanor would run the place day-to-day, and Maggie would be more of a silent partner helping when she had time away from Memorial Library. The other deal they made that day was about Connor. Eleanor and Maggie agreed they were friends first, and if Connor wanted to take them both on dates, they could accept it in the short term. Neither would interfere in the other's relationship, but once he made a choice, they would respect the decision.

That was a disaster waiting to happen! It's one thing to go into business with a friend. You might have a few fights, but usually there's a way to work through the tension. Add in the drama of both women dating the same man, and Braxton might become the center of World War III. I knew better than to talk them out of it, so I just congratulated them, confirmed Eleanor would still meet Cecilia and Emma, and listened to their renovation plans.

By the time they finished telling me about the new diner, I had to return to campus to teach my last class before the big announcement about the new president. On the walk back, I realized not only did it mean Maggie and Eleanor were both dating the same guy, but it also meant Connor and I were possibly dating the same girl. I still hadn't decided whether my dinner with Maggie would be an official date or a relaxing meal with a friend, but I knew my old feelings had been stirred up.

As if that weren't enough to ruin my afternoon, I also didn't get a free lunch out of my trip to the Pick-Me-Up Diner. I grabbed a bag of salt and vinegar potato chips from the snack machine and quickly shoveled them into my mouth. What had I done to myself? Whatever it was, I couldn't get sidetracked as the students settled in the classroom for my final lecture of the day. Three hours later, the entire school gathered in Paddington's Play House for the big announcement. My father had reserved a seat for me by the stage since they'd be publicizing both his new role and mine. I looked around for my mother, but she was busy in a conversation with Dean Terry. I suspected my father asked her to keep the dean distracted since losing the Braxton presidency would upset her.

When I finally reached the front row, I ran into Myriam. She was dressed to the nines and had the silliest grin on her face. I honestly thought she might have just come from the plastic surgeon. I suddenly felt a tremor grow inside my stomach that she would be named the new president, but I was certain an outside candidate had ultimately been awarded the prominent position.

"Good day, Myriam. You look excited to be here," I said, hoping to keep the conversation civil. I'd had enough words with her the last few days to last a lifetime. I also didn't want to bring up her discovery of Bridget's underhanded role in the grade changes.

"Kellan, I didn't expect to see you here today. I thought you were only sticking around for a few weeks. Since they've selected the new department chair, I'm certain we'll find a replacement for Abby in the next few days, and you can head back to Los Angeles." As Myriam finished speaking, the goddess I'd met at Abby's funeral joined her side.

"It's Kellan, right?" asked Ursula with a sparkle in her eyes.

I wasn't attracted to her as much as her elegance and poise impressed me. I was in awe of what I suspected might be as close to perfection as a person could get. "Yes, and you're Ursula Power. I met you at the funeral parlor this week. I'm a little surprised to see you here today." Unless she was our new department chair, which would make her both Myriam's and my boss. Interesting theory.

"Ursula is my wife, Kellan. I thought your father would have told you that already," Myriam replied. Her smile grew even larger. Not that I thought such a thing was remotely possible given the elasticity of a human being's mouth. Then again, she was part monster.

Wow! I would never have guessed Myriam and Ursula were a couple. A sourpuss and a goddess. If Ursula was Myriam's wife, there's no way she could also be the new chair of the department. I still didn't understand why she was present at my father's big meeting. Just as I was about to respond, someone on the stage asked everyone to take their seats, so the president could begin speaking. I leaned over to Myriam as we sat. "Do you know our new department chair's identity?"

"Yes."

"Are you going to share that news with me?" *It's wrong to hit a woman. Even Myriam Castle.*

"I'm your new *temporary* boss, Kellan," Myriam replied with a sinister look on her face.

I could do nothing but sink into my seat, wishing to disappear into its crack at the thought of my new queen bee. Not only would I have to obey my father for anything with the new Braxton University, but while I was teaching classes at the existing college, Myriam would have control over everything I did.

My father gripped the microphone and began his speech. After thanking us for attending, he informed everyone that the Board of Trustees had gone through a long and arduous search for a new president. He mentioned how it was a close race, and the runner-up was an amazing and brilliant candidate, but they'd chosen someone else to assume leadership as Braxton's next commander-in-chief. "It is my privilege to welcome our new president, Ursula Power, who...."

Now I understood why she was here. Not as Myriam's wife. Not as a new faculty member. But as the new head of the college. Even with Myriam being promoted to chair of the communications department, Myriam still reported to Dean Mulligan as the Dean of Academics, so it didn't violate any policies. Ultimately, the dean reported to the president and the Board of Trustees, which meant at that level, there were fewer concerns about people's relationships. I tuned out my father's speech while reflecting on all the repercussions of the changes going on in Braxton. When I found myself alert again, I caught wind of his change in topics on the stage.

"And it gives me immense pleasure to announce who will work with me to lead the new Braxton University. Please come to the stage, Professor Kellan Ayrwick and Dean Fern Terry," my father stated.

As I stood, Myriam's excruciatingly annoying grin finally receded. I found the strength to join Dean Terry, and together we marched up the stage steps and faced the crowd. All I could think about at that moment was that I'd gotten myself in way too deep with the stupid, ridiculous mistake of a move back home to Braxton. How could so much change in only two weeks? Dean Terry first took the microphone, sharing her excitement about Braxton's future direction. "Sometimes life throws you lemons. And then everyone tells you to make lemonade. But I don't like lemonade. Usually, it's too sweet. Other times it's too sour. When life throws me a lemon-size curveball, I throw it right back into the universe and forget about it. Kind of like our remarkable baseball team who's won all their games so far this year. Last year's failures are this year's wins. I have infinite plans for expanding our amazing institution, and nothing will stop us from achieving greatness."

I admired her ability to pick herself up by the bootstraps—not that she was wearing any mind you—and trudge forward despite initial setbacks. Should I look to her for how to handle my old, sourpuss spitfire lemon better known as Dr. Myriam Castle? Was Dean Terry motivating me to mix up some lemonade and douse it over my enemy-turned-boss? As I pictured the possibilities, she handed me the microphone. *Please don't let me screw this up!*

"I'm honored to be here. Before I say anything, let me get the obvious out of the way, right? You're probably thinking... *Not another stuffy Ayrwick running the show at Braxton. They're like pesky rabbits popping up all over the place...* " I caught both my parents staring at me with fear consuming their expressions. Then I heard laughter from the crowd. "Or maybe you're worried I'm not quite committed to this new role? Let me assure you, I don't decide on a whim, and I never say *no* to a challenge. How else could I survive being the middle child of Wesley and Violet Ayrwick?"

My mother held my father back as he approached the center of the stage. I nodded at him and whispered, '*Trust me*', which seemed to hold him at bay. "My parents gave me all their strengths, and I'm confident that I've learned from the best. I look forward to serving all of you as we take Dean Terry's lemons and kick them to the curb." The room erupted with a boisterous applause, and for a moment, I felt on top of the world despite everything that had happened or that I'd lost in the last few days.

Once the announcements were finished, I stepped backstage to steal a moment to myself. I wanted to stick around to talk to a few people, but Emma would arrive any minute, and she was exactly what I needed to make myself feel better and to find normalcy again. I heard my phone vibrate and retrieved it from my pocket. It was Eleanor.

"Hey, please tell me Emma is here, and all is right with the world again," I said.

"Yes, but we have a problem, Kellan."

"What's wrong? I worried Emma wasn't feeling well or Cecilia was being difficult about the extended stay in Braxton." I stepped into an offstage dressing room to better hear our conversation.

"I'm not exactly sure how to say this," Eleanor replied.

"Out with it. If this is about my daughter, don't keep me in suspense." Eleanor could be overly dramatic. I'd been through enough already today.

"She's not alone."

"What do you mean?" I contained a mounting annoyance with my sister.

"Francesca's here too. It seems your dead wife might not be so dead, after all."

About the Author

James is my given name, but most folks call me Jay. I live in New York City, grew up on Long Island, and graduated from Moravian College with a degree in English literature. I spent fifteen years building a technology career in the retail, sports, media, and entertainment industries. I enjoyed my job, but a passion for books and stories had been missing for far too long. I'm a voracious reader in my favorite genres (thriller, suspense, contemporary, mystery, and historical fiction), as books transport me to a different world where I can immerse myself in so many fantastic cultures and places. I'm an avid genealogist who hopes to visit all the German, Scottish, Irish, and British villages my ancestors emigrated from in the 18th and 19th centuries. I write a daily blog and publish book reviews on everything I read at ThisIsMyTruthNow via WordPress.

Writing has been a part of my life as much as my heart, my mind, and my body. I pursued my passion by dusting off the creativity inside my head and drafting outlines for several novels. I quickly realized I was back in my element, growing happier and more excited about life each day. When I completed the first book, *Watching Glass Shatter*, I knew I'd stumbled upon my passion again, suddenly dreaming up characters, plots, and settings all day long. I chose my second novel, *Father Figure*, through a poll on my blog where I let everyone vote for their favorite plot and character summaries. My goal in writing is to connect with readers who want to be part of great stories and who enjoy interacting with authors. To get a strong picture of who I am, check out my author website or my blog. It's full of humor and eccentricity, sharing connections with everyone I follow—all hoping to build a network of friends across the world.

List of Books & Blog

Watching Glass Shatter (October 2017)
Father Figure (April 2018)
Braxton Campus Mysteries
   Academic Curveball - #1 (October 2018)
   Broken Heart Attack - #2 (January 2019)

Websites & Blog
Website: https://jamesjcudney.com/
Next Chapter author page:
https://www.nextchapter.pub/authors/james-j-cudney
Blog: https://thisismytruthnow.com/

Social Media Links
Amazon:
https://www.amazon.com/James-J.-Cudney/e/B076B6PB3M/
Twitter: https://twitter.com/jamescudney4
Facebook: https://www.facebook.com/JamesJCudneyIVAuthor/
Pinterest: https://www.pinterest.com/jamescudney4/
Instagram: https://www.instagram.com/jamescudney4/
Goodreads: https://www.goodreads.com/jamescudney4
LinkedIn: https://www.linkedin.com/in/jamescudney4

Dear reader,

Thank you for taking time to read *Academic Curveball*. Word of mouth is an author's best friend and much appreciated. If you enjoyed it, please consider supporting this author:

- Leave a book review on Amazon US, Amazon (also your own country if different), Goodreads, BookBub, and any other book site you use to help market and promote this book

- Tell your friends, family, and colleagues all about this author and his books

- Share brief posts on your social media platforms and tag (#AcademicCurveball or #BraxtonMysteries) the book or author (#JamesJCudney) on Twitter, Facebook, Instagram, Pinterest, LinkedIn, WordPress, Google+, YouTube, Bloglovin, and SnapChat

- Suggest the book for book clubs, to bookstores, or to any libraries you know

You might also like:

Broken Heart Attack by James J. Cudney

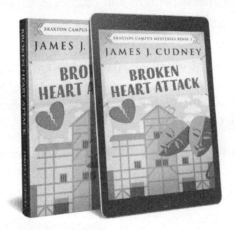

To read first chapter for free, please head to:
https://www.nextchapter.pub/books/broken-heart-attack